Yasmin gulped

It was too soon for them to be this close. Her trepidation allayed as he caressed her back. His touch set her heart at ease. Longing melted her resolve and the only way Yasmin was ever going to get him out of her mind was to kiss him. Once she got it out of her system, she could forget him. Lifting her chin to receive his kiss, she waited anxiously for him to accept her invitation.

A bolt of electricity shot through her as their lips met. To her surprise, the kiss felt like the most natural thing in the world. She tuned out the voices around them and focused her entire mind and body on the experience. Entangled by the sheer intensity of the kiss, she lost all sense of time and place. His mouth was soft, sweet, inviting, and he kissed her as if they had all the time in the world. Yasmin liked that. He wasn't in a rush and he wasn't aggressive. She curved into the arch of his body, savoring the feel of his warm embrace.

Rashawn abandoned her lips and kissed the side of her neck. He touched a hand to her cheek then fingered a lock of her hair. "Nice technique, doc."

Yasmin licked her lips. If a kiss could leave her with erect nipples and shaky legs, there was no telling what would happen if they ever made love.

He nibbled on her earlobe before returning to her lips. This time the kiss was long, deeply intense and fraught with passion.

D1636233

Books by Pamela Yaye

Kimani Romance

Other People's Business
The Trouble with Luv'
Her Kind of Man
Love T.K.O.

PAMELA YAYE

has a bachelor's degree in Christian education and has been writing short stories since elementary school. Her love for African-American fiction and literature prompted her to actively pursue a career writing romance. When she's not reading or working on her latest novel, she's watching basketball, cooking or planning her next vacation. Pamela lives in Calgary, Canada, with her handsome husband and adorable daughter.

Love **T.K.O.**

pamela yaye

KIMANI™
ROMANCE

KIMANI PRESS™

ISBN-13: 978-0-373-86091-3
ISBN-10:   0-373-86091-9

LOVE T.K.O.

Copyright © 2008 by Pamela Sadadi

Dear Reader,

Do you believe everyone has a soul mate? Is there one, special person created to love you and only you? That question, posed by one of my man-happy girlfriends, got me thinking. I hope you're not expecting me to tell you the answer, because the jury is still out on that one! But what I do know is that physical chemistry is a potent, mind-numbing drug that can't be faked. Either you have it or you don't!

Opposites *don't* attract. At least that's what clinical psychologist Dr. Yasmin Ohaji has discovered while counseling embittered couples for years. Overcoming the pain of losing her fiancé and the struggle of getting her private practice off the ground leaves the South African beauty little time to even consider dating again. Yet after a chance meeting with hometown hero Rashawn "The Glove" Bishop, she can't seem to get his luscious smile and bed-me voice out of her mind. But the championship boxer is more than a set of six-pack abs and a chiseled body. He's smart, savvy and before it's all said and done, he'll turn Yasmin's quiet, uneventful life upside down! *A Love T.K.O.* indeed!

Happy reading and be blessed,

Pamela Yaye

Love is that condition in which the happiness
of another person is essential to your own.
—Robert A. Heinlein

To my super-fine hubby, Jean-Claude: You are my real-life
hero! I love you more than chocolate and there is no one I'd
rather call my husband. Thank you for being patient with me
and being the shoulder I can lean on.

Daniel and Gwendolyn Odidison: Not only do you spoil me
(I LOVE when you come visit and cook, clean and shop!) you
give great advice, support me wholeheartedly and encourage
me to dream big. I love you both with all my heart.

Bettey: Where would I be without you? You're the wind
beneath my wings, the gin in my juice (ha, ha) and the best
sister a girl could have. You're my rock, and I'm a more loving,
more patient and less stubborn woman because you keep me in
check. Love ya!

Kenny: You're always there when I need you and I'm proud
to call you my big brother. Keep doing your thing. Your hard
work and perseverance are going to pay off one day soon. Just
don't forget the family when you make it big!

Sha-Shana Crichton: You work tirelessly on my behalf and
help me to become a better writer. Thank you for your honest
feedback, your great suggestions and for calling to check up
on me if we haven't spoken in a while. You're like a big sister,
a friend and an agent all rolled up in one!

Kelli Martin: We haven't worked together long, but I already
respect and admire you. You're prompt and thorough in
everything you do. Thanks for all the time you put into
improving the manuscript. It's SO much better
than the first draft (smile)!

To my fabulous critique partners, Donna Tunney,
Sherilee Reilly and Lecia Cornwall. I don't know where
I'd be without you girls! You critique with love, force me to dig
deeper and I come away from our sessions feeling even more
excited about the story. I appreciate your advice and
I'm incredibly thankful we found each other when we did.

Chapter 1

Yasmin Ohaji hated blind dates. Suffering through stilted conversation and dressing up to impress some man she'd probably never see again was not her idea of a good time, but when her sister had said she had the "perfect guy" for her, Yasmin had reluctantly given in. Imani had never steered her wrong and since she could spot a playboy a mile away, Yasmin had decided to give it a shot.

After playing phone tag for a month, she had agreed to meet Cecil Manning at the Laurdel Lounge. The city councilman, like most up-and-coming politicians, talked a good game, but Yasmin had her doubts about the divorced bachelor from Boston. She wasn't pessimistic by nature, but she wasn't expecting much to come of their date. Some good conversation and a nice meal would suffice. Anything more would be icing on the cake.

Yasmin followed the hostess past the smoky bar toward the dining area. Ignoring the tingling in her feet, she lifted her head and arched her shoulders. There was no telling who was watching and she didn't want anyone to know the high heels were sucking the life out of her. But that's what she got for listening to a commission-hungry shoe salesman with pretty-boy looks.

Her thick bangles jingled as she walked, drawing the attention of every single man in the restaurant. Lifting a hand to smooth her hair, she soaked up all the stares of the professional men in the lounge. Healthy smiles welcomed her, but Yasmin was careful not to make eye contact with anyone. Cecil was waiting for her and she was late.

Wanting to know exactly what she was getting into, Yasmin had done a thorough background check on Cecil Manning. Twice married, no kids, a house in South Tampa, properties in Miami and Fort Lauderdale. The son of a barber and an emergency room nurse, he had done well for himself and had a vaulting ambition to one day make it to the White House.

A dapper man in a black suit stood as she approached. A smile overwhelmed Yasmin's mouth. *Not bad, not bad at all,* she thought, licking her lips. The picture she had seen of him on the city council home page had not done him justice. He was fit, lean and had medium-dark-brown skin. Yasmin liked clean-cut intellectuals and, based on his appearance, Cecil Manning could be the next president of the United States.

Smiling widely, she prepared to meet her date. If Cecil turned out to be as interesting as he was fine, she would owe her sister big-time.

"You must be Yasmin. It's a pleasure to finally meet you."

Yasmin thought Cecil was going to hug her or at the very least give her a peck on the cheek, but he stuck out his hand and pumped hers with all his might. He was clearly in politician mode. Handshake, smile, turn to the cameras. "I hope you haven't been waiting long," she said, taking her seat. "I got stuck in traffic."

"Ten minutes, perhaps. I used the time to check in at the office. We are on the verge of passing a new bill that would ban smoking in all public areas," he explained.

"It's about time. I for one am sick of going out with my girl-friends and coming home smelling like an astray. It's infuriating."

Riotous laughter filled the room. All heads swiveled toward the sound. Yasmin turned around, annoyance written all over her face. A few feet away from their intimate table for two, a group of youths cackled like hyenas. Pitchers of beer and enormous platters of chicken fingers, potato skins and quesadillas crowded their table. The hefty guy with the hoop earrings winked at Yasmin and she snapped her head straight ahead. Embarrassed at being caught staring, she picked up the menu and perused the beverage list.

The Oliveiras had been her last couple of the day and their constant bickering and name-calling had left her physically spent. A cocktail, rich with alcohol and ice, would perk her up. But if she drank on an empty stomach she'd regret it later. When the shaggy-haired waiter arrived, she ordered something light, a lemon daiquiri.

Cecil adjusted his tie. "I am glad our schedules finally permitted us to meet."

"Me, too. This is my first time here, but it definitely won't be my last." Yasmin had been surprised when he had suggested they meet at the Laurdel Lounge but had decided to reserve judgment until she had seen the place for herself. The restaurant was west of Fenwick Avenue, a few blocks north of Rakine Park, one of Tampa's dangerous inner-city neighborhoods. The establishment had obviously not been affected by its close proximity to the crime-ridden area. All of the tables and booths were occupied, the lounge was packed, and servers shuttled back and forth to the kitchen at a frenetic pace. It was a fun, happening spot and, though the menu was mediocre at best, the laid-back atmosphere attracted plenty of hungry diners.

"How long have you been a city councilman?" she asked.

"Five years. I always knew I wanted to be a politician. My mom says when I was seven, I solicited neighbors for money so I could go to science camp. In high school, I was class president, leader of the debate team, on the student council committee and voted most likely to succeed. I graduated at the top of my class and went on to study political science at Boston University. It wasn't easy working to put myself through school, but I did. While the other kids were partying, I was in my dorm room…"

Yasmin was just making conversation. She hadn't expected Cecil to give her a blow-by-blow account of his life, spanning some twenty-odd years. To keep from dozing off, she sipped her cocktail and tried to listen to what he was saying, just in case there would be a test. Like the men and women she counseled, he talked until he was short of breath and only paused long enough to gather his thoughts.

Bored out of her mind, she entertained thoughts of excusing herself from the table and ducking out one of the emergency-exit doors. Cecil asked her what she thought of Mayor Keirstead's proposed tax hike, but before she could answer, he launched into a lengthy speech about the significant downsides of the plan.

"Baby got b-b-b-ack!"

"Yeah, she's got ass for days!"

"And I bet she knows how to work those big, juicy lips."

Yasmin's eyes tapered. The hood in her almost slipped out when she heard someone use the term *fine-ass ho*, but she forced herself to remain in her seat. *Those clowns better not still be talking about me!* she thought, tossing a menacing look over her shoulder. She had assumed, based on the gold chains and oversize basketball jerseys, that they were teenagers, but upon closer inspection she could tell they were all in their early twenties. Young, but old enough to know better. The stony-faced man with the tattoos on his neck said something, and everyone at the table roared.

"Clam linguine with shrimp?" The waiter set the plate down in front of Yasmin, momentarily drawing her attention away from the delinquents behind her. Picking up her fork, she ran her tongue over her lips. The tantalizing aroma of the pasta was nothing compared to the taste. Yasmin was so busy savoring the first bite, she didn't hear the question Cecil posed to her.

"How long have you had your own practice?" he repeated, slicing his steak into long, thin strips.

"Three years." Yasmin loved talking shop, especially now that A Better Way Counseling Services was thriving, but she didn't want to discuss work now. Good food needed to be eaten in silence. And she had a feeling if she answered Cecil's questions, it would give him license to make his own counseling critiques babble even more. Yasmin twirled a string of linguine on her fork, swirled it around the thick, creamy sauce, then put it into her mouth. Her eyes closed in silent appreciation of chefs everywhere.

"Do you have any other siblings besides Imani?"

"A brother."

"I'm an only child. I can't say I mind, though. My parents are both retired and are helping me run my campaign. Elections are a year away but you would be amazed at all the work that needs to be done. There are phone calls to make, letters to send out, money to raise and I'm in the process of…"

Between Cecil's nattering and the men guffawing behind her, Yasmin couldn't enjoy her meal in peace. The quartet had been running their mouths ever since she had entered the Laurdel Lounge and, after an hour of their senseless chatter, she was losing her patience. Initially, she had paid them no mind. Their comments, though juvenile, had been harmless. But now she was finished eating, and they were still on the same topic: her. Her stylish, backless dress was daring but tasteful, sexy but classy, but that didn't stop them from undressing her with their beady little eyes. And when the gap-toothed ringleader began making sexual references, like I-know-what-I-would-do-with-her-if-she-was-my-woman, Yasmin lost it.

Cecil was an uptight, by-the-book type of man, but that didn't mean he couldn't intervene. Too busy listening to himself talk about crooked city council members and archaic state laws, Cecil didn't have the presence of mind to come to her defense.

Interrupting him midsentence, she asked, "Are you going to say something to them, or are you waiting for them to come over here and sexually assault me before you take action?"

Cecil stared down at his Frappuccino. "Yasmin, I'm sure they don't mean anything by it," he told her, his voice lined with apprehension. "They're just teasing you. Ignore them and they will move on to something else."

"Teasing?" The word shot out of her mouth like a bullet. "The guy with the gold teeth said I have a sexy mouth and the one with the hoop earrings said he'd like to take me from behind. That's teasing?" Yasmin didn't know why she was surprised. No-backbone Cecil was simply showing his true color: sissy pink.

"Keep your voice down. I do not want to cause a scene. Do you?"

Yasmin crossed her legs to keep from kicking Cecil in the shin. Fighting to maintain her composure, she took a deep, soothing breath and repeated words of affirmation to herself. Aloud she warned. "Do something, Cecil, or I will."

"Sista', look like she could give a brotha' a real nice time," came the booming voice of the man in the Adidas hoodie. "I could go a few rounds with ma'."

"Me, too," agreed the cross-eyed one. "That's a bad-ass bitch over there."

Something inside Yasmin snapped. Her parents had raised her to let bygones be bygones, but she couldn't let this go. Forgetting she was an educated woman, with a Ph.D. from one of the finest schools in the country, she leapt up from her chair. Blood pumping, chest heaving and hands clenched, she charged over to their booth. A thousand thoughts raced through her mind and all of them were illegal. *I'm going to kill them! How dare they talk about me like I'm a prostitute standing out on the street corner?* But before Yasmin could connect her fist with a face, a broad-shouldered man stepped in front of her, obscuring her view.

"Apologize, *now*," the stranger ordered. Folding his arms across his chest, he shot a murderous stare at the foursome.

The men looked warily at each other, clearly intimidated by his imposing size. Other patrons glanced over, interested in the exchange, anxious to see how the confrontation would play out. The hostess rushed to the scene, her strawberry-blond hair flapping wildly behind her.

"Is there a problem, Bishop?" she asked, dividing her gaze between her favorite patron and the black men in the booth. No one replied. Desperate to resolve the situation, she tried again. "Is there anything I can do to help?"

Shrugging his puny shoulders, the ringleader stood abruptly and stepped away from the booth. "We don't want any trouble, Bishop."

"Yeah, we were jus' messin' 'round, homes," explained the pimple-faced Latino guy. "It was nothin'. I swear."

"She's waiting for that apology," he repeated. His voice was smooth, like aged cognac, not what Yasmin expected for a man of his size or stature. "You can apologize now or after we have a few words outside. It's your choice."

The ill-mannered men mumbled apologies, then scurried out of the dining area before the stranger could make good on his threat. The situation defused, the hostess followed them out of the dining area and the patrons resumed eating as if nothing had happened.

Rashawn Bishop turned around and felt a stab of guilt. He sympathized with the guys he had just chased out of the restaurant. It wasn't their fault the woman in the curve-hitting dress was stunning, was it? He was ogling her, making a complete and utter fool of himself, but he didn't avert his gaze. She probably thought he was just as corrupt as those young men were, but her photogenic smile was irresistible and he couldn't pull his eyes away.

The look of annoyance on her face didn't impede her beauty. She was exquisite. A Nubian princess straight from the motherland. Her mink-black skin reminded him of whipped cocoa. She had thin eyebrows, a delicate nose and the biggest, brightest eyes he had ever seen. They were as deep as the Atlantic, round and bright. Under the subdued overhead lights, her eyes glittered like diamonds. Beaded earrings dangled from her ears, a chocker graced her neck and gold bangles hung from her wrists. She had a one-of-a-kind look that made her stand out in a roomful of women who were trying too damn hard. Her vibrant, copper-brown hair was an abundance of twists and Rashawn had to fight the urge to reach out and touch them. Her locks weren't as wild as Lauryn Hill's, but they were just as thick. The definition and tone of her arms and her healthy figure told him she was no stranger to diet and exercise. She had the kind of body he liked, all curves, all woman.

"I'm sorry about that, Miss. They obviously don't know better."

Yasmin eyed her defender. The stranger had a gravity about him that intrigued her. He had to be of mixed heritage, as his skin was more beige than brown. She couldn't see beyond his steel-blue suit, but the way his jacket gripped his shoulders and draped casually over his chest told her everything she needed to know. He had a solid upper body, a flat stomach and not an ounce of fat. He was either a regular at a fitness club or had damn good genes. Either way, he was appealing in every sense of the word. His hair was cornrowed in an intricate crisscross design. He wore a cologne that smelled like the great outdoors and reminded her of the carefree summer days of the past. Yasmin loved his goatee, the quickness of his smile and the sensual tone of his voice. Unlike Cecil, she could listen to him talk all night. He had a host of attractive physical qualities, but his dreamy baritone was definitely his greatest charm. She shattered the silence by saying, "Thank you. I really appreciate that."

"No problem. I would have done something sooner, but…" Rashawn trailed off when he noticed her date was standing behind her, scowling. "Again, it was my pleasure." With that, he turned and stalked away.

Her eyes followed him back across the room. Two Hispanic men in dark suits were awaiting his return. When the stranger sat down and resumed eating, Yasmin wheeled around to face Cecil. The coward had the nerve to smile. Pulling out her chair, he said, "Let's get back to our date. I think I was in the middle of telling you about the city charter rules when—"

"This date is over and don't you *dare* think of calling me for another one. Since I'm not worthy of your respect, there's no reason for us to continue seeing each other."

"You are upset, and rightly so, but don't let this, ah, misunderstanding ruin our evening." Cecil fed a smile to some senior citizens sitting nearby. "Why don't I order you another cocktail? Or would you prefer a glass of wine?"

Ignoring him, she grabbed her purse and draped her jacket over her arm. Remembering that Cecil was an acquaintance of her sister's, she said, "Enjoy the rest of your evening."

Head high, she strolled out of the dining room, through the lounge and into the lobby. Cecil scampered behind her. He paused at the entrance, assured the hostess he would be back and followed Yasmin outside.

It was the end of March but the air was warm. Long streaks of wispy clouds hung in the otherwise clear sky. The street was packed with partiers looking for some action. On Saturday nights, downtown Tampa hummed with life, activity and excitement. Groups of single women, couples and university students ambled around, stopping in at clubs, bars and cafés.

Yasmin was in front of the restaurant, checking her cell phone for missed calls, when Cecil caught up with her. Stepping onto the curb, she extended her hand and signaled an approaching taxicab. Ignoring her, the driver continued down the street.

"Yasmin, what did you expect me to do?" Cecil asked, glancing around to ensure no one was listening in. "Take on four gangbangers by myself?"

"That's ludicrous," she said, rolling her eyes skyward. "None of them was a day over twenty-five. They were kids, Cecil. *Kids.* Boys who needed to be put in their place."

His second and third apology fell on deaf ears. "It won't look good if I return inside without you." Jamming his hands into his pockets, his eyes pleading for understanding, he said, "I had a special night planned for us. I thought after we finished here we could have dessert at the Grand Hyatt."

Yasmin shot him a not-on-your-life look. This would be the first and last time she went out with Cecil Manning. "Good night, Councilman."

"Fine, have it your way." With a shrug, he ambled away.

Rashawn glanced out the window. He had almost suffered whiplash when the dark-skinned woman had stormed out of the restaurant a few seconds earlier. When her date returned inside looking dejected, Rashawn excused himself from his table for the second time in minutes. When he got outside, the mystery woman was stepping into a taxicab.

"Let me call you another one," he said, extending his hand. "The driver looks buzzed."

Yasmin smiled knowingly. Puzzled, yet intrigued by where this was going, she stepped out of the taxicab and slammed the door. The driver sped off, leaving behind a trail of dust.

"I didn't catch your name."

"That's because I didn't give it to you."

He gestured toward the restaurant. "What happened with your man? You break up with him over what happened in there?"

"He's *not* my man. He was a blind date." Yasmin spoke her mind as if she were talking to one of her girlfriends, rather than a man she had known all of ten seconds. "Can you believe he wanted me to ignore them? As loud as they were? My mother raised me to be a strong black woman and I'm not about to let a bunch of knuckleheads disrespect me."

"I hear you. Looked like you were ready to rumble in there!"

Laughing, she tucked her clutch purse under her arm. "I was. Thank God you stepped in when you did, ah…" She waited for him to volunteer his name.

"Rashawn."

She repeated his name, liking the way it sounded to her ears. It was unique, unlike anything she had ever heard and fit him perfectly. "I like it."

"Glad you approve."

Yasmin flirted back. "I do."

Chasing down women wasn't his style, but he had a feeling this Afrocentric sister with the no-nonsense attitude would be worth the chase. She glowed like an angel under the decorative streetlights, and her eyes shimmered with humor. "What's your name, beautiful?"

"Yasmin Ohaji."

"You're South African."

She didn't hide her surprise. Very few people were able to surmise where she was from just by the mention of her name. "How did you know?"

"I read a lot about the history of the country before I traveled there."

"*You've* been to South Africa?"

"Twice." Rashawn extended his hand. "It's nice to meet you."

Yasmin's heart stood still when he touched her. Her hand slipped easily into his and the heat of his touch warmed her down to her toes. The man had a magazine-worthy smile, a solid physique and he smelled positively divine.

Rashawn wanted to talk to Yasmin some more but he had to get back inside. He had some important business to discuss with a Las Vegas boxing promoter and he couldn't afford to blow this opportunity. If he could convince Mr. Alvarez to give him a chance, he would be one step closer to a title match and all the perks that came with being a top contender. Rashawn had the drive, the talent and the motivation. He just needed a break. "Maybe we can get together next week for drinks."

"Won't your girlfriend, fiancée, wife mind?" she asked, prodding openly. "I don't want to break up a happy home."

"I'm as single as they come."

After the night she'd had, the last thing Yasmin wanted to do was go on another blind date. Rashawn looked good, but so did Cecil. No, she was better off at home planning the charity fundraiser than wasting another evening with a good-looking man of little substance. A taxicab pulled up and she opened the door. "Sorry, I can't."

"Can I at least have your number in case you change your mind?"

Yasmin opened her mouth to decline, but stopped herself. She was drawn to him, and that scared her. The smart thing to do would be to brush him off, but she didn't feel right shooting him down. After all, he had stood up for her. If it hadn't been for him defending her, she would still be inside listening to lewd and sexist comments. "I guess that would be okay." Yasmin opened her purse, retrieved one of her business cards and handed it to him. "Here you go."

Rashawn took the card. "Hold on, your home number isn't on here."

"I know," she said, wearing a cheeky smile. Before Rashawn could reply, Yasmin was in the backseat of the cab, waving good-bye.

Chapter 2

Curling his body toward the heavy bag, Rashawn threw a swift uppercut punch. The sound of gloved fists pounding against leather mingled with the grunts and groans drifting in from the weight room. Tupac blared from a portable stereo, giving fighters that extra boost of energy when their bodies begged to quit. It was a paltry fifty-eight degrees outside but the high-energy atmosphere, coupled with the overcrowded gym, made Rashawn feel like he was in a sauna.

The stifling air in the Boxing Institute of Champions was inundated with testosterone, and the women sparring in the ring were anything but feminine. Not like the African beauty he had met last week. Yasmin Ohaji. Baby girl had it going on.

He liked that she had none of the vanity or arrogance often associated with beautiful women. She was real, honest, refreshing. And she had one hell of a smile. Rashawn tried not to think about her, tried not to relive their meeting, but he did.

Their five-minute conversation had left an indelible impression on him, and she crept into his thoughts during his workouts.

The moment she'd stormed out of the Laurdel Lounge, he knew he had to see her again. Rashawn had always been crazy for sophisticated, elegant chicks. One look at Yasmin and he was sprung. He had been calling her office since Monday, but a week later still hadn't connected with her. Every time he called, her terse-sounding assistant told him Ms. Ohaji was with clients and would contact him at her earliest convenience. Rashawn was hopeful she would come around because she was too fine for him not to keep trying.

Adrenaline pumping, he completed his set, then tugged off his gloves. Wiping the sweat from his face with a towel, he exited the workout area and went into the back office. Signed photographs of Muhammad Ali, Tommy "The Hit Man" Hearns and Lennox Lewis dressed the walls, papers and invoices obscured the desk and garbage flowed onto the floor. The windows were open, ushering in a healthy mixture of fresh air and sunshine. Guzzling from his ice-cold water bottle, he sunk onto one of the plastic chairs and dropped his elbows on his knees.

"You finished your workout already?"

"Already?" Rashawn didn't bother to look up. He knew Kori Gallanger was watching him, her thin ruby-painted lips twisted in a scowl. The scent of cheap perfume, nicotine and Listerine engulfed the office like flames. "I've been here for six hours. Hell yeah, I'm done."

"Boss man's gonna be pissed when he comes back and you're not here."

"Oh, well. I've got things to do."

Flopping down on the armchair, she steered it over to the wooden desk. "Suit yourself. It's your funeral."

Glancing up at Kori, he slowly began unraveling his hand wraps. "Where's your old man anyways? He said he'd be right back."

Shrugging a shoulder, she started cleaning the papers off the desk. "Beats me. He said he had some errands to run. Didn't say when he'd be back."

When the last piece of material fell away, Rashawn massaged the tenderness in his hands. He'd run, lifted weights, sparred off and on all afternoon and jumped rope until but his calves ached. Not only were his hands blistered, his feet were tender and his back was stiff. Standing, he stretched his weary arms above his head. "See you tomorrow. Tell Brody to call me."

"Whatever. I'm not your message girl." The ugly edge in her voice fell away when she answered the ringing telephone, "The Boxing Institute of Champions."

Rashawn shook his head. For someone who had a mouth like a trucker, she sure knew how to turn on the charm when it was necessary. Her voice was cheerful and bright. She sounded less like herself and more like the office manager she was paid to be.

Kori finished her call and replaced the receiver. "I thought you were getting out of here. Thought you had things to do."

"Listening to you gave me an idea." A crafty expression came over his face as he scratched the stubble on his chin. "Could you do me a favor?"

"Why would I help you?"

Rashawn strolled over to where she was sitting, bent down and wrapped his arms around her. He had known Kori ever since junior high and, though they bickered relentlessly, he loved her like a sister. "Because we're practically family."

"It's gonna cost you."

"Name your price."

Typing her password into the computer, she smiled at him over her shoulder. "I'll have to think about it."

"I don't have all day, Kori."

"All right, fifty bucks."

He muttered a string of curses. "Fifty bucks to make a phone call? Are you out of your damn mind?"

"Do you want my help or not?"

"Okay, okay, it's a deal," he said between clenched teeth. He hated parting ways with his money, especially when his savings account was in the black, but Yasmin was worth it. Rashawn met beautiful women every day, but there was something about her that appealed to him on a personal level. And it didn't hurt that she had a body that wouldn't quit. "I'll bring the money tomorrow."

"You better. Or I'll tell my dad you've been shaving time off your workouts." Feeding him a sickly sweet-smile, she patted his cheek with a bony hand. "Now, what do you need me to do, honey?"

"My husband's an egotistical bastard who only thinks about himself. If it wasn't for the kids, I'd kill him and bury his body in the backyard."

Coughing, Yasmin shifted in her chair. Sophie Kolodenko, a Russian-born immigrant with a heavy accent, was by far her most colorful client. The overworked, underappreciated mother of five didn't mince words when it came to her husband, a sometime plumber, and called him everything from a louse to a freeloader. If Yasmin hadn't been biting the inside of her lip, she would have laughed.

"Have you told him how his selfishness makes you feel?"

"Yes, but he doesn't listen to what I have to say." Sophie wrung her hands in her lap, stress lines forming across her brow. "I've even threatened to take the kids and leave but every time I start packing my stuff, he apologizes and promises to change. A week later, he's back to ordering me around."

"What can Igor do to make things better?"

"You mean besides die?"

Laughing inwardly but remaining stoic on the outside, Yasmin took off her silver-framed eyeglasses and rested them on the glass table to her right. "Let's be honest with each other, Sophie. You don't want your husband to die. You want to know that he appreciates you and values you as a wife and a mother. Isn't that what this is all about? Validation?"

Staring out the window, Sophie dragged her fingernails through the ends of her ash-blond hair. "I guess so."

"Have you spoken to Igor about joining our sessions? We've

been working together for almost three months and I think at this point it would be beneficial for him to join in. How do you feel about him taking part in this discussion?"

"I guess that would be okay."

"Excellent," Yasmin said, uncrossing her legs and standing. "That's our time for today, but don't forget to book an appointment with Niobie on your way out."

Shrugging into her lint-infested coat, Sophie stood. "About what I said earlier—"

Yasmin put a comforting hand on the older woman's shoulder. "What we discuss during our session is private. Don't worry, I won't repeat anything you've said to me in front of your husband."

Relief flooded her face. She ambled over to the door, but didn't open it. "You asked me what Igor could do to make things better. It would be nice if he said thank you. He doesn't say thank you anymore. He just expects me to do stuff, you know?"

"Maybe you should tell him what you just told me."

Nodding, Sophie opened the door and exited the room.

Closing her office door, Yasmin returned to her desk and sat down. Plagued by a headache all afternoon, she picked up her remote control, selected disk number five, and sighed softly when the rich, soulful voice of Anthony Hamilton eased the tension flowing through her body. Yasmin couldn't stop her eyelids from drooping. It was if they had a mind of their own. Kicking off her shoes, she rested back in her leather armchair.

This was very quickly turning out to be the day from hell. Talking with Mrs. Kolodenko had been the only bright spot of the afternoon. First, her sister had called wearing a funky attitude. Imani had been in a mood ever since Yasmin had walked out on her favorite councilman and reminded her every chance she got that Cecil Manning was a terrific catch. Her session with the Fujiyamas had been going well until she suggested Mrs. Fujiyama foster her independence by getting a part-time job. It had taken her ten minutes to calm down her husband and another five to convince him not to cancel their remaining sessions. And if that wasn't bad enough, the caterer she had hired for the charity fund-raiser had cancelled. It was the first time since Yasmin had arrived at the office that she had had a moment to herself, and it was long overdue.

Yasmin was singing along with Anthony when she heard someone clear his throat. Her eyes shot open. Without her glasses, all Yasmin could make out was the shape of a man. Squinting, she pushed back her chair and sprang to her feet. Where the hell was Niobie? And who was this man in her office, smelling like soap and baby powder?

Rashawn took his time appraising Yasmin. Her twists were pulled up off her face and drew attention to her delicate cheekbones. The charcoal-gray suit gave her an older, more mature look, and though he liked the way it fit her, he wished she was wearing something that showcased her sexy arms and legs. When she ran her fingers through her hair, he caught a breath of her perfume and forced his hands into his pockets. He didn't know Yasmin well enough to touch her, but hell if the desire wasn't crushing. "I hope you don't mind me letting myself in. There was no one out front."

"It's no problem at all," she lied, grabbing the stereo remote. But instead of turning off the CD player, Yasmin increased the volume. The music blared so loud her ears throbbed. Grimacing, she marched over to the bookshelf and jabbed the power button. Smoothing a hand over her blazer, she gave the stranger a shaky smile. "I'm sorry about that."

"It's no problem. These things happen, right, Doc?"

Yasmin retrieved her glasses from the end table and slipped them on. Now that the room was in focus, she was able to match the voice with the face, and what a face it was. Heavy eyebrows, sensuous mouth, built-to-last physique. Her usual calm deserted her as she stared at Rashawn. He was more handsome than she had remembered.

He wore large diamond studs in each ear, a wide-link chain on his neck and a platinum watch encrusted in diamonds on his wrist. A large tattoo of a cross with two daggers knitted together covered his arm. Only the strong survive was written in fine, black script. Faded blue jeans hung from his waist and his sneakers were spotless.

"This is a pleasant surprise," Yasmin said, pulling her gaze back up to his face. The man had sleepy, bedroom eyes. Eyes so deep and mysterious a woman could easily get lost in them.

"I'm glad to hear that, because it took a lot of work tracking you down." His eyes bore down on her, robbing her of speech. "When you didn't return my calls, I didn't know what to think. Thought maybe you were avoiding me."

Yasmin laughed. It was either that or confirm his suspicions.

"Nice setup you got here," Rashawn said, noticing the framed diplomas, leather furniture and flower-filled vases. A saltwater aquarium filled with vibrantly colored fish and seashells sat against the far wall. The fish tank gave the otherwise ordinary room a much-needed punch of color. "I just bought a house in Clearwater. Maybe you can help me decorate."

Locking a smile into place, she leaned against her desk. The man had a killer voice. It was heavy with masculinity and touched with just the right amount of sensuality. Getting rid of Rashawn wouldn't be easy, but her last session of the day was about to start and she wanted to read over Mr. Gallagher's file. "I wish we could talk further, but I'm expecting my next client any minute now. It's his first time here and I want to be prepared when he arrives."

"Cool. Don't mind me." Rashawn stepped back, stretched out on the tan-colored couch and crossed his legs at the ankles. "Do what you have to do. I'll wait right here until you're ready."

"You're not Brody Gallagher."

"I know, his assistant made the appointment on my behalf."

"I see." Yasmin swallowed. She could do this. She was a trained professional, equipped to help clients resolve their personal issues and achieve self-awareness. It didn't matter that Rashawn had a dreamy voice and rippling muscles. This was business and Yasmin refused to let anything stand in the way of doing her job. "I need a few minutes to get myself together and then we can begin."

He closed his eyes and folded his hands across his chest. "Like I said, Doc, take as much time as you need."

Yasmin was behind her desk, gathering assessment forms, when there was a knock on the door. "Come in," she called, glancing at Rashawn, who was still lounging on the sofa.

Her assistant came in, an apologetic look on her face. Niobie Slade had been with her from the first day she had opened the doors of A Better Way Counseling Services three years earlier, and though the twenty-three-year-old single mom still had a lot to learn, Yasmin could always count on her to be affable and efficient.

"Yes, what is it?" she asked, trying to squelch her frustration. Niobie had a penchant for see-through tops, miniskirts and stilettos and, though Yasmin had spoken to her at length just last week about her wardrobe, she had shown up today in a getup straight out of a music video. If it weren't for all the work that had to be done for the fund-raiser, Yasmin would have sent her home. The slinky tomato-red dress was a soft, lightweight material but looked very expensive. Yasmin liked it, but not on Niobie. Her assistant was literally busting out of it. Her breasts were on display like a Ferrari in a showroom and the sides bunched up in layers when she walked. The outfit was clearly intended for a woman with height and curves and Niobie was short on one and had too much of the other.

"Sorry to disturb you, but Ms. Dubois called from Pastries and Stuff Catering. They're booked the first Saturday in June, but when I explained it's a charity event for inner-city children, she said they could squeeze us in," Niobie explained, tucking a lock of golden-brown hair behind her ears. "The only catch is they can't decorate or provide servers. We'll have to take care of that ourselves."

"That's fine. I think it would be a nice touch if we had the kids serve the guests." Pleased that things were finally starting to fall into place, Yasmin said, "Did she leave a number where I can reach her?"

"Yes. She asked that you call by five and let her know either way."

"Great. Thanks."

"No problem." Niobie turned toward the door but stopped abruptly when she saw the man stretched out on the couch. A pudgy hand flew to her mouth. "Oh, my God! It's Rashawn Bishop!" The words came out muffled, but there was no mistaking her excitement. "I'm your biggest fan!"

Rashawn sat up and swung his legs out in front of him. Seven years ago he had been an amateur boxer with only a handful of fights under his belt. Winning the Golden Gloves and then placing well at nationals had catapulted him from obscurity into the local spotlight. And after his record improved to thirty-seven wins, his celebrity had grown and offers started rolling in. Better management, more exposure and a professional debut had soon followed. These days he was recognized more often than not, and he was receiving more and more female attention. Except from Yasmin Ohaji.

"Could you autograph something for my son? He's only seven but he already has dreams of becoming a boxer. Crazy, huh? I'm saving up so I can send Miles to one of those junior boxing camps. He's good and I'm not just saying that because I'm his mom."

Rashawn chuckled. "How about I swing by tomorrow and drop off an autographed picture for your boy?"

"That would be awesome!"

Yasmin cleared her throat, which snapped Niobie out of fan mode and into work mode. "Sorry for the interruption, Ms. Ohaji. If you need anything I'll be at my desk."

"Thank you, Niobie. That will be all."

Waving good-bye at Rashawn, she proceeded through the open door and shut it behind her. They could hear Niobie giggling, then the sound and her footsteps faded.

"I apologize for my assistant's behavior. It was—"

"No problem. I love meeting fans."

"You're a boxer? I don't watch a lot of sports but you must be pretty popular if people recognize you."

"I do all right."

"How long have you been boxing?"

"Since I was fifteen. I got decent grades but I was always

getting into trouble at school. My phys ed teacher took pity on me and started letting me hang out at his father's gym. I've been hooked on boxing ever since I threw my first punch."

Boxing was a violent, barbaric sport and Yasmin would never understand why someone would subject himself to such abuse. Shuffling the papers on her desk, she collected her clipboard and sat in the chair across from Rashawn. He could fill out the assessment sheets later. The clock was ticking and Yasmin didn't want him to feel short-changed. After all, he was paying a hundred and fifty dollars an hour. "What brings you here today, Mr. Bishop?"

"You, Dr. Ohaji. And please, call me Rashawn."

Chapter 3

Yasmin shifted in her chair, convinced the man sitting across from her liked making her sweat. Rashawn wasn't her only male client, but he had a way of looking at her that made her feel nauseated, dizzy and nervous all at the same time. The long, steady looks, the way he wet his lips and the naughty gleam in his eyes troubled her.

Shoving aside her trepidation of being alone in her office with a man with whom she shared a sheer, almost magnetic chemistry, Yasmin made notes on her client assessment sheet. "Our relationship is strictly a patient–doctor one, so let's stick to what brought you here and the issues you're dealing with in your life right now."

"Does that mean I can't ask you out again?"

Yasmin dodged the question. "Why don't you tell me about yourself?"

"You first."

"What would you like to know?"

"Tell me about your educational background."

No one had ever asked her that before. People from all walks of life came into A Better Way Counseling Services for her help, assuming everything they had heard about her was true. Yasmin didn't know if she should be impressed or offended by his request. "I graduated from the University of Miami with a degree in psychology, then got my master's degree in marriage and family therapy the following year."

"I bet you got good grades. You strike me as someone who wouldn't settle for anything but a perfect GPA."

Rashawn was right. Proud that she had coasted through her studies and made the dean's list four consecutive years, but not wanting to sound arrogant, Yasmin stuck to the facts. "After a brief stint working in a public health clinic, I finished graduate school and received my doctoral degree in clinical psychology."

"A savvy, young sister with a successful practice? Impressive."

Uneasy with the way he was staring at her, she said, "Thank you, but I'm sure you didn't come all this way to discuss my credentials. Let's talk about you."

"I'm single. Never been married. No children that I'm aware of. I'm a loving, sensitive brother searching for the right woman to spend my life with." Rashawn saw her eyes soften and chuckled lightly. Extending his arms along the couch, he said, "I'm just playing, Doc. But women love to hear that sensitive crap, don't they?"

Yasmin refused to be pulled into the conversation. Regardless of what he thought, this was not a two-way discussion. "Why don't we discuss your family history?"

"What do you want to know?"

"Tell me whatever you feel comfortable sharing."

"My mom raised me and my brothers by herself. My dad wasn't around much, so she shouldered most of the responsibility. I have three loudmouth brothers and I'm the oldest of the brood. They have girlfriends and kids and still live in the old neighborhood."

"What's your ethnic background?"

"Sounds like a personal question."

It was and Yasmin felt guilty for asking it. Her curiosity had gotten the best of her and she was blurring the lines between professional and personal interest. "You don't have to answer—"

"I'm just teasing, Doc." A humming sound came from inside his jeans pocket, but he ignored it. "I came to see you, so feel free to ask me anything. My mom's half black, a quarter white and a quarter Mexican, and my dad is Puerto Rican."

"That's quite a mix."

"I know. I'm always teasing her that she should work for the United Nations!"

Laughing, she loosened her grip on the clipboard. "And maybe you should be a comedian instead of a boxer."

"Then would you go out with me?"

Yasmin shied away from his gaze. If she wasn't careful, she'd succumb to the boxer's advances and destroy her credibility as a respectable therapist. "Do you have a relationship with your father?"

For the next half hour, Yasmin asked Rashawn about his upbringing, background and career. He was engaging, straightforward and humorous. Yasmin tried to remain unaffected by what he told her, but Rashawn was so easy to be with, when he asked her about growing up in South Africa, she spoke freely.

"My family came to the States when I was nine, but I still remember playing in the cornfields with my younger brother and sister. We lived in Duthasa, a remote village only accessible by car. It was tough living out there, away from the city and my relatives, but at a very young age I learned how to fish, how to climb peach trees and I could swim better than kids twice my age."

"When was the last time you went home?"

"I'm ashamed to say," she admitted, tapping her pen absently on her clipboard. "It's been almost ten years."

Rashawn shared what had led him to South Africa and Yasmin was so caught up in his story, she lost track of time. If Niobie hadn't buzzed with Ms. Dubois on line two, they would have continued talking.

"That went well," Rashawn said, watching Yasmin. She stood and adjusted her suit. Grinning mischievously, he imagined what was underneath the crisp polyester material. Something told him this therapist was going to be a tough woman to crack. But Rashawn loved a challenge, especially one with curves. "We should continue this conversation tomorrow night."

"You don't give up, do you?"

"I wouldn't be undefeated if I did."

Yasmin raised her eyebrows, her face the picture of doubt. He talked a good game, but he was no different than any of the other guys who hit on her. "Thanks for asking, but I'm not interested in going for dinner and a movie. It's become a cliché, don't you think?"

"No doubt. That's why I thought we'd do something original like drive down to the pier and spend the night checking out our great city on a boat. Ever been on the evening boat cruise?"

"No, I've always wanted to go but my fia—" Yasmin stopped herself midword. Returning to her desk, she fought the emotion crawling up her throat. Now was not the time to have an emotional breakdown. She had work to do and a charity fund-raiser to plan. Forcing a smile, Yasmin put a hand on the phone and said, "I hope you don't mind, but I really have to take this call."

"No problem. Do what you gotta do."

"I look forward to seeing you next week."

"That makes two of us. Bye, Doc." Rashawn strolled over to the door and tossed one last look over his shoulder before leaving.

Yasmin sat down on her chair. Closing her eyes, she took a moment to collect herself. Eric had been gone for over two years, but she felt guilty for lusting over another man. Life had been empty since her fiancé's death, but she was finally starting to feel like her old self. Work had filled the void Eric had left and now she was near the apex of her career. After only three years of business, A Better Way Counseling Services was flourishing. Yasmin had more work than she could handle, but she still couldn't shake the feeling that something was missing.

The memory of better days brought tears to Yasmin's eyes. Life with Eric. Nights at the symphony. Poetry readings at the Soul Café. Family barbecues. The night he had proposed. No, she wouldn't betray Eric's family or cause them any more pain. What would Eric's parents think if they knew she was dating? Her relationship with the Iwenofus was as important to her as her relationship with her own family.

They had lost their son and brother and she had promised to help them through the ordeal. Pushing aside all thoughts of dating Rashawn and overpowering feelings of guilt, Yasmin picked up the phone and said, "Ms. Dubois, I'm sorry to have kept you waiting."

Yasmin pulled her Volvo into the garage. Grabbing her purse off the passenger seat, she clicked the power lock button and entered the house through the side door. The elegant book- and art-filled home was in Carrollwood, an upper-middle-class neighborhood in north Tampa. Young executives and stay-at-home moms frequented the boutiques, specialty shops and five-star restaurants in the local plaza.

Flicking on lights as she strode through the main floor, she unbuttoned her blazer, shrugged it off and then draped it over one of the chairs at the kitchen table. Wanting their place to have a chic look, but not wanting to do the work herself, Imani had insisted they hire an interior designer. The sisters had sat down with renowned decorator Essence Gilbert-Clark, told her what they wanted and left their house in her hands. The end result was a stylish, urban decor with low-hanging ceiling lights, large suede area rugs and rich, vibrant paint. The open-concept kitchen, like the rest of the house, had walnut-stained flooring and plenty of bay windows ushering in natural light. Maple cupboards tinted in sable brown, granite countertops and dainty glass chairs accented the wide, luxurious space. Beyond the kitchen were a half bathroom and laundry room that led to the heated double garage.

Opening the fridge, Yasmin selected a bottle of her favorite wine. Once the pinot blanc was uncorked, she poured herself a glass, opened the back door and stepped outside onto the patio. Since Eric's death, she had found herself more appreciative of the beauty of the great outdoors. The fresh air, the stars, the gentle passing of the night. It was in these quiet moments that Yasmin did the most thinking. Sitting down on a wicker chair, she propped her feet up on an ottoman and slowly sipped her drink.

Yasmin spotted *Anna Karenina* on the table, but didn't reach for it. Tonight she just wanted to be alone with her thoughts. The extra hours she had put in at the office after quitting time had been well spent. The fifth annual Parkland Community Center Charity Fund-raiser was starting to come together. It had taken some convincing, but Yasmin had booked the caterer, wrangled up a five-piece orchestra and organized a decorating and cleanup crew. There were eighty confirmed guests and, if they wanted to break even, they had to sell another forty tickets. All she needed now was a celebrity emcee. Last year, P. Diddy had been scheduled to appear, but a snowstorm in New York had prevented him from attending. It had been a huge letdown, but the music mogul later sent a donation and enough Sean John T-shirts for all of the children at the community center.

This year's fund-raiser had to be a success. The well-being of a hundred inner-city children and their families was at stake. If she wanted to draw more attention to the event, she had to find a celebrity guest. Nothing attracted people to an event like an actor. Or a singer. Or an athlete.

Yasmin tilted her head to the right, an idea taking shape in her mind. There was someone she could ask. Someone popular enough to draw a huge crowd and raise thousands of dollars for the center. A man so charismatic he would make female guests swoon and male guests cheer. Rashawn Bishop was a hometown boy who'd made good, and that was a story anyone could admire. The only questions now were whether he would do it and what it would take.

"Hey, girl."

Yasmin turned at the sound of her sister's voice. Imani stepped onto the patio, the bottle of pinot blanc at her lips. "What are you doing home? Shouldn't you be at Dean's?" Yasmin asked.

"He had to work late so I decided to come home and catch up on some work."

"I see."

"Did you have a good day?"

"You mean before or after you reamed me out?"

Imani plunked down on the chair beside Yasmin. Her long legs poked out from underneath her money-green wrap dress, which emphasized her small bust and size-six waist. Kicking off her heels, she crossed her legs and adopted a matter-of-fact attitude. "You have no right to be mad at me. *You* blew off one of my biggest clients. Cecil Manning is not only poised to be our next mayor, he's making major moves in the real estate industry, as well. We have a solid business relationship and I'd like to keep it that way."

Yasmin took a deep breath and blew it out. When it came to her sister, she had no choice but to take the bitter with the sweet. She was annoyed with Imani, but decided not to speak on it. She had come out on the patio to clear her mind, not get into a discussion about that wimp Cecil. He had been calling her office nonstop since their blind date and had even gone as far as sending lavish bouquets of roses. Unlike Rashawn, he didn't have a creative bone in his body. Exploring the city by boat sounded romantic. Flowers? As clichéd as a box of chocolates on Valentine's Day.

Imani must have sensed her frustration, because she dropped the subject. "How are things coming along with the fund-raiser? I sold tickets to everyone in my office and all of the prospective buyers I met with today."

"Thanks. Things are going a lot better now that I've booked the entertainment and found a caterer."

"That's great. Have you found an emcee yet? I mentioned it to Cecil and he was more than happy to volunteer. He said—"

"I have someone in mind."

Imani took a swig from the wine bottle. "Really, who?"

"Ever heard of Rashawn Bishop?"

"That fine-ass boxer with the six-pack? Of course, who hasn't?"

"Me, I guess." Yasmin told her about what had happened at the Laurdel Lounge and his surprise visit to the clinic that afternoon. "He asked me out again. He said we could drive down to the pier and spend the night on one of those evening boat cruises."

"Damn, girl! Why didn't you tell me?" Imani asked, smacking her sister's leg. "I wouldn't be pushing Cecil on you if I knew you were interested in someone else."

"I'm not interested in Rashawn. I just want him to emcee the fund-raiser."

"You guys aren't going out?"

Yasmin shook her head. "I can't think about dating anyone until I'm over Eric."

"When does this self-imposed grief period end? It's been over two years and you've turned down every single guy who's asked you out. You need to jump-start your love life and maybe this Rashawn guy is the one to help you do it."

"Leave it alone, Imani. I'm not ready." Her eyes watered and everything went out of focus. "I need more time."

"Yassie, I know you loved Eric but who's to say there isn't someone else out there for you?"

When silence settled over the patio, Imani put the bottle of wine on the table, stood and headed back into the house. Returning with her laptop under her arm and a can of tuna and a spoon in the other, she said, "I know how much you like to look people up on Google, so let's check out this Rashawn guy together." While she waited for the computer to load, she opened the tuna and ate it straight out of the can.

Light flooded the patio as the computer came to life. Yasmin watched her sister type Rashawn's name into the search bar, convinced this late-night investigation wouldn't garner any useful information.

"Imani, don't waste your time. I'm not ready to start dating, and even if I was, it wouldn't be with someone like Rashawn

Bishop. He's pierced and tattooed and he's a boxer, for God's sake! He doesn't even have his college degree." Shifting in her chair, she averted her gaze. He was all wrong for her. He looked like a player, like the kind of man who lied, cheated and dogged women out. But, Yasmin knew that wasn't true. Rashawn had stood up for her and only a gentleman would do that.

"Bingo!" A picture of Rashawn, bare-chested and glistening, filled the eighteen-inch screen. His Web site was loaded with pictures, newspaper articles and had expensive, high-powered graphics. Imani leaned forward, her nose practically touching the monitor. She read his bio out loud and shared any information she thought would interest her. "I'd go ten rounds with him any day!"

Yasmin didn't doubt the truth of her sister's words. Imani was in a committed, long-term relationship, but her gutsy style and carefree spirit attracted men in droves. "And what about Dean? What would you tell him?"

"Please, he'd probably ask if he could watch!"

Yasmin laughed, her narrow shoulders shuddering. Imani and Dean took spontaneity to a whole new level. They'd tried it all, strip clubs, bondage, threesomes, and still managed to maintain a healthy, committed relationship. Yasmin would never advise a female client to fulfill her man's every wish or sexual fantasy, but Imani and Dean's arrangement worked for them, period.

Imani tapped a manicured nail on the screen. "According to his bio, he just turned twenty-seven. You found yourself a hot young boxer! Way to go, Sis!"

"I didn't know. I thought he was my age," she protested, peering at the computer screen. Yasmin never would have guessed he was five years younger. He was mature, responsible and had an air of authority about him. Definitely not the average twenty-something guy. "I don't care how old he is. Like I said, he's not my type."

"Don't be so quick to write him off, Yassie. You know my motto. Keep an open mind and jump at every opportunity that comes your way. Before meeting Dean, I went out with anyone who asked. Why not? It's a free meal, a chance to get dressed up, and half the time, decent conversation."

"I've never looked at it that way," Yasmin admitted. As usual, her sister had given her something to think about. No one said she had to marry the guy.

Imani turned away from the computer screen, the expression on her face a serious one. "Give it some thought, Yassie. You never know when love may come knocking."

Chapter 4

Parkland Community Center was located in downtown Tampa. Drug addicts and prostitutes frequented the area, often scoring crack across the street from where toddlers played. At-risk youth under eighteen enjoyed computer classes, tutoring, group and individual counseling and job-readiness training. The center consisted of conference rooms, learning centers, a cafeteria and a full-size gymnasium. Parkland Community Center was an integral part of the neighborhood, but the twenty-five-year old building was falling apart. The roof had pot-size cracks, concrete crumbled from the walls and the floors were colored with stains.

"It's huge in here," Rashawn commented, as he followed Niobie through the lobby. Staff and volunteers milled about, talking to kids and answering phones, and a group of people were watching Judge Mathias on the thirty-two-inch TV in the lounge area.

"Thanks for giving me a ride down here."

"No sweat." As promised, Rashawn had dropped by the office with an autographed picture for Niobie's son. Yasmin had left for the day, so when Niobie had suggested they go by the community center, where Miles was playing, Rashawn had agreed. He'd left the gym early and wasn't anxious to return.

"The kids are going to flip when they see you!"

Rashawn could hear laughter, children's voices and the sound of chairs scraping against the floor. They entered the learning center and found teens arm wrestling, a handful of kids playing board games and girls braiding hair.

"Mom!" A chunky boy ran across the room and threw himself into Niobie's arms. "Did you bring me something?"

"You know I did, baby." Niobie smoothed a hand over his plump face before reaching into her purse and pulling out a king-size chocolate bar.

"Thanks, Mom!" He ripped off the wrapping paper and took a bite. Chewing, he bobbed his head to the beat of his swallows.

The last thing the child needed was candy, but Rashawn kept his observations to himself. He wasn't a single parent and he didn't want Niobie to think he was judging her. As a young mother, she probably got her fair share of criticism. Her son was cute, in a Nutty Professor kind of way, but it was obvious he needed more exercise and less junk food. To his amazement, the seven-year-old demolished the candy bar in three bites.

It wasn't until Miles was finished eating that he noticed the man standing beside his mom. "Who are you?"

Yanking her son to her chest, Niobie cupped a hand over his mouth. "Miles, don't be silly. You know who that is. It's Rashawn "the Glove" Bishop."

Squirming out of his mom's arms, he said, "Are you a basketball player? Do you know T-Mac? He's my favorite."

"No, I'm a boxer. Your mom told me you want to be a boxer, too."

"No way! I'm going to be a race-car driver!"

Niobie's laugh was tinged with anxiety. "Kids. One day he wants to be a boxer, the next day he wants to be a race car driver."

Rashawn had a feeling this trip to the community center had little to do with Miles and everything to do with Niobie. This wasn't the first time a woman had feigned interest in his career to get close to him. Most of the time he was flattered, but what Niobie had done cool wasn't cool.

"Hey, it's the Glove!" shouted a squeaky voice.

Within seconds, Rashawn had a group of children around him, asking for handshakes, autographs and money. Laughing, he opened his wallet and handed a fifty-dollar bill to the tallest kid in the group. "Run up the block and get everyone a fruit smoothie."

"Yay!"

"Thanks, champ!"

"You're the best!"

Children raced out of the room behind the boy with the money.

"That was a nice thing to do," Niobie said, flashing a toothy smile. She coiled a hand around his arm like a python. "Why don't I give you a quick tour while we wait for Miles and the others to come back?"

"Sure, why not?"

Niobie showed Rashawn the facility, introduced him to staff, volunteers and parents and told him interesting pieces of information about the people who worked there, the counseling sessions Yasmin oversaw and why the fund-raiser was so important to the families who frequented the community center.

"How much do you guys need to raise?"

"I don't know the exact figure, but I'd guess about twenty-five thousand. The center receives support from local churches and other outreach programs, but we never have enough volunteers or supplies. Not to mention the extensive renovations that need to be done. The planning committee is hoping we raise enough to…"

Boisterous applause drowned out the rest of her sentence.

"Sounds like something's going on in the gym."

"It's always crazy in there when the teenagers take on staff."

"Why aren't they playing out on the field?" he wondered out loud. It was a sunny day and he couldn't understand why kids would want to be cooped up inside. Rain was expected tomorrow and most residents were taking advantage of the weather while it lasted. Beyond the community center doors, people were gardening, mowing their lawns and clearing the trash off their properties.

"Too many needles and drug paraphernalia."

Shaking his head, Rashawn opened the door and allowed Niobie to precede him into the gymnasium. Sprinting full speed toward the soccer net in a blue tank top, shorts, kneepads and sneakers, was Dr. Yasmin Ohaji. She kicked the ball and spectators cheered the impending goal. The robust goalie blocked the shot and the soccer ball sailed through the air and smacked Yasmin hard in the face. The blow stunned her temporarily, but once the ball hit the ground, she was off and running again.

Propping a foot behind him against the wall, Rashawn crossed an arm across his chest. Smiling broadly, he watched Yasmin move effortlessly around the court. The therapist was unlike anyone he had ever met. Not only did she leave every man she passed breathless, she stood up for herself, demanded respect and had one hell of a front kick. Rashawn knew a lot of professional women, but he didn't know any who played soccer with such tenacity. Yasmin was competitive, aggressive and seemed bent on scoring a goal before the time on the scoreboard ran out.

"Ready to finish the rest of the tour?"

Caught up in his thoughts, he'd forgotten that Niobie was standing beside him.

"Maybe later." Rashawn wasn't leaving until he saw how the match played out. Yasmin and her teammates had five minutes to tie the game and something told him she would be the one to score the goal her team needed.

Niobie chatted beside him, but Rashawn wasn't listening. He was focused on Yasmin and when she shot down the court toward the goal, he cheered along with the crowd. She kicked the ball to a lanky man, who outran his defender, dodged the goalie and scored in the open net. The buzzer sounded, signaling the end of the game and, once the teams had shaken hands, the audience filed out of the gym.

Niobie touched a hand to his forearm. "We should go. I'm sure Miles and the others are back now."

"You go on. I'm going to hang back."

"Are you sure?"

"Positive," he said, momentarily pulling his attention away from the court. Appreciative of the time she had spent showing him around and introducing him to the staff, he said, "Thanks for the tour. See you later?"

"Ah, okay, bye."

Rashawn caught Yasmin's eye. Her sweat-drenched T-shirt clung to her body, outlining each and every luscious curve. She would look good in a brown paper bag, he speculated, admiring her thick, childbearing hips. Clapping his hands, he gave her a hearty smile. "You got one hell of a kick, Doc. Who knew a therapist could play soccer like a pro? You're going to have to teach me some of your fancy footwork."

Smiling, she smoothed the base of her ponytail. "Don't let the business suits fool you. I played volleyball, soccer and basketball throughout high school."

"I thought you said you didn't like sports?"

"No, I said I didn't *watch* sports. I'd much rather play than watch, especially football. It's a great feeling chasing someone down and tackling them."

"Damn, Doc! I'm scared of you." His eyes were wide with admiration, conveying just how impressed he was. "And for the record, you can tackle me anytime."

He licked his lips and Yasmin felt her legs go weak. Not only was Rashawn handsome, he had a likeable nature and a winning smile. If she could stop drooling over him long enough to speak, she could ask him to emcee the fund-raiser. This was the perfect time. He was in a good mood and it was unlikely he would turn her down, especially once she showed him all the repairs that needed to be done. "Are you going to be here for a while? Once I get changed I'd love to give you a tour."

Rashawn thought of telling her that Niobie had beat her to it, but decided against it. Quality time spent with Yasmin would help her see him in another light. Based on his initial observations, he sensed she was an optimistic, fun-loving woman who knew how to take care of herself. He liked that. Soft on the inside but tough on the outside. He loved the rise and fall of her voice, the femininity of her laugh and the quickness of her smile. They would get along great. All he had to do was show her he posed no harm. If she could see that he was a good guy, with no ulterior motives, she would say yes when he asked her out.

"I'd like that. But don't change," he said, his gaze sliding down the slant of her hips. "I like your shorts."

A tiny, frizzy-haired black woman in a crumpled apron interrupted their conversation. "There you are, Yasmin. I've been looking all over for you!"

"What is it, Ms. McClure?" A gentle and caring woman, Melba McClure planned and prepared all of the meals at the community center and donated more time than any other volunteer. A retired postal worker, she was the grandmother of six, dated regularly and was a stern but loving presence. "I thought you'd be in the kitchen getting things ready for dinner."

"I was until Mr. Santos came down with a fever. I begged him to stay until the end of the six o'clock session but he could hardly stand. His wife came to pick him up a few minutes ago."

Yasmin's face crumpled. "B-b-but he's facilitating the M.O.I. session tonight! Who's going to lead the group now that he's gone?"

"I've called and left messages for Walter, Tarik and Emilio, but I haven't heard back from any of them."

Yasmin knew Melba was trying to help, but she secretly hoped her calls weren't returned. Walter was a pleasant middle-aged man who spoke in a dull monotone and was known to put the kids to sleep, Tarik was a recovering drug addict, fresh out of rehab, and Emilio flirted relentlessly with the female staff. No, she would just have to chair the meeting herself. "Thanks for giving me the heads-up, Melba. Let the boys in the Men of Initiative program know that—"

"Men of Initiative? What's that?" Rashawn asked.

"It's a new program designed to get teenage boys off the

street," she explained. "The purpose is to help kids between the ages of thirteen and eighteen develop a positive sense of self and to set high education goals. Tonight's was supposed to be an open forum, basically a question-and-answer period where the boys could speak freely about the struggles they're having at school, at home and on the streets."

"I don't mind helping out," he said, directing his comment to Yasmin.

Melba eyed him warily. "Normally we do an extensive background check before we let anyone around the kids, but since we're understaffed and Yasmin will be supervising, I guess it would be okay. What's your name, son?"

"Rashawn."

"You're not a drug dealer are you?"

"No, ma'am."

"Don't smoke pot, do you?"

"No."

"Do you abuse or exploit women?"

"No. Never."

Melba stared into his eyes to judge his sincerity. Confident he was telling the truth, she said, "Don't mind me, Rashawn. I'm just mighty careful about who I let around these boys. As you can see we're short-staffed and we could really use your help." Clapping her hands together, her eyes expanded to the size of cue balls. "This is going to be swell! I can feel it in my bones. Why don't you follow me to the kitchen? We'll get some food into you before the session starts. Do you like red beans and rice?"

Yasmin glanced at her watch, amazed that a five-minute discussion about respect could last three-quarters of an hour. At the back of the room, away from the group, she wrote a brief outline of the goals, objectives and purpose of the Men of Initiative program. The more teens who joined the program, the more government funding the center would receive.

Counting the number of teenagers seated in the semicircle,

she noticed the intense expression on each young face. Rashawn easily held the attention of his young audience. Not only did the man have a way with women, he appealed to children and teenagers, as well. Affable and laid-back, he had the type of personality people took to immediately. In the cafeteria, kids had crammed onto his bench and more than half of the adults had made their way over to chitchat. Yasmin had sat across from the charismatic boxer, in the hopes of discussing the charity fund-raiser, but every time she opened her mouth, they were interrupted by an adoring fan. Eating dinner with Rashawn had been an eye-opener. Strangers clamored for his attention and made utter fools of themselves just to have ten seconds of his time.

Yasmin watched him now, sitting in the middle of the circle. His arms dangled between his legs and he had a relaxed, carefree expression on his face. His body language suggested he was open, bare, willing to share himself with the world. And he was.

Yasmin had learned some shocking truths about Rashawn Bishop, facts that further underlined just how different they were. His father had abandoned the family when he was five, his mother had raised him and his three brothers single-handedly and had struggled to provide food and shelter. But it was the story of his life on the streets that had left her slack-jawed. He'd stolen cars, went joyriding with his crew and had a lengthy rap sheet by the time he was thirteen.

Tate, one of her favorite kids at the center, lifted his hand and waited for the discussion to die down before he spoke. "Did you ever sling rock?"

Rashawn locked eyes with Yasmin. He couldn't read the expression on her face. Trepidation fell upon him. Was she regretting her decision to let him lead the session? Or disappointed about what she had learned about him? This was not how she was supposed to find out about his past, but he couldn't let this opportunity to share with these teenagers pass him by. If Yasmin couldn't appreciate the fact that he'd changed his life and made something of himself, then she wasn't the right woman for him anyway. "I didn't sell dope, but I used to run errands for the local drug dealer. I'm not proud of it, but I did what I had to do to survive. I was the oldest and had to help my mom take care of my brothers. Everyone else was doing it and I wanted to fit in with my crew. They were my family."

Nods and murmurs of assent filled the room.

"In tenth grade I discovered boxing and that changed my life for the better. Boxing was my ticket out of the 'hood and I took advantage of all the opportunities afforded to me."

"But what if you ain't got no talent?" asked an unsmiling kid with buck teeth. "What if all you know how to do is jack cars and beat down punks for what they got?"

"I don't believe that, Chaz. Everyone's good at something."

The boy shook his head. "Not me. I hate school, I suck at sports and I don't get along with my step-dad."

"Ever tried boxing, martial arts or wrestling?"

"Naw, that's not my thing."

"How do you know unless you try? You look strong, you could probably be one hell of a wrestler. "

He shrugged a shoulder. "I ain't got money for shit like that."

"Chaz, you can come by the Boxing Institute of Champions and work out with me whenever you want." Standing, Rashawn said, "Anyone else want to get in shape, look good and impress the honeys?"

Chuckles broke out.

"If you're interested in a serious workout, meet me at the gym tomorrow at three. If you're late, I'm starting without you."

One by one, participants stood and approached Rashawn. Some of the younger kids even hugged him. Conversation was put on hold while tables were returned to their rightful place and chairs were stacked against the wall.

As the teens trickled out into the hall, Yasmin gathered her things. She wanted to talk to Rashawn privately but he was speaking to Tate and Brandon. Remembering that she had wanted to leave a note for the health nurse regarding the new date for the next health and nutrition clinic, she exited the room.

"You're not leaving without me, are you, Doc?"

Yasmin slowed her pace and did a half turn.

"What'd you think of the session?" he asked, as they continued down the hall.

"I think you really connected with the kids."

"I don't know about all that, but I hope they give some thought to what I said. Far too many kids are getting killed and it's up to us to put a stop to it."

"I couldn't agree more." Deciding she would call the health nurse in the morning, she tucked a hand into her pocket and pulled out her keys. Rashawn pushed open the door, and her shoulder brushed his chest as she passed by. Yasmin felt like she'd been zapped with a stun gun. Her pulse quickened. She glanced at Rashawn and was surprised to find him watching her. He must have felt it, too, she decided, tearing her gaze away.

Outside, the sky was clear. It was quiet on Keeler Street, but Yasmin knew from experience that could change at any minute. A week earlier, a father of three had been mugged on his way to his night job. Luckily, some of the center's volunteers had heard the commotion and come to his aid. Thanks to their bravery, he hadn't been seriously injured.

"Bye, Dr. Ohaji."

Yasmin turned at the sound of her name. A group of boys were standing on the curb, talking. Broken bottles, cigarette butts and food wrappers littered the sidewalk. Tomorrow she would have to ask the caretaker to clean up the mess. Waving, she smiled at the teens. "Bye, boys. Get home safe."

"Catch you later, Bishop."

"Bye, champ," another hollered.

"See you next Thursday!"

Yasmin glanced at Rashawn. "You're coming back?"

"Sure, why not?"

"I don't know, I just thought this was a one-time thing. Mr. Santos should be back by the end of the week."

"That's cool. Then he can lead the discussion and I can listen in. I promised the kids I'd be back and I always keep my word."

Rashawn motioned toward the silver Volvo S80 parked beside his Mustang. "Is that you?"

"Yeah."

"Figured as much."

"What's that supposed to mean?"

Rashawn chuckled. "It's safe, practical and probably gets great gas mileage."

"You're right, it does." Yasmin didn't like him teasing her, especially when his car was decades old. She guessed the coral-blue two-seater was a late seventies model, and though it was in pristine condition with chrome wheels, leather seats and flashy front and rear spoilers, it was still old. "Do you have a minute? There's something I've been meaning to ask you."

"Go ahead, ask away," he told her, leaning against the bumper of his car.

"How would you feel about emceeing the charity fund-raiser? I know this is short notice, but all my calls to other celebrities have been ignored. Your involvement could mean hundreds, if not thousands, of dollars raised for the center and—"

"Oh, I get it, I'm sloppy seconds. You couldn't get Steve Harvey or Cedric the Entertainer so you decided to ask me."

Yasmin was caught so off-guard by his remark, she didn't notice the twinkle in his eyes. "No, no, it's nothing like that," she insisted, raising her voice. "If I had known how popular you are around Tampa, I would have contacted you first."

"Sure, sure, Doc."

"It's the truth."

"Why don't we discuss this tomorrow when we have more time? There's a boat leaving the pier at seven-thirty." Rashawn leaned forward, his breath against her ear. "Let me take you out. You already know I'll take good care of you."

Yasmin resisted the urge to smile. The reference to how they'd met wasn't lost on her. He was her knight in shining armor and she would always be grateful for what he had done that night at the Laurdel Lounge. Courage was damn sexy, and he personified the word in more ways then one. "Now's not a good time," she told him. "I have a lot of work to do for the fund-raiser and very little time. The program needs to be planned and I have silent auction prizes to organize."

"We'll brainstorm together. I've done this sort of thing before and it's really not as hard as you're making it sound." Rashawn hoped Yasmin couldn't see his nose growing. Aside from helping plan his mom's surprise birthday party last year, he had never planned a major event like a charity fund-raiser. How hard could it be? As long as there was food, wine and music, it would be great.

"Why don't we meet at the clinic?" she suggested, her tone light. He was flirtatious and straightforward, but in an unexpectedly disarming way. Going on a cruise was much too romantic and there would be other couples. The last thing Yasmin wanted was to be seduced by him in the presence of other people. Pleased that she had come up with a suitable alternative, she said, "I'll order in some sandwiches from the deli up the block."

"No offense, Doc, but your office is kinda stuffy. I want to go somewhere we can kick back and relax."

"I'd be a lot more comfortable at my office."

"Do you have a little old lady living inside you?" he joked, a grin on his lips. "If it'll make you feel better we'll call it a business dinner, okay?"

"I still don't think it's a good idea."

"I do," he countered, his eyes beating down at her with the intensity of the sun. "I read somewhere that Puerto Rico ranks as one of the happiest places on earth. Most people live below the poverty line, the crime rate is ridiculously high and the average family survives on just pennies a day, but you know why they're so happy?"

Intrigued, Yasmin asked, "No, why?"

"The motto in Puerto Rico is simple, 'Don't take life too seriously. Eat, drink and be merry!'" Signaling the end of the discussion he strolled confidently over to the driver's-side door. "I'll pick you up at six."

"No!" Yasmin coughed to clear the panic in her voice. There was no reason to overreact. This was a business date. Sure, they were going to be surrounded by candlelight, champagne and soft music, but that didn't mean she had to get caught up in the magic of it all. "I'll just meet you there."

Grinning, he slid into his car, revved the engine and backed out of the space. "See you tomorrow, Doc."

Chapter 5

Yasmin spotted Rashawn as soon as she pulled into the Bahia Mar Dock. It was hard to miss him. He was surrounded by a bevy of attractive women. All weaves galore and heavy makeup, the buxom quartet resembled high-class call girls. Not wanting to give him the wrong idea about tonight, Yasmin had selected a loose, flowing blouse, slim-fitted pants and sandals. But as she watched stylishly-dressed couples exit their vehicles and head toward the boat, she had second thoughts about her conservative attire.

Once the car was locked, she walked briskly through the parking lot and joined the throng of sightseers. A slight breeze rose and with it the scent of spring flowers. Dark, somber clouds drifted peacefully across the sky. The air was thick with rain and mingled with the perfume of the sea.

Yasmin saw Rashawn glance around the harbor. His admirers were trying fruitlessly to hold his attention, but his mind was obviously somewhere else. He probably thought she'd stood him up. He wouldn't be far from wrong. The idea had crossed her mind more than once, but blowing him off wouldn't be right, especially since she needed his help. He hadn't agreed to host the fund-raiser yet, but she was confident he would.

Rashawn's face broke out into a grin when he spotted her. Mumbling good-bye to the cosmetology students, he strolled down the pier toward his date. A flabby Hispanic man acknowledged him, but Rashawn didn't stop. Tonight wasn't about meeting fans or signing autographs; it was about spending time with Yasmin.

"You're late," he said, when they were a few feet apart.

"I know. I'm sorry."

His eyes gleamed. "I was about to come looking for you. Thought maybe you weren't going to show."

Yasmin looked at the beddable and willing women standing behind him. "I'm sure you would have been in good hands."

"Hardly." He leaned in and whispered, "They're not my type. I like sophisticated women who know how to leave things to the imagination."

"…Said the man with the harem," she teased, raising her eyebrows.

Rashawn took her hand, pressed it to his chest and said, "Did you feel that?"

"Feel what?"

"My heart skipped a beat."

Yasmin melted like an ice cube in the sun. Rashawn definitely had a way with words. On the drive over, she had told herself nothing was going to happen between them, but deep down she knew something would. Rashawn wasn't her type, but she was drawn to him.

It was his sensual bedroom tone, his sexy swagger and his killer smile. Or maybe it was the fact that he couldn't be more different from the men she usually dated. Eric had been a plastic surgeon, owned a lavish six-bedroom home and had a fleet of luxury cars. Rashawn was from the inner city, made his money beating his opponents to a pulp and drove a Mustang. But God help her if she didn't want him. When he was around, she had that walk-on-water feeling and was short of breath. Like now.

"You're lookin' good, Doc. Real good."

"Thanks. I hope it's not cold tonight because I forgot my jacket in the car."

His eyes sparkled with lust. "Don't worry. I'll keep you warm," he promised, admiring her classy outfit. Rashawn liked how Yasmin had a different look every time he saw her. She kept him guessing and it didn't matter if she was wearing a dress, a business suit or gym shorts, she always looked sexy.

"You know what we should do?"

"No, what?"

"Kiss now, so we're not thinking about it all night." Resting a hand on her lower back, he gently pulled her toward him. A whiff of her perfume tickled his nose and elicited images of them making love on a bed of roses. "One kiss, that's all I want, but if you'd like to go further, I won't stop you."

Desire zipped up her spine. A wave of excitement swept over her as she leveled a hand over her stomach. His confidence bordered on arrogance but made him even more appealing. "I, um…"

"All aboard!"

The gray-haired captain stood at the portal of the boat, his hands propped on his hips like Long John Silver. Behind him was a smiling crew of both male and female stewards.

Rashawn broke the silence with a soft chuckle. "Looks like that kiss is gonna have to wait until later. Ready to go inside, Doc?"

"Can I interest you in a Bahama Breeze?"

Rashawn glanced up at the waiter. "Sure, what's in it?"

"Coconut rum, pineapple juice and a splash of tequila. It's our most popular drink," he finished, setting the cocktails down on the table.

Yasmin tasted it. "This is delicious."

"Yeah, keep them coming!"

The server pulled out his pen and notepad. "Do you need a few more minutes to look over the menu or have you decided on the ribs-and-chicken buffet?"

Rashawn and Yasmin spoke at once, drawing a light chuckle

from the twenty-something waiter. "I'll give you guys a couple of minutes to decide."

When he departed, Rashawn put his menu off to the side. "You've gotta have the buffet. Ribs, chicken and three-cheese lasagna. It's a meat lover's paradise."

"I'm a vegetarian. You'll be picking me up off the floor if I eat all that food."

"For real? What made you come to that decision?"

"When I was ten I saw a pig slaughtered on my grandfather's farm. I quit eating meat that same day."

"That's brutal. You don't mind if I have the buffet, do you?"

"Of course not. Don't worry, I'm not one of those vegetarians who make meat-eaters feel bad."

"Good, 'cause I've been dreaming about ribs all week!"

While they waited for the server to return, they discussed the Men of Initiative program. Conversation came easily and they shared the same opinion on many prevailing issues. Politics, like religion and sex, weren't topics to discuss on a first date, but when the discussion turned to the state of black America, Rashawn couldn't resist weighing in.

"Police brutality, racial profiling and the AIDS epidemic in the African-American community are topics that should be addressed by all of the presidential candidates but will probably be ignored. That said, I still think Senator Obama has a good chance of becoming president," he told her, picking up a piece of rib with his hands. "Most people would rather see a black man in power than leave the country in the hands of a woman."

Yasmin nodded. "You're right. The United States might be the land of the free and the home of the brave, but when it comes to equality for women, we lag behind less prosperous nations."

"We like to think we're an elite superpower and that other countries should learn from us, but it's often the other way around. Finland, Mozambique and the Philippines all have female presidents, but we've never had one in our two-hundred-and-thirty-year history."

"Is that how old America is?" she asked. Yasmin was surprised that Rashawn knew who all of the political candidates were and the pressing issues dividing the country.

"Someone needs a refresher course on American history," he teased.

Yasmin hid her frown behind her napkin. This was mind-blowing. If she had been standing up, she would have toppled over onto the floor. She had her doctorate. She had graduated at the top of her class. She should be the one schooling him, not the other way around. "How do you know so much about history and politics?"

"I'm a news junkie. When I was a kid my mom worked at the local TV station and me and my brothers used to hang out there after school." Rashawn tasted his drink, a pensive expression on his face. "Mom always dreamed of working her way up from the mailroom and being the first woman of color in the anchor chair, but it never happened."

"Do you see your dad now?"

"From time to time. Now that my career's taken off, he comes around a lot more."

"And that doesn't bother you?"

Rashawn drew a deep breath before answering. "Hugo was only nineteen when my mom got pregnant with me. He was a high school dropout and didn't know the first thing about taking care of a baby. No one ever taught him what it means to be a man, so how could I blame him for the mistakes he made?"

After she had peppered him with more personal questions for what seemed like hours, but wasn't more than a few minutes, he said, "This feels like another therapy session!"

They laughed together. The ambiance of the ship, coupled with the starlit sky and the stunning view spread before them in all directions, made for a romantic setting.

"I can't believe how beautiful this boat is. I never imagined it would be this nice," Yasmin confessed, glancing around the dining room. Upon entering the boat, they'd followed the other passengers to the upper deck. There they'd sipped wine, admired the collection of skyscrapers and vivid blue-green water and listened to the gentle lapping of the waves. After meeting the captain and his crew, they retired to the dining room and found a table near the piano. A short, stocky man had been playing since the ship had set sail, but now the raspy voice of Michael Bolton was purring from the overhead speakers.

"I brought you another helping of ribs, sir."

"You must have read my mind!"

The waiter replaced Rashawn's empty plate and set down one heaping with ribs, chicken and potatoes. "Enjoy," he said, before departing.

Shaking her head in awe, she finished what was left of her cocktail. The heat from the fireplace wrapped itself around her, warming her body. "You eat a lot. I figured you'd have a very strict diet, being a boxer and all."

"My workouts run anywhere from four to six hours." Rashawn picked up a slab of ribs and ripped the meat off the bones, leaving nothing behind. "I have to eat enough so I have the energy to train. I snack during the day and load up on carbohydrates and protein in the evening." He devoured the plate of food in minutes and when the waiter returned told him it was the best meal he'd had all day.

Yasmin watched Rashawn over the rim of her glass. His deep, masculine voice, his soft eyes and athletic physique made her mouth water, but he was more than just a handsome face. He was interesting, entertaining and just plain old funny.

"I'm gonna have to skip my morning workout because there's no way I can run five miles after eating three plates of ribs."

"Do you train every day?"

"Yup, except for Christmas and Easter. My mom'll kill me if I miss mass." He rested back in his chair, watching her. "I'm having a good time."

"Me, too," she confessed, surprised by her admission.

"I'd like to see you again. If you're free tomorrow night we could go bowling or shoot pool or something."

"I can't, I'm going to a wine-tasting party."

"A wine-tasting party?" he repeated, clearly amused. "What's that all about?"

"Once a month, my friends and I get together and sample various wines. It's really an excuse to gossip and get drunk, but we like to think it's cultured and high-class."

Rashawn liked beer better than wine, but he would sip Merlot and discuss fashion trends if it meant spending more time with Yasmin. If he was going to pull this off, he'd have to educate himself on the different flavors, textures and aromas. He'd stay up all night if he had to. It was a small price to pay for having another date with this beautiful appealing woman. "Is this thing just for the ladies or can fellas come, too?"

"It's a good mix of singles and couples. Actually, my best friend is hosting tomorrow. She just moved into her new place so it's more of a housewarming party."

"Mind if I tag along?"

Yasmin didn't know how she felt about Rashawn meeting her friends. Katherine could be a snob sometimes and her pretentious, upper-middle-class colleagues weren't any better. But how could she tell Rashawn she didn't want him to come because she was scared he wouldn't fit in? Sure, he was well read, but what did he know about Wall Street, trust funds and vacationing in the south of France?

Rashawn must have sensed her inner turmoil, because he said, "Two dates in one week is too much, huh? Getting sick of me already, Doc?"

"No, no, it's nothing like that. I want you to come, I just don't think you'll have a good time. We're a pretty boring group and—"

"Let me be the judge of that. Besides, it's not about anyone else, it's about being with you." His eyes revealed nothing, but there was no mistaking the heat in his voice.

Yasmin didn't know what she was doing. Inviting Rashawn to the party was a bad idea. He was a twenty-seven-year-old boxer from the inner city. What would he talk about with a room full of executives, doctors and millionaires who lived in gated communities? But instead of dissuading him from coming, she heard herself say, "It starts at seven o'clock."

"Cool." Wiping his mouth with his napkin, he pushed back his chair. "Do you want anything else?"

Her stomach rebelled at the thought of more food. Yasmin stole a glance at the dessert table. Guests were sampling cakes, pies and other high-calorie treats. The strawberry shortcake looked tempting, but Yasmin wouldn't be able to forgive herself if she overindulged. The fund-raiser was weeks away and she had a designer gown to fit into. "No, thanks. I've had enough for one night."

"We should walk off some of this food." Rashawn punctuated his sentence with a smile. He wanted to be alone with her. Her eyes sparkled under the soft lights and the more time they spent together, the more she impressed him. "How about we take a stroll around the deck?"

"But we haven't discussed the charity fund-raiser yet."

"No, problem. We'll talk outside." Rashawn directed his eyes to the back of the room. "Let's get out of here. Rhythmically challenged people are starting to dance."

Giggling, Yasmin allowed him to help her to her feet. Swayed by his smile, she took the hand he offered. It was a simple gesture, but one that made her feel warm and tingly inside. Eric thought hand-holding was juvenile. According to him, professional people didn't act "common," but being this close to Rashawn was as natural as breathing.

Brushing past a burly man in a high cowboy hat, Yasmin cast a bemused glance at the couples "dancing" to Miami Sound Machine. "You sure you don't want to stay? I'd love to see you out on the dance floor."

Rashawn grinned. "And I'd love to have you in my arms."

Chapter 6

"It's a beautiful night," Yasmin said, as they exited the side doors. Darkness swallowed them, but the light from the moon illuminated their faces. Their eyes aligned. Then Rashawn released her hand and slipped an arm around her waist. It felt strange being so close so soon, but she didn't pull away. His touch was warm, welcome and made her feel soft and pretty. It had been months since she'd felt that way.

"I'm surprised there aren't more people out here."

"Would you believe I paid everyone to stay away?"

Yasmin laughed. "I wouldn't put it past you."

"It's great that we're alone. We can discuss the fund-raiser without any interruptions." He held her tighter. "What else needs to be done and how can I help?"

Just when Yasmin was ready to write him off, he surprised her. He really did care about the kids at the community center. She widened the smile that had already found its way onto her lips. "Niobie and I got a lot done today. We ordered the decorations for the hall and finalized the menu with the caterer. After a lot of begging, I convinced a local restaurant and a five-star hotel to donate gift certificates for the silent auction."

"Gift certificates?"

"Yeah, people love them and the two-night stay at the Seminole Hard Rock Hotel & Casino always gets the most bids. Last year we made five hundred dollars."

"Why not offer something big like a Pro Bowl package or Wimbledon tickets?"

"Because those things cost money and we're strapped for cash as it is."

Nodding, he mulled over the idea forming in his mind. Tomorrow he'd ask Brody to get him a pair of Pro Bowl tickets. They were hard to come by, but his trainer knew a lot of athletes and entertainers. If anyone could score a deal on the package, it would be Brody. Rashawn thought of sharing his plan with Yasmin, but decided against it. No use getting her hopes up. If he came through he'd be hailed as a hero, but if he didn't he'd look like a bigmouth who couldn't deliver.

"Have you given any more thought to hosting the fund-raiser?"

Rashawn had made up in his mind to emcee the charity fund-raiser the moment she had asked him. He pitied the families who lived in the slums and if it weren't for Brody taking him under his wing, he'd still be running the streets with his friends. "I'll do it."

"You will?"

"Yeah, as long as you agree to be my date."

"I already have a date," she told him. "Does that mean you won't do it?"

"No. I'd love to help out and it'll make my mom proud. Who's the guy?"

"A friend of the family." How could she tell him it was her deceased fiancé's brother? He wouldn't understand. Hell, she didn't either.

Eric's older brother, Julius, had been a steady presence in her life ever since the funeral. They talked regularly and met for lunch a few times a month. In the beginning, she had valued his company. He had shared his fondest memories of Eric, had taken care of her those first few weeks after his death and had been a shoulder she could cry on. But lately he had started hinting at them being more than friends, and Yasmin dreaded the day they'd have to have "that talk." He was a great guy, just not the right guy for her.

"I can't thank you enough, Rashawn. This year's theme is 'Transforming our neighborhood, one child at a time,' and you're a symbol of hope for the kids at the center."

"I like the theme. Sounds good. Let me guess, you thought of it, right?" Rashawn teased, winking. "It has your name written all over it."

"Some of the other committee members think it's corny. I've held off on having the banner made because…"

In the corner of his mind, he thought about kissing her. Yasmin was a stunner. Big smile, long legs, curves galore. A dime if he'd ever seen one. But she had more going for her than just her looks. He was captivated by the quickness of her mind and, although she had an Ivy League education and a host of degrees, she didn't act like she was better than him. She took on causes and people and had a successful practice. Yasmin Ohaji was a charming, generous spirit who, as far as he could see, was loved and admired by everyone who knew her, including him.

"What do you think?"

He abandoned his thoughts at the sound of her voice. He stared at her, surprised to find her watching him expectantly. The last thing he'd heard her say was something about changing the slogan. "I'd leave it, but if you want something shorter, cut out the first part. 'One child at a time' is still a very powerful message."

"That's good, but I like mine better."

"All right, Sister Souljah! Keep your slogan and tell the other committee members it's your way or the highway!"

They laughed together, their voices floating on the evening breeze. When they reached the topmast of the ship, Yasmin walked over to the railing and stared out at the burnt-blue sky. It was a clear summer night, filled with romance and laughter. The ship would be docking soon, and they had made it through the night without crossing the line. Her biggest fear was giving in to her desires, but she had worried for nothing. Rashawn was a perfect gentleman and it was refreshing being with a man who kept his word.

Closing her eyes, she hugged her arms to her chest. The wind whistled, water lapped against the ship and the faint sound of music drifted from the dining room. The once-empty deck had quickly filled with couples, and she could hear the shouts and chatter of people standing nearby.

"This is nice, huh?"

Her breathing accelerated. The sound of Rashawn's deep, oh-so-cool voice made ripples soar up her back. Yasmin didn't have to turn around to know he was standing behind her, but she did. "I have a confession to make."

"Don't look so serious, Doc. Whatever it is can't be that bad."

"I'm older than you." She examined his face to gauge his reaction. No change. "I'll be thirty-two in December."

He slipped a muscular arm around her waist. "That's cool. I like mature women. Now, if you'd said you were forty-two, we might have a problem!"

Yasmin laughed freely. "You're too much."

"And you're absolutely stunning."

"You think so?"

He tightened his hold. "Yeah, Doc. I do." To further prove his point, he lowered his head and kissed the side of her neck.

Yasmin gulped. It was too soon for them to be this close. Her trepidation fell away as he caressed her back. His touch set her heart at ease. Longing melted her resolve and filled her with desire. Their connection had been growing since the night they had met, and the only way Yasmin was ever going to get him out of her mind was to kiss him. Once she got it out of her system, she could forget him. Lifting her chin to receive his kiss, she waited anxiously for him to accept her invitation.

A bolt of electricity shot through her as their lips met. To her surprise, the kiss felt like the most natural thing in the world. She tuned out the voices around them and focused her entire mind and body on the experience. Entangled in the sheer intensity of the kiss, she lost all sense of time and place. His mouth was soft, sweet, inviting and he kissed her as if they had all the time in the world. Yasmin liked that. He wasn't in a rush and he wasn't aggressive. She curved into the arch of his body, savoring the feel of his warm embrace.

Rashawn abandoned her lips and kissed the side of her neck. He touched a hand to her cheek, then fingered a lock of her hair. "Nice technique, Doc."

Yasmin licked her lips. If a kiss could leave her with erect nipples and shaky legs, there was no telling what would happen if they ever made love.

He nibbled on her earlobe before returning to her lips. This time the kiss was long, deeply intense and fraught with passion.

"Rashawn, is that you?"

Yasmin pulled away midkiss. Forcing her eyes to focus, she turned in the direction of the voice. Her desire waned at the sight of the young woman with a café au lait complexion. She wore a gold tube top and a pair of skintight shorts that were probably bought in the junior girls section of a department store. Draped in accessories from head to toe, she was the quintessential around-the-way girl LL Cool J had once paid homage to.

Rashawn coughed. "Hey, Teagan. What's up?"

"Not much, just here with my girls, celebrating Mydeisha's birthday."

"That's cool." Rashawn didn't want to introduce Yasmin to Teagan, but if he didn't, she'd think he was hiding something. Things were going well between them, and he didn't want to ruin their date. "Teagan, this is my friend, *Dr.* Yasmin Ohaji."

Yasmin snuck a look at Rashawn. The tiny muscles around his eyes twitched but he was wearing a proud smile. He'd emphasized the word *doctor*, cueing her that Teagan had either once rejected him or was an ex-girlfriend. Only a blind woman would turn him down, so she suspected the latter was true.

The women greeted each other, then an awkward silence settled in.

"Seeing you here brings back old memories," Teagan said,

tossing her dark, bone-straight hair over her shoulders. She addressed Yasmin, her smile as cheap as silicone. "He brought me here on our first date, too."

Yasmin stared at Rashawn. Under his goatee he wore an angry frown. Adopting a light, playful tone, she said, "Oh, he did, did he?"

"Yeah, it was superromantic. We spent the whole night on the lower deck making out. But girl, that's nothing. Wait until he takes you to the—"

Rashawn cut in. "It was nice seeing you again, Teagan. Catch you later." He slipped an arm around Yasmin's waist. It was time to go. Teagan's mouth was liable to get him in trouble. "Take care."

Steering Yasmin in the opposite direction, he prayed the ship would dock without another run-in with Teagan. Rashawn hated to admit it, but seeing his ex left him rattled. Teagan Vargas was his first girlfriend. His first love. His first everything. Nostalgia washed over him, but he grabbed hold of himself before he slipped into the past. He was with Yasmin now. And if she let him into her life, he wouldn't mess it up like he had in the past.

Yasmin waited until they were a safe distance away before saying, "Pretty girl. How long were you guys together?"

"A couple years."

"Must have been serious."

His eyes revealed nothing. "Not really. We dated for a while in college, but it didn't work out…We, ah, wanted different things."

"You went to college?"

"Yeah, but I dropped out my sophomore year to focus on boxing."

"Ever think of going back?"

"Maybe when my career's over. I'd like to open a management firm, you know, to help other athletes navigate the business world, but no one's going to take me seriously unless I have a degree."

Yasmin wanted to find out more about his relationship with Teagan, but now was not the time. She'd been questioning him since they'd boarded the ship and she didn't want Rashawn to think she was grilling him. There would be plenty of time later to find out about his past loves.

"What's next?"

Her forehead creased. "You mean tonight?"

"The night's still young. What do you want to do after this?"

"Go home and go to bed."

"Want some company?"

Yasmin laughed. "No, I think I'll manage just fine."

Rashawn trailed a finger along her collarbone. It felt good hearing her laugh. He was scared that running into Teagan had spoiled their night. Yasmin was special to him and, if he wanted to keep seeing her, he had to address what his ex had said earlier. "I don't want you to get the wrong picture of me. I took Teagan on a dinner cruise, but we came with a group of friends. When you told me you'd never been, I thought it would be a new experience for you." His gaze was strong, steady, piercing. "I'm not playing games with you, Doc. I'm for real."

"I understand. Thanks for being honest with me." He caressed her fingers, then her arms. His touch triggered a chain reaction of pleasure throughout her body and Yasmin could actually feel her blood pressure rise. Curiosity pushed her to ask, "Um… where are you planning to take me on our second date?"

He kissed the side of her neck. "I'll take you anywhere you want."

"Ma, where are you?" The next day Rashawn slipped his keys into his pocket and closed the door. After a three-hour workout, he needed to unwind and there was no place he'd rather be than his mom's house. The aroma of chili stew elicited a grumble from his unruly stomach. He'd eaten a chicken sandwich an hour ago, but the smell of his favorite dish made him smack his lips in anticipation. "Ma?"

Inside was cool. As he strolled through the main floor, he noticed that all of the windows were open. He peeked into the den, confident he'd find her knitting in the recliner or combing through photo albums, but she wasn't there. The three-bedroom house was small but attractive and decorated with a mother's touch. Family photographs highlighting birthdays, graduations and holidays dominated the walls; worn-out couches were situated in front of the TV, and the bookshelf was lined with greeting cards.

Rashawn expected to find his mom in the kitchen preparing her famous tamale pie, but she wasn't there. After a quick sweep of the house, he returned to the kitchen. The stove was on low, the microwave was on and the table was set. She had to be nearby.

On the table, next to the day's newspapers, was a stack of bills in Armondo's name. All credit cards Rashawn didn't have to open the envelopes to know they were past due.

Rashawn took a glass from the dish rack, opened the fridge and poured himself some lemonade. Leaning against the counter, he rubbed a hand over his face. The curtains flapped in the breeze, ushering in the cool afternoon air. As he drank, he spotted a figure moving around the backyard. He should have known his mom was outside. She loved to feel the sun on her face, the wind in her hair and the aroma of the season. Popping a blueberry muffin into his mouth, he made his way to the back of the house. Using his left shoulder, he pushed open the screen door and strode across the lawn.

Rashawn found his mom knee-deep in weeds, singing an off-key rendition of a popular '80s Lionel Richie song. To keep from startling her, he touched her shoulder. "Ma, I've been looking all over for you."

Johanna Bishop adjusted her straw hat so she could get a better look at her oldest son. "Hijo. What are you doing here? I didn't know you were stopping by."

Chuckling, he bent down and pecked her cheek. He came by every day but she was always surprised to see him. "Ma, you have food on the stove. You shouldn't be out here gardening. What if the kitchen catches on fire?"

Shaking her head, she waved a gloved hand at him. "You

worry too much, Hijo. Besides, I'm done cooking. The stew's just simmering." Johanna examined his mouth for any signs of chili. "I hope you weren't inside tasting the food."

"No, I'm not hungry." Leaning against the brown picket fence, he watched her pull up a row of dandelions. His mom had a weary look on her face. Years of working long hours and skimping on sleep had prematurely aged her. Her skin was dry, wrinkles lined her eyes and her once-lustrous black hair was infused with gray.

"Have you talked to Armondo? He said he's been calling you but you haven't returned any of his calls. He needs your help, Hijo."

"I know. I saw the bills on the table."

"He asked me to talk to you."

"Stay out of it, Ma."

Johanna's head jerked back. "But he's your brother!" she protested. "If I taught you boys anything it's that family sticks together."

"Are you forgetting this isn't the first time he's gotten into trouble? Six months ago he racked up five grand in credit card debt buying rims and expensive crap for his car. I paid it off and he swore he'd stay out of trouble. Now he's back at it. I'm not doing it again, Ma. If Armondo's old enough to spend it, he's old enough to pay it."

"But he's a baby. He's only nineteen!"

"A baby, my ass," Rashawn muttered, folding his arms across his chest. "When I was Armondo's age, I juggled school, a part-time job and I trained six days a week. If I could be responsible at nineteen so can he."

"He's not as mature as you were at that age."

"That's because we're always bailing him out! It's time for Armondo to grow up and stand on his own two feet."

She turned to Rashawn, her face pinched with grief. "Do it for me, Hijo. I'm begging you. I cosigned on the applications so if he doesn't pay I'll be held responsible. Creditors have been calling, threatening to take me to court and repossses the house."

Rashawn had to tread slowly. His mom had to be handled with care. She was very sensitive and cried easily, especially when it had to do with her children. It had been stressful raising four boys single-handedly, and even now, at forty-six, she was still taking care of the family. "Don't worry about it, Ma. I'll talk to him."

"You'll pay the bills?"

"No, but I'll see what I can do. Maybe I can get him a job. I know a guy who owns an auto body shop. He's always looking for—"

"Armondo can't work right now. He was helping one of his friends move and sprained his ankle. The doctor said he should rest it for four to six weeks."

Rashawn tasted his drink. His brother was such an arrant liar that he had a hard time believing anything he said. "Like I said, Ma. I'll handle it."

Johanna resumed digging. "I'd help him out, but I don't have much left in my savings account. Fenton hasn't repaid the money I lent him during the holidays and yesterday I gave Vincente a thousand dollars to pay his rent."

"Son of a bitch!"

"Watch your mouth, Hijo."

"Ma, why do you keep giving them money?" he demanded, the veins in his neck popping. Bitterness settled into his stomach, stealing his good mood. His brothers were never satisfied. If they weren't borrowing money from him, they were begging his mom. Johanna had been retired for years and her pension was barely enough to buy groceries. His brothers and their families ate dinner at her house most nights and it was costly feeding twelve or more people on a fixed income.

"The money I put into your account is in case of an emergency. Not to help Vincente, Fenton and Armondo." Rashawn examined her face. Her eyes were watering and her lips trembled. Her sullen expression made him want to hug her. All she wanted in life was to see her children happy. She was generous to a fault and his brothers took advantage of that. Governing his mouth, he said, "Next time they ask you for a loan, send them to me. Okay, Ma?"

Johanna motioned for him to help her up and, when he did, she slid an arm around his waist. "You're a good boy, Hijo. Always taking care of me and making sure I have everything I need."

They stood arm in arm for a few minutes, the sounds of summer inundating the air. Kids shrieked, skateboards rolled across the pavement and birds tweeted. Heady perfumes of the season drifted on the breeze and surrounded the yard.

"Guess who's emceeing the Parkland Community Center Fund-raiser?"

"Hijo, I'm so proud of you! I can't believe it. My son the humanitarian." Squeezing his waist, she rested her head on his chest. "We'll celebrate tonight during dinner. I think I have a bottle of that Mexican brandy you like so much."

"I can't stay, *ma*. I'm going to a wine-tasting party."

Johanna's girlish giggle belied her age. "What do you know about wine?"

"Nothing. That's why I'm here," Rashawn confessed, steering her in the direction of the house. "I need you to bring me up to speed."

Her face clouded in confusion. "I've never been to a wine-tasting party."

"Ma, you're practically an expert when it comes to wine."

"Just because I've been to the vineyard a few times doesn't make me an expert, Hijo."

"Come on, Ma, I really need your help."

"Okay," she conceded, his broad, infectious grin finally wearing her down. "Where should we begin?"

"Well, you can start by telling me everything you know about Bordeaux, Chablis and Sauvignon Blanc."

Chapter 7

River Tower Condos were in an enviable part of downtown Tampa. The pixel glass building had an over-the-trees view of the city's skyline, a uniform-clad doorman who opened doors and buzzed elevators, and a sunlit lobby furnished with suede armchairs, overgrown plants and European art.

When Yasmin and Rashawn stepped off the elevator, they could hear the refined sounds of classical music coming from the end of the hall. Yasmin dragged her feet as if she were going to the electric chair, rather than to a wine-tasting party. It was important to her that her best friend like Rashawn. Katherine Duke, an only child born into an upper-middle-class family, traveled the world acquiring rare pieces of art for the Tampa Museum. Yasmin admired the curator's vivaciousness and she had a lot of insight about the opposite sex. The women had met in graduate school and, though their friendship was only five years old, Katherine was someone Yasmin could always depend on.

"It's quiet in there. Are you sure we're at the right place?"

Too nervous to speak, Yasmin nodded. What was she thinking

bringing Rashawn with her? Her friends could be seen as a stuffy, uptight bunch and, though she loved them dearly, they weren't the most down-to-earth people. Hopefully, conversation would center on the weather or the economy and not what Rashawn did for a living. Smiling at Rashawn, she rang the doorbell for a second time. "Maybe I should call," she said, groping in her clutch purse for her cell phone. "It's taking a long time for someone to answer."

"It's cool. It's not like we're going anywhere." He winked at her and she sighed inwardly. His suave, smooth nature made her think of an old Isley Brothers song. And the more time she spent with him, the stronger their attraction grew. There was something about the boxer that made her want to dive into his arms and kiss him until she was breathless. It was the lethal combination of good looks, self-assurance and honesty that left her feeling scatterbrained whenever he was around. And Yasmin suspected he had this effect on other women. Her girlfriends might think he was a thug, but they'd be slobbering all over their cocktail dresses. Rashawn certainly had his own sense of style and, like his down-home vibe and anything-goes personality, she liked it. He'd paired a sports jacket with a perfectly white, wrinkle-free dress shirt, blue jeans and sneakers. It was a look straight out of *Vibe* Magazine and he wore it well.

"I hope we're not going to be listening to Mozart all night because I want to dance with you," Rashawn said, licking his lips. She was hot and his eyes let her know it. "You look much too good to be standing around sipping wine."

"If you wanted to dance you picked the wrong place."

"Then, I guess I'll just have to take you to Bar 21 when this is over."

"I don't go to nightclubs," she told him. "Sorry."

"No problem. We can go back to my place." Leaning over, he rested a hand on the small of her back. "I just bought the new Anthony Hamilton CD."

Her heart raced. The suggestive look in his eyes conveyed more than his words. No, when the party was over, she was going home, alone. Dancing with Rashawn would lead to touching, then kissing and who knew what else. Just because she was attracted to him didn't mean she had to act on her feelings. It was bad enough she'd kissed him. She didn't want to push the boundaries of their relationship any further.

The apartment door swung open. A slender woman in a mauve strapless dress smiled at them. "I thought I heard the buzzer."

"Hi, Morgan. It's been a long time. What have you been up to?"

"I studied French in Clermont-Ferrand for six months and then traveled across France with some of my girlfriends. I just got back a few days ago." Morgan stepped aside. "Where are my manners? Please come in."

"Thanks."

"You're looking great, Yasmin. How have you been?"

"Busy. I'm organizing the Parkland Community Center Fundraiser and it's taking up a lot of my time. If you don't have plans for June fourteenth I'd love it if you could come."

"I won't make any promises, but I'll try."

Yasmin introduced Rashawn to Katherine's cousin.

"Are you a doctor, too?" she asked, brushing her hair off her shoulders.

Yasmin knew the question was coming. People naturally assumed that she would end up with another doctor because Eric had been a surgeon. "No," she replied, trying to keep the hostility out of her voice, "he's not in the medical field."

Morgan raised her eyebrows. "What do you do for a living?"

"I'm a boxer."

Her faced brightened with interest. "Like Mike Tyson?"

"Better."

"Remind me to give you my business card later. I'm an entertainment lawyer and you never know when you might need someone with my skills and expertise."

"Cool. I need more reliable people in my corner."

Staring adoringly at him, she smiled, her hazel contacts glittering like emeralds. "Well, it was very nice meeting you, Rashawn. I do hope we have a chance to talk later."

Yasmin led Rashawn into the living room, hoping that everyone would be as friendly as Morgan had been. The whole gang was there: Terri-Lynn and DeWitt were cuddling on the sofa-loveseat; Bianca, Noreen and Iris were standing by the punch bowl; Wellington and Lars were on the balcony, and Pierce, Katherine's man-of-the-month, was talking on his cell phone.

Rashawn whistled. "This place is tight! I wish my place looked like this."

"Katherine did an amazing job fixing it up. I almost don't recognize it." Allowing her eyes to wander, she openly admired the rich carpet, teal walls and ornamental light fixtures. The last time Yasmin had been to the apartment it had streaky windows, an ungodly odor and bargain-store furniture. Now quiet lighting, crystal floor lamps and knee-high pallid candles created a cozy atmosphere and highlighted the many delights of the recently renovated condo.

Parading into the room like a beauty contestant, Katherine tapped her wineglass with a dainty silver spoon. "We're ready to begin! The servers are handing out the tasting cards as we speak. Record your initial impressions and thoughts, including things like appearance, texture and aroma. There is bread to clear your palate and dump buckets for you diehard wine hobbyists. *Commençons!*"

Rashawn took the index card the male server offered him. "I thought you said this party was an excuse to get drunk. Looks like your friend takes this wine-tasting thing very seriously."

"She does, but everyone else will lighten up once they have a few drinks."

"I sure hope so, because I'm having flashbacks of being in high school!"

Yasmin laughed. "It's not that bad. We'll do it together and if you have any questions just ask."

For the next hour they sampled wine and nibbled on Swiss cheese. Rashawn pretended to be interested in what Lars was saying about the recent slump of the Dow Jones, but it was hard to stay alert on an empty stomach. The cheese made him thirsty, the Riesling was dry and the bite-size tuna rolls only made him hungrier. Wishing he'd eaten dinner before coming, he downed the rest of his glass and handed it to server passing by. "Where's the bathroom?" he asked, whispering in Yasmin's ear.

It was an innocent question, but the heat of his breath aroused her. Fingering her turquoise-hued chain, she cleared the desire from her throat and said, "It's down the hall to the left."

"Cool. Be right back."

Iris watched Rashawn leave. "I understand your boxer friend is hosting the charity fund-raiser. That's, um, interesting."

"He's a boxer? I'm embarrassed to say I've never heard of him," DeWitt confessed, with a shrug. "The kid must be a local talent or something."

The others murmured in agreement.

"Why don't you try to get a real star like Bill Cosby, Sidney Poitier or Oprah? They all do a lot of work for inner-city projects and organizations that benefit African-American children," Wellington explained. "I know someone who plays golf with Oprah's third cousin on her mother's side. Do you want me to inquire if she's available?"

Rolling her eyes, she stared balefully at Wellington. The university professor had no clue what it took to organize a charity event. As philanthropic as Oprah Winfrey was, Yasmin didn't have the time or the energy to chase the self-made woman down. Besides, she was confident Rashawn would charm the pants off the audience and raise thousands of dollars for the center. "Just because you guys don't know who Rashawn is, doesn't mean he's not popular." To further emphasize her point, she told them what had happened at the community center weeks earlier. "I've never seen the kids so happy! He chaired the Men of Initiative session and the boys really took what he said to heart."

DeWitt shrugged. "I hope the audience likes him because most of the guests are professional, white-collar people, not low-income families from the 'hood."

Yasmin sipped her wine. The Chianti was definitely having its way with her. She knew the only way to know whether or not the wine was good was to finish it all, so instead of dumping the contents after each tasting, she had drained her glass. Now she had a slight buzz and felt completely relaxed. So much so, she didn't care what her friends had to say. "Well, what's done is done. The most important thing is that we raise a ton of money for the center."

Noreen wrinkled her nose. "I do hope you're not using the same caterer from last year. Down-home cooking has no place at an upscale charity event. The chicken was greasy, the potatoes were soggy and…"

Bored with the conversation and tired of hearing Noreen complain, Yasmin searched the room for Rashawn. He wasn't back from the bathroom, but her face brightened when she spotted Katherine alone at one of the wine tables. Not bothering to excuse herself, she walked purposefully toward her best friend. "Where have you been hiding? I've been trying to talk to you all night!"

Katherine tossed a look over her shoulder. "You, my friend, are a liar. You've been too busy with your boy toy to pay me any mind!"

Laughing, they refilled their glasses and went out onto the balcony. It was a clear night. Trees rustled in the wind and a collection of stars surrounded the moon. "Great party and the Chianti is the best thing I've ever tasted."

"Forget the wine. Let's talk about junior."

"Not you, too, Katherine."

"He's five years younger than you. Those are the facts." The look on her face was a serious one. "Yasmin, do you know what you're getting yourself into?"

"It's nothing, really. We're just—"

Katherine cut in. "Just what? Hanging out? If I had a penny for every time I heard a woman say that, I'd be on the cover of *Forbes* magazine."

"We have fun together. Is that a crime? It's nice having a little male attention," she confessed, desire seeping into her tone. "We've been out a few times, that's it."

"That's how it starts, then the next thing you know you're

lending him money, spending nights at his place and letting him drive your car."

Yasmin didn't see things getting that far, but she couldn't deny their growing attraction. Over the course of the night, he'd flirted with her, held her hand and even fed her blue cheese. Rashawn was very open about his feelings and it felt good knowing he found her desirable. "I don't see anything wrong with us going out."

"Me, neither, as long as you're prepared when he loses interest and moves on to someone else. Someone younger."

Yasmin stared out into the sky. This is what she was afraid of. Her best friend was projecting her biases onto her. Against the advice of her friends and family, Katherine had started dating a truck driver at one of her father's moving companies. Within weeks, she had been lending Dejaun money, paying his rent and even cosigned on a car loan. Before the ink had dried on the application, he had gone back with his baby's mother and Katherine's once exemplary credit report had been ruined.

"Don't get me wrong, Yasmin. I'm not trying to dissuade you from dating him."

"You're not?"

"No. Go out with the young buck, just don't fall in love."

"There's no chance of that ever happening," she said, sighing deeply. "When Eric died, I lost more than a lover. A small part of me died, too. I'm not saying I'm going to be alone for the rest of my life, but what if I never have another love of a lifetime?"

"You really believe that?"

"True love only comes along once," Yasmin said, sighing wistfully. "Not a day goes by that I don't think about him."

Katherine gave her a hug. "That's understandable. You guys were together for years. It's going to take time for you to heal, Yasmin. Be gentle with yourself and don't feel like you have to minimize your feelings."

"Sometimes I feel so hopeless, you know? Like I'm watching life pass me by."

"I hear you, girl. I don't know where my soul mate is, but I wish he'd hurry the hell up because I'm tired of dating these losers!"

Laughing, the two women clinked wineglasses.

"How are things going with Pierce?" Yasmin asked, flipping her hair over her shoulders. "Are you getting along better now?"

"I'm dumping him tomorrow."

"Why? What did he do now?"

An amused expression fell over Katherine's face. "Let's just say he doesn't take instruction well."

"Which man does?"

More laughter passed between them.

"I bet you won't have any problems in the bedroom with the boxer," Katherine teased, bumping Yasmin with her hips. "By the way, when do I get to meet him?"

"How about now?"

Yasmin whipped around, spilling some wine on the ground. "Rashawn, how long have you been standing there?" the question sounded like an accusation.

"Long enough." Wearing his trademark smile, he extended a hand to the impeccably dressed, full-figured woman. "You're the only person here I haven't met. You must be Katherine."

"And you must be Rashawn. Welcome to my home."

"Thanks for having me." Smiling, he tucked a hand into his jeans pocket. "This place is gorgeous and the view is out of this world. When I make it big, I'm going to buy my mom a condo just like this."

The friends shared a skeptical look.

"That's very generous of you. Most athletes spend their earnings on cars, jewelry and clothes."

"My mom sacrificed a lot for me and my brothers. The least I can do is take care of her. She deserves it."

"That's admirable, Rashawn. It's too bad there aren't more men like you around." Katherine finished her wine. "If you'll excuse me, I have to check on my other guests. Enjoy the rest of the evening."

Rashawn moved toward Yasmin. Behind his back, Katherine nodded emphatically and mouthed, "Nice ass," before escaping inside.

"You look tipsy," he said, resting his hands against the railing. Yasmin was trapped. The only way out was to duck under his arms. But how would she look wiggling around in a designer dress? His spicy, fresh cologne wrapped itself around her in a sensuous embrace and brought images of their first kiss to mind.

"Do you know what I want to do right now?" he asked.

"No."

"Guess."

"I have no idea," she lied, staring back at him. Rashawn was just inches from her face. So close she could smell the Merlot on his breath. His eyes gleamed with lust and his voice was thick with bravado. He wanted to kiss her and she wanted it, too. Just not here. She peeked over his shoulder. Good, no one was watching them. Yasmin wouldn't pigeonhole herself as prim, but there was a time and place for everything and Katherine's balcony was definitely not the place for kiss number two. "We should get back inside. Guests are getting ready to share their observations."

Rashawn rubbed his chin against her bare shoulder. "I didn't come here to discuss the texture of the Riesling or the aroma of the zinfandel. I came to be with you."

His lips flittered over her ear. Yasmin shivered. Who knew such a simple act could leave her breathless? And when he stroked her back, her knees buckled. His touch was sweeter than wine, soft and tender. Making love to Rashawn or anyone else on a second date was unthinkable, but she was more tempted than she'd ever been before. Keenly aware of their environment and not wanting to give her friends an R-rated show, she lifted his arms and freed herself from his grasp. Yasmin felt silly running away, but what other choice did she have? It was either put some distance between them or fall victim to her desire.

"Down, boy," she teased, sauntering past him. Stepping through the glass door, she flashed him a coy smile over her shoulder. "Meet me inside when you've *cooled* down."

Chapter 8

Niobie slid the April issue of *Cosmopolitan* magazine into the drawer, tossed the empty box of Twinkies on top and dusted the crumbs inside before slamming it shut. Her compulsive, anal-retentive boss would lecture her if her workstation looked anything but perfect. Spraying rose-scented air freshener around her desk, she put on her headset and pretended to be talking to a prospective client.

"Thanks for calling A Better Way Counseling Services. Have a nice day," she said to the make-believe caller. Wearing a too-bright smile, she moved the mouthpiece away from her lips and said, "Good morning, Dr. Ohaji. How are you?"

"I'm fine, thanks. I see you're already hard at work."

"I'm just trying to keep on top of things." Standing, she handed her boss a copy of the day's schedule. "Mr. Tibbs rescheduled for next Wednesday, so you have an extended lunch today. Your coffee is on your desk, along with the alphabetized client list you requested and the tentative program for the charity fund-raiser."

"Thank you, Niobie. I wasn't expecting you to have the

program typed up so soon." Yasmin smiled. "You've done a lot this morning and you've only been here for an hour. Great work."

"No time spent like the present," she sang, her eyes filled with phony admiration. "Isn't that what you're always telling me?"

"I like your attitude."

"I learned from the best."

Smiling proudly, Yasmin continued through the reception area. Niobie watched her, wondering why such an attractive woman would often wear dark, drab outfits. Sure, the business suit was a designer brand, but it did nothing to flatter her body. You could barely tell she had an hourglass figure underneath all those clothes. Flopping down onto her chair, Niobie shook her head. If she had firm hips and toned legs, she'd be in tube tops and Daisy Duke shorts all day long. Her mom always said no one was born with a full deck of cards and she was right. Dr. Ohaji was beautiful, educated and financially stable, but she didn't know how to dress.

Niobie waited until her boss closed her office door before she resumed reading the titillating article about groupies who catered to professional athletes. Propping her elbows up on the table, she studied the ten ways to seduce a wealthy, high-profile man. Grabbing a yellow highlighter from the pen jar, she underlined each step and quickly committed them to memory.

Closing her eyes, she envisioned what her life could be like. A rich man would solve all of her problems. Instead of working long hours at a job she hated, she could shop at trendy, upscale boutiques where the sales personnel offered customers champagne and waited on them hand and foot. A live-in nanny could look after Miles, her overdue bills would be paid and she could finally afford to buy a car. No more long, depressing rides on the city bus. She'd drive the Lexus during the week, the Jag on the weekends and the Bentley when the mood struck.

Niobie dated regularly but she was no closer to snagging a rich man than a gold digger with a neon sign on her back. Every Saturday she dropped Miles off at her mom's house and set out in search of the hottest party in town. At the end of the night all she had to show for her effort was a phone number or two, blistered feet and an empty wallet. On the rare occasion that she did meet someone, she'd give him her number and, after determining exactly what he could do for her, decide whether or not he was worth her time. More often than not, he wasn't.

The phone rang, interrupting her musings. "A Better Way Counseling Services."

When Niobie heard Rashawn's voice, she perked up. There could only be one reason for this call. He was finally going to ask her out! Niobie was so excited she could barely sit still. "How have you been? I haven't seen you in a while."

"I'm good. Been busy training for my next fight. How are you and Miles doing?"

"Can't complain. His pediatrician thinks I should put him on a diet. Says he's considered obese for his height and weight. Can you believe that?"

"Maybe you should sign him up for baseball, soccer or basketball."

"But he gets plenty of exercise at the community center."

"Kids can never get enough."

"You're right," she conceded, staring down at the magazine. According to the article, a groupie was never afraid to make the first move. Taking the writer's advice, she said, "I was just sitting here thinking about you."

"Ah, okay." A pause, then, "I was hoping to talk to Yasmin. Is she free?"

"That depends, is this a personal or private call?"

"It's personal."

Niobie's eyes darkened. What the hell? What would Rashawn want with her stuffy, uptight boss? He needed someone like *her*. A woman from the same neighborhood who knew what it was like to grow up in the inner city. "I'm sorry, but she's with a client."

"Is she free for lunch?"

"Dr. Ohaji is fully booked."

"How about I bring you guys something to eat. Help me out, Niobie. What does she like?"

"I wouldn't bother coming by if I were you…Dr. Ohaji

usually goes out with friends." She added, "A very *close* male friend."

Silence settled over the line.

Niobie's confidence returned. If she wanted Rashawn to take her seriously, she had to be more assertive. "Do you have a date for the charity fund-raiser?"

"I'm taking my mom. Hey, do you know who Yasmin's going with?"

What was with all the questions about Dr. Ohaji? Didn't he know they were completely wrong for each other? It was up to her to put an end to his infatuation with her boss. Niobie was looking for a man who could take care of her and, for now, Rashawn Bishop was all she had. "Her date is a brain surgeon, I think. God, Dr. Ohaji dates so many different guys it's hard to keep them all straight."

"She does?"

"Yeah, she has a *very* active social life. Dr. Ohaji really has a thing for doctors, lawyers and entrepreneurs. You know, rich, white-collar men who drive a different convertible every week and vacation in Europe. According to her, the only thing a regular guy can offer her is sex and she has a vibrator for that."

More silence. And the longer it lasted, the wider Niobie smiled. Rashawn's gullibility worked to her advantage. Her boss was more interested in working than dating and turned down everyone who asked her out. Sneering, Niobie adjusted her push-up bra. It was a wonder she hadn't cracked up when she'd mentioned the sex toy. Her boss had said no such thing, but he didn't have to know that. Now she could pursue Rashawn without Dr. Ohaji distracting him. "Do you have plans tonight?" she asked, her tone rich with sensuality. "I was hoping we could check out Food Fest. It's international cuisine at its finest. There'll be Italian, Polish, Jamaican and—"

"I can't. I'm training."

Niobie drummed her fingernails on the desk. Was he brushing her off or telling the truth? Would he have turned down Dr. Ohaji? Instead of asking the questions running through her mind, she said, "No problem. Maybe another time?"

"Sure. Is Yasmin still with clients?"

"I'm afraid so."

"Will you tell her I called?" he asked, his voice a combination of disappointment and concern. "It's important that I speak to her."

"Of course."

Rashawn hung up. Yasmin had never mentioned she was dating anyone. He didn't know why he was surprised. A woman like her was bound to have men beating down her door. Hell, it was a wonder she wasn't married. Scratching his head, he exited the office and returned to the gym. How was he supposed to compete with a brain surgeon? Powerful, accomplished women liked powerful, accomplished men. Not guys like him. Younger women appreciated dinner and a movie, but he couldn't take Yasmin to the local diner. She was a doctor, a therapist at that. She liked wine, imported cheese and caviar. He had a thousand dollars in his bank account and Armondo was breathing down his neck for yet another loan. He knew what he had to do: If he wanted to date Yasmin, he'd have to dip into his emergency stash and romance her Donald Trump–style.

He was next in line to spar with Ortiz, but he liked to jump rope when he needed to clear his mind. It was Friday afternoon and there were only a handful of fighters in the gym. Only diehard boxers trained in this kind of heat. It was a searing ninety-eight degrees outside and ceiling fans circulated the thick, muggy air drifting in through the open windows.

Rashawn lined up his feet and started skipping. Pain shot up his calf, but he ignored it. Lately, he'd been pushing himself too hard. Sore arms, an aching back and blistered feet made routine tasks excruciating. If he continued his intense workout regimen, he'd be defeated before he even stepped into the ring with Luis "AK-47" Lipenski.

His gaze slid to the clock. Yasmin's session was over, but if he called back and left another message, she'd think he was sweating her. And there was nothing worse than trying too hard. He wanted to see her again, but how? As he racked his brain for ideas, he thought over his conversation with Niobie. He couldn't believe she'd asked him out. She knew he was checking for Yasmin, so why had she invited him to Food Fest? His face broke out into a slow, lazy grin. He'd never attended the three-day event, but from what his mom told him it was well attended, with plenty of food and live entertainment. Now that he had the venue, all he needed was to persuade Yasmin to go out with him.

Rashawn returned the rope to the wall. He would finish his workout, then head home. The only question now was whether he should call Yasmin or wait for her to call him back. Deep in thought, he entered the weight room and sank down onto a bench. Across the room, Brody was collecting dirty towels.

"Where the hell've you been?" Brody asked, casting a smoldering look over his shoulder. "Been lookin' all over for you."

"Had a call to make."

"Hope you ain't wastin' your time callin' that therapist woman."

Rashawn's head shot up. He should have known better than to trust Kori. "Your daughter has a big mouth."

"Why do you think I keep her around?"

Both men chuckled.

Brody strode over to the bench, added ten pounds to the barbell and waited until Rashawn was in position before he lowered it. "Who's this new chick you're sweet on?"

"Her name's Yasmin."

"Another island girl?"

"No, she's South African."

Brody whistled. "Oo-wee! Bet she has booty on her!"

"Watch it, Brody." His tone was sharp. "Yasmin's sophisticated and classy, not like the gold diggers I've dated in the past. She has her own therapy clinic, plenty of money and she doesn't need shit from me."

"I hear you, but there's a downside to dating a successful woman."

Rashawn felt a burning sensation in his chest as he pumped

the bar over his head. If he didn't finish the set, Brody would tear into him, and they had been butting heads all week. Rashawn felt he needed more rest; his manager thought he was bellyaching. Brody was the only father he'd ever known and he didn't want to disappoint him. The pain was unbearable but he pushed past it. "What downside? I can't think of a single one."

"You can't afford to take her to expensive restaurants and shit. You have a family to take care of. Dating this therapist lady will send you straight to the poorhouse."

"I ain't got anyone to take care of but my mom."

The older man stroked his beard. "What about your brothers? Armondo came by here yesterday asking some of the guys for money. Said he was in trouble and—"

"Armondo can go to hell! I've been taking care of him for years and the more I give, the more he wants. I'm sick of his crap." Rashawn gripped the bar, imagining it was his brother's neck. "If Vincente and Fenton can work, so can he. At least they're trying to make something of themselves."

"Is this Yasmin woman the reason you shelled out all that money for those tickets? You takin' her to Hawaii?"

"No, the Pro Bowl tickets are for charity."

"She's going to leave you high and dry. Don't say I didn't warn you. I've seen it happen before and this girl ain't gonna be no different."

Rashawn dropped the barbell on the weight rests, the clanging sound underlining his frustration. "Thanks, old man, but I'll take my chances."

"Enough woman talk. Keep your eyes on the goal, you hear me?" Brody chucked a towel at Rashawn. "You have a match to get ready for. You're fighting Lipenski and in case you forgot he's a former heavyweight champion."

Shrugging, he cleaned the sweat from his face. "I'm not worried. He's a washed-up boxer who's out of shape."

"True," Brody agreed, heading for the door, "but he still has that lethal roundhouse uppercut. Back to the ring, champ. We have work to do!"

* * *

"Let's take pole-dancing lessons."

Yasmin's head whipped up. Propped against her office door wearing a cheek-to-cheek smile was her sister. Dressed to impress in a vermilion pantsuit and heels, Imani looked every bit the part of the tenacious real estate developer at the top of her firm.

"Thanks, but no thanks."

"What about capoeira?"

Yasmin's forehead creased. "Capahoo?"

"Ca-po-eira. It's a high-energy aerobic workout that fuses martial arts and dance with African and Brazilian music," Imani explained, shaking her hips to an inaudible beat. "It's the latest exercise craze, Yassie. Everyone's doing it."

"Sounds like fun, but I think I'll pass."

"At least give it some thought. It's become really popular and the women in my yoga class swear by it."

"All right, all right. I'll give it some thought." Yasmin beckoned Imani inside. Feeling lethargic, she welcomed the distraction she was sure her sister would provide. "What brings you by?"

"We haven't seen each other much the last few weeks, so I figured I'd stop by to see how you're doing. Want to go for lunch?"

"Sure, if you don't mind waiting while I finish up. Tomorrow's the annual midyear meeting at the community center and I need to present this—" she held up a bulky report "—to the board of directors."

"No problem."

Buzzing telephones and the hum of the air conditioner didn't bother Yasmin half as much as the heat radiating from her sister's eyes. Dean could be married to Imani for fifty years and he still wouldn't know her as well as Yasmin did. Her sister's invitation to lunch had nothing to do with food. She was hungry all right. Hungry for gossip.

Realizing it was impossible to finish her work with Imani the sleuth breathing down her neck, Yasmin set the report aside. "Where do you want to go? I don't have much time, so let's make it somewhere nearby."

"No problem. Let's go to the Garden Rose Café. I'm in the mood for their spicy Cajun chicken… Speaking of spicy, I ran into Bianca this morning at Spa Dreams and she told me you brought Rashawn to Katherine's party. You've been holding out on me, Sis. What happened to him being all wrong for you?"

"I had a change of heart." She felt compelled to add, "And just because we hang out every now and then doesn't mean we're dating."

Imani pressed her palms down on the desk. "Every now and then? You've gone out three times in a matter of weeks and now you're lying about it. You wouldn't be keeping secrets if something wasn't going on between the two of you."

"We went to Katherine's party, big deal." Standing, Yasmin shuffled the papers on her desk into one neat pile. "And as for me keeping secrets, that's ludicrous. I'm not hiding anything. I would have told you, but you haven't been around."

"You can deny it all you want, but I know there's a lot more going on between you and the boxer than you're willing to admit." Imani nudged her sister with her hips. "I'll let you off the hook this time, but the next time something happens I want to know about it *first*."

"Okay, mother hen. Can we go now?"

"Have you guys done anything besides kissing?"

"How did you know we kissed?" Yasmin asked, her eyes tapered. Imani's face broke out into a smirk. "I didn't. You just told me!"

"You're intolerable." Shaking her head, she marched through the open door. "Let's go, Imani."

"Good for you, Sis! It's high time you got yourself some!"

Ignoring her, Yasmin approached the reception area, told Niobie to hold her calls and proceeded through the lobby. She opened her purse, found her sunglasses and slipped them on. As she lifted her head, she spotted Rashawn through the front window. What was he doing here? Her first impulse was to hustle back into her office, but Imani was behind her. Before Yasmin could collect herself, he was standing in front of her. "Hey, Doc."

"Rashawn," she said, loud enough for people outside to hear.

He wore an easy smile. His blue T-shirt and cargo shorts flaunted his solid arms and legs. Shifting her feet, she smoothed a hand over her belted dress. Her mouth was dry and she felt a raging thirst. What was it about him that made her nervous?

Rashawn leaned in and kissed her cheek. "You look amazing, Doc."

Yasmin inhaled his scent. It wrapped itself around her, squeezing her most intimate parts. "What brings you by?" she queried, when he stepped back.

"I have some news that just couldn't wait."

"Oh, really? What is it?" Why did her voice sound squeaky? Yasmin heard a peal of laughter and groaned inwardly. Obviously, Imani had noticed, too.

"You'll have to forgive her, she hasn't been getting much sleep lately." Imani spoke in a sultry tone. "Hot, sleepless nights can wreak havoc on one's mind *and* body."

Rashawn chuckled. He didn't know this firecracker with the short, chic hairstyle, but he liked her instantly. "I'm a friend of—"

"Oh, I know who you are," Imani said, openly admiring him. "And I must admit that I'm impressed. You've managed to do something others have tried and failed."

"And what's that?"

"Take Yassie out on a second date."

"Yassie?" he repeated, clearly amused. Winking at Yasmin, he dropped an arm casually around her waist. "Cute name. Can I call you Yassie, too?"

Unsettled by his gaze, Yasmin dipped her hands into her oversize handbag and pulled out her car keys. She wasn't driving to the restaurant, but she needed a diversion. Rashawn's dreamy look, coupled with the butterflies in her stomach and Imani listening in, made her temperature soar. Adjusting her purse strap fussily, she said, "You said you had something to tell me? What is it?"

"Do you have plans tonight?" he asked, sidestepping the question.

"No, she's free."

Yasmin shot her sister a look that would shatter glass. "Imani, could you give us a minute, please?"

"There's no need. I'll just come by your place tonight, say eight o'clock?" Rashawn gave her his best smile. "And save your appetite."

"I'd prefer if we—"

"Oh, give the man a break," Imani snapped, examining all six feet of him. He was built to be an athlete, and an aura of sexual confidence surrounded him. Rashawn couldn't be more right for Yasmin. Her sister needed an adventurous guy who wouldn't buckle under her strength, and something told her the boxer was the right man for the job. Smiling, she fluttered her long, naturally thick eyelashes. "What do you have planned for my sister tonight, Rashawn?"

"We're going to check out Food Fest, then kick it at my place for a while. How does that sound?"

"Like a date," Imani replied brightly. "She'll be ready and waiting."

Chuckling, he shifted his attention to Yasmin. "See you later, Doc."

Speechless, the Ohaji sisters watched him swagger out the office door.

Imani rushed over to the window and pressed her face against it. "Good God! Does he ever have a body on him!"

Chapter 9

Food enthusiasts strolled around the Tampa Bay Civic Center, sampling international cuisines from over sixty countries. A combination of spices, blends and aromas seasoned the air, arousing the appetites of visitors. Individual tents displayed the name of each restaurant and employees wore vibrant costumes reflecting their nationalities.

"Let's check out Chocolate Delights," Rashawn suggested, leading the way toward a red-and-white-striped booth. Glancing over his shoulder, he winked. "I suddenly have a taste for something sweet."

Handing the brunette attendant eight tickets, he draped an arm around Yasmin's waist. "Let's try the chocolate fondue."

Yasmin stared down at the counter. A container filled with chocolate sat amid tubs of whipped cream, sprinkles, candy and fruit. She had never tried the sexy dessert, but it looked downright sinful. And messy. "I don't know, I'm wearing white…"

"No problem," the attendant said, flashing a friendly smile. She handed Yasmin a bib and a pack of wet naps. Selecting strawberries and green grapes, she set down the platter and poured some of the melted chocolate into a heart-shaped ceramic bowl. "Here at Chocolate Delights we use only the richest dark chocolate imported directly from Berne, Switzerland. Now, the trick to eating fondue is that you have to do it fast. Swirl the fruit around the bowl until it's completely covered, like this."

Demonstrating, she lifted the straw and popped the chocolate-covered strawberry into her mouth. "It's your turn," she announced, cleaning her hands on her apron.

"It doesn't look hard, does it?" Rashawn secured his bib, then helped Yasmin with hers. "There, we're all set."

"We look like a couple of kids," she joked, taking a fleeting look over her shoulder. "Are you sure you want to do this?"

Nodding, he popped a bite-size kiwi into his mouth. "What do you want to try first? Angel food cake, strawberries, banana chunks?"

Inspecting what was on the platter, she quickly determined what would make the least amount of mess. Yasmin liked trying new things, but she didn't want to spend the rest of the night walking around the civic center with a giant stain on her blouse. "The angel food cake."

While Yasmin waited for him to get further instructions from the attendant, she grabbed some gummy bears from a silver tin. When she had finished what was in her hands, she reached for more.

"Looks like someone has a sweet tooth."

"All my teeth are sweet," she joked, "I'm a junk-food addict and proud of it."

"Then let me hurry up and feed you your cake!" Rashawn picked up a piece of cake and dipped it into the fondue. When he lifted the straw, the cake was gone.

Yasmin patted him on the back. "I think you need more practice!"

"Oh, yeah?" Rashawn dipped his finger into the batter and dotted her nose.

"I'm going to get you for that!"

"Bring it on, Doc."

Behind them, a black elderly couple laughed. Rashawn and Yasmin took turns feeding each other and chuckled every time they lost a piece of fruit in the batter. When they finished their bowl of fondue, they wiped their mouths and continued their promenade. For the next hour, they walked through a park under the glow of the stars.

Yasmin didn't know much about boxing, but she liked hearing how Rashawn had turned a hobby into a successful career and commended his future aspirations of returning to the university for his business degree.

A man of African descent strolled past them and her thoughts turned to Eric. He never would have taken her to Food Fest. He hated crowds and, moreover, he liked to socialize with people of the same socioeconomic background. Although he hadn't liked all the time she spent at the center, he'd tried his best to be supportive. Sadness threatened to come back, but she shook it off. Rashawn was great company and the least she could do was listen to what he was saying.

She studied his profile, awed by the creaminess of his skin and the sensual slope of his lips. They made an odd couple and she couldn't help wondering what people thought as they passed by. Rashawn was a light-skinned Hispanic man and she was a dark, curvaceous African. That made for one hell of a conversation.

The sat down on a bench, under a tall streetlamp.

"I don't understand why you're still single," he said, a puzzled expression on his face. "Unless you haven't been straight up with me."

"No, I'm telling you the truth. I've never been married."

"Engaged?"

"Once."

"What happened?"

Yasmin swung her legs out in front of her. "I don't want to talk about it."

"Did he cheat on you or something?"

"No. Relationships don't always end because someone's been unfaithful."

"That's true. What happened?"

Rashawn touched her cheek. Sadness flickered in her eyes, communicating the depth of her pain. "Talk to me, Doc."

"I don't know what to say."

"There's no pressure. Tell me as much or as little as you want."

Seconds passed, then minutes. Gazing into the sky, she blinked back tears. Yasmin was so used to listening to other people's problems, she had forgotten how cleansing it could be to unburden the soul. And for some reason, she could open up her heart to Rashawn in a way she couldn't to anyone else. "Eric and I met at the university. He was with a bunch of friends and I was with mine. The two groups decided to have lunch and after spending the day with him, I knew he was the man I wanted to marry."

Rashawn arched an eyebrow. "For real? That's kinda fast, don't you think?"

"When you meet the right person, you just know. At least that's what happened in our case." Yasmin sighed, her face losing some of its sadness. "We had a fairy-tale relationship. Eric lavished me with gifts and money and loved showing me off. And I really loved him."

Jealousy crawled up Rashawn's skin. It was hard hearing her talk about another man. Cursing himself for asking about her ex-boyfriend in the first place, he smoothed a hand over his goatee. "Sounds like he had it bad. What happened next?"

"We got engaged after graduation. Eric kept asking me to set a wedding date, but I wasn't ready. I wanted to wait until I got my practice off the ground."

"Did he get tired of waiting and split?"

"No, no, Eric would never do something like that." Her lips trembled as she pushed the words out of her mouth. "He died two years ago of a brain aneurysm. I tried to give him CPR, but he was…he was already gone."

"Damn." Rashawn gathered her in his arms. "I'm a jerk. I shouldn't have asked."

"It's not your fault. How were you supposed to know what happened?" Yasmin brushed away her tears. Her family and friends were supportive, but there was something about being in Rashawn's arms that quieted her soul. "I'm doing better now. I've come to terms with his passing and I don't blame myself anymore."

"I'm glad to hear that. I lost my best friend to gang violence and as much as I like to think I could've saved him, I couldn't." Rashawn lifted her chin and held her gaze. His respect for her was boundless. She was a fighter who bested every trouble as it came. Losing her fiancé had been a devastating loss, but she hadn't let it destroy her. She had picked herself up, nursed her wounds and kept going. "If we have faith, we shouldn't be afraid of death because it brings us closer to God."

"That's beautiful, Rashawn."

"I heard someone say that at Culley's funeral and it stuck with me."

"I can't believe I'm crying," she said, lowering her eyes. "The two-year anniversary of his death was last week and I managed to get through the day without breaking down. I thought I was coping with everything okay, but sometimes I'm so sad, I just can't hold it in."

"Say no more." Reassuring her with a smile, he tightened his grip around her waist. "I know how it is. I'm just glad I could be here for you."

"Me, too." She sat up but didn't move out of his arms. "Thanks for listening, Rashawn. I really needed that."

"Anytime, Doc." Rashawn wore a small smile. What he had to tell her would boost her mood. Determined to put the sparkle back in her eyes, he said, "I bet you're wondering what I have to tell you."

"Not really." Sniffling, she cleaned her face with the back of her hands. Thinking about Eric opened old wounds, but she enjoyed spending time with Rashawn. He had some kind of hold on her and it felt good being with him. "Actually, I forgot about it."

"Good."

"But, now that you mention it, I *am* curious."

Rashawn reached into his back pocket, pulled out a manila envelope and handed it to her. "This is for you." Reading the bewildered expression on her face, he said, "Don't ask any questions, just open it."

Yasmin did as she was told. Inside the envelope was a letter and two Pro Bowl tickets. Her mouth fell open. "Oh, my God!" The paper shook in her hands as she scanned the letter. "You…you got them!"

"I sure did."

"B-but how?"

Rashawn shrugged. "I made some calls to the powers that be and told them about the community center. Told them all the good things that were happening down there and that we needed a donation."

Her face came to life. "And that worked?"

"No. I had to beg like a convict before the parole board!" He chuckled lightly. "I wish I could've done more but—"

Interrupting him, she said, "Done more? Rashawn, this is amazing!" She didn't have on her reading glasses, but managed to read the letter without difficulty. "It says here that guests will have press passes, arena access, a chance to meet the captains from both teams, signed jerseys and seats in the press box." Yasmin broke off, too excited to continue. Raffling off this once-in-a-lifetime Pro Bowl package would not only help the community center reach its financial goal, but would put them above and beyond the target.

Overcome with gratitude, she flung her arms around his neck. "Rashawn, thank you so much! You don't know how much this means to me and the kids at the center."

"You're wrong, I do." Tonight, his admiration for Yasmin was boundless. She was passionate about the projects being developed at the center and had a host of ideas for how to make things better. "I'm glad I can help. It's time I stopped complaining about what's wrong with our community and started being part of the change."

Yasmin pulled away, a radiant smile on her lips. "I feel like I should do something special for you. I mean, you've done so much for me…and the kids."

His eyes bore down on her, robbing her of thought and speech. "I know something you could do."

Her smile slipped. Why did men always ruin a perfectly good moment by making things sexual? Rashawn had come through for her and single-handedly ensured the success of the fundraiser, but that didn't mean she was going to sleep with him. If his donation came with strings, then she wasn't interested. She didn't appreciate what he was implying, but before she could set him straight, he said, "I know it's short notice, but I'm taking my nieces and nephews to Magic Mountain tomorrow and I'd like it if you could come. They're a handful, especially the twins, and I could use another set of eyes."

A slow smile formed on her lips. Rashawn never ceased to amaze her. He was unpredictable and knew how to keep things interesting. Yasmin had plans to go shopping with her mom tomorrow, but she could always reschedule.

"I'd love to tag along."

Rashawn helped Yasmin to her feet. "I had a good time."

"Me too."

"Are you for real or are you just saying that?"

"I'm serious."

"Show me."

She leaned over and pecked his cheek. "There. Now do you believe me?"

"How about another one, over to the right?"

Laughing, they resumed their walk, their arms wrapped tightly around each other.

Chapter 10

Rashawn slid open the van door. During the hour-long drive, he'd implored his nieces and nephews to behave when they reached the park, but he wanted to give them one last reminder. Every year, he brought the kids to Six Flags and every year, their disobedience resulted in the group leaving early. This year, he wanted things to be different. He wanted to hang out with Yasmin and let her see another side of him. A sensitive side. In his experience, nothing impressed a woman more than a man who was good with kids.

"Okay, gang, we're here. We're sticking together, so no one run off. It's a huge park and I don't want anyone to get lost. Or worse—" he glanced around the parking lot and dropping his voice to a spine-chilling whisper, he murmured "—kidnapped."

Behind him, Yasmin cleared her throat.

One by one, the kids filed out of the van. Their voices bubbled with excitement as they sprinted toward the amusement park entrance.

Rashawn locked the doors, tucked the keys into his pocket and fell in step with Yasmin. He perused the multitude of thrill-seekers and immediately spotted his nieces and nephews. Anticipating the mass of visitors and not wanting to repeat what had happened last year, he'd bought neon-green shirts and had the logo Team Bishop splashed across the front and back. The girls had made a fuss about putting the shirts on over their sundresses, but Rashawn had insisted they wear them.

"Did you like my speech?"

"If you were trying to scare them into behaving, I'd say you probably achieved your goal. Using the word *kidnapped* is a bit extreme, don't you think?"

"Nope. The world's changed a lot since I was a kid. I just want them to be safe."

"That's understandable," she conceded, pushing her sunglasses up the bridge of her nose. Spotting the kids, Yasmin stifled a laugh. "Looks like I spoke too soon. The twins are trying to scale the fence!"

Cursing under his breath, he grabbed her hand and shouldered his way through the slow-moving crowd. High-pitched voices and squeals of terror pierced the air. The scent of hot dogs, caramel popcorn and roasted peanuts drifted on the afternoon breeze.

For the rest of the afternoon, Yasmin followed the Bishop family around Magic Mountain, amazed they had the energy to run in the scorching heat. Anna Belle and Porsha, the youngest of the brood, stuck to her side like glue. The six-year-old divas-in-training were more worried about messing up their hair than joining their cousins on the waterslides.

"Let's go on the Gyro Drop," Miguel suggested, dumping his empty drink container in the garbage. "My homeboys told me it's the scariest ride in the park. I gotta check it out!"

Carlito raced ahead. He stopped in front of the gate and pointed to the sign. "It says anyone under sixteen must be accompanied by an adult."

"Then I guess you can't go," Rashawn said, his voice firm.

"Please, Uncle? My boys will diss me if I tell them I didn't go on the ride."

Rashawn rumpled the twelve-year-old's hair. "Sorry, Miguel. Maybe next time."

Yasmin stepped forward. "The kids have been great today. They deserve a reward. You go on and I'll stay with the younger ones."

"Why don't we all go?" Vincente Jr. suggested.

"Yay!"

"Awesome!"

"I want to go, too!"

"That's a good idea," Yasmin agreed. "It's been years since I was here, but I remember the Gyro Drop being a real screamer. I'm in."

Rashawn coughed. "I'll stay behind. You know, in case something happens."

Yasmin studied his face. As a therapist, she often had to look beyond the surface to find the truth, but the expression on Rashawn's was one of all-out fear. He was sweating profusely and his eyes were lined with panic. Either he was scared of heights or he'd suddenly come down with a case of the flu. "Are you okay?" she asked, when he dragged a hand down the length of his face. "You look like you're going to be sick."

"Me? Naw, I'm fine." Rashawn plucked at his T-shirt. "It's hot out here, that's all." He didn't mind swimming with the kids or losing money at arcade games, but he hated extreme rides, especially ones that catapulted participants fifty feet in the air. Rashawn didn't want Yasmin to think he was soft, but he didn't want to die, either.

"You're not scared are you, uncle?" Miguel asked, staring up at him.

"Of an amusement park ride?" Chucking off the comment, he thumped a hand to his chest. "I'm undefeated, remember? A championship contender, no less. Trust me, I've tackled far scarier things."

"Then it's settled. We're all going on the ride." Yasmin counted out the necessary number of tickets and handed them to the operator.

Rashawn was bound to get sick, but he wasn't about to punk out in front of Yasmin. If she could stomach the staggering height, so could he.

"Uncle, do they have those sick bags in case I puke?" Smirking, Carlito knocked elbows with Vincente Jr. "I don't know if I can handle it. My knees are shaking!"

"Cut it out, you guys, or we won't be going." His doubts returned with a vengeance. Swallowing his fear, he glanced warily at the ride dubbed the Shot of Terror. The only way to save himself was to persuade one of the younger kids to back out. "Are you sure you want to go on this ride, girls? It looks pretty scary." His voice cracked but he quickly recovered. "Once they strap us in, there's no turning back."

"Let's go!" Porsha seized his hand and dragged him through the gate.

Twenty minutes later, Rashawn stumbled off the Gyro Drop, with a headache and an upset stomach. The kids asked if they could take a spin on the Ultimate Ferris Wheel and he managed a weak nod. He didn't care what the kids did, as long as he didn't have to participate. His eyes were out of focus and his mouth was dry. It took all of his effort to remain upright, but when Yasmin asked him what he thought of the ride, he said, "Loved it."

"Really?" She clutched his arm. "Me, too! Let's do it again!"

His jaw went slack and the little color he had left in his cheeks drained.

Laughing, she rubbed a hand across his back. "I'm just teasing you, Rashawn. One ride on the Gyro Drop is more than enough for me."

"There it is. My secret is out. I'm scared of heights."

"That's nothing to be ashamed of," she told him. "Everyone's afraid of something. It's only human."

"Really? What are you afraid of?"

Yasmin paused. Rashawn had proven to be trustworthy and she felt comfortable talking to him. They had shared an intimate moment last night at Food Fest, one that had brought them closer together and she felt they were on the threshold of something special. Something real. "Promise you won't laugh?"

"Cross my heart and hope to die."

"You're silly."

"And you're stalling. Come on, what is it?"

"I'm scared of being home alone."

"Really?"

Yasmin channeled her gaze. "When Imani's not home, I double-check all the locks and windows at least five times before I go to bed. I wasn't always this way, but after Eric died…" Her voice faded.

"You don't have to worry about being alone anymore. You've got me now and I'm not going anywhere." Rashawn stopped. He stared down at her, a tender look in his eyes. Aligning his head to the left, he skillfully and carefully dipped his tongue into her mouth. Her skin was warm and her body responsive. Oblivious to the activity around them, he enjoyed the sweet taste of her lips. Seconds passed, then minutes, with no end of the kiss in sight.

"Look! Uncle's kissing Yasmin!"

Yasmin recognized Anna Belle's squeaky voice. Embarrassed, she tried to break away but Rashawn wouldn't release his hold. Nuzzling his face against the side of her neck, he buried his fingers in her hair. "That was…nice." Like Usher, he had it bad, and wasn't ashamed to admit it. "I'm feelin' you in a big way, Doc."

"I like you, too."

"This is more than just like."

Concealing her smile, she said, "I don't know what to say."

"Say you'll have dinner with me tonight."

"Okay."

"I was hoping you'd say that." Remembering they weren't alone, he glanced over at his nieces and nephews. They were swiping change out of a wishing pond. "Let's get out of here before these little deviants get into trouble!"

Over the next month, Yasmin divided her time between the office and the community center. When she wasn't counseling patients, she was on the phone with the caterer, the decorating crew or administration. Costs for the event had ballooned and she had been ordered by the planning committee to rein in the budget. With only days left before the fund-raiser, stress levels were high and the patience of volunteers was running low.

Turning right onto Staler Avenue, Yasmin took a sip of her hazelnut coffee. She needed caffeine and lots of it. Between the last-minute problems that crept up at the center and her issues with Niobie, it was turning into another tiresome week. Her assistant was one miniskirt away from a pink slip and utterly clueless about how her actions were affecting the business. Clients came into A Better Way Counseling Services to have their emotional and psychological needs met and being attended to by a heavyset girl playing dress-up like a video vixen scared them off.

In the past three weeks, not only had Niobie started wearing less and complaining more, her productivity had begun to suffer, as well. Just that morning, she had showed up an hour late. She didn't apologize for her tardiness and offered no explanation. Then, when she was leaving at the end of the day, she asked for Friday off. She suspected her son had an ear infection and wanted to take him to see their family doctor. To keep from losing her temper, Yasmin had continued reading the Medical Report Journal and channeled positive thoughts. It was either that or reach across her desk and shake some sense into the twenty-three-year-old. Had Niobie dressed in the dark? What had she been thinking when she'd left her house that morning? A therapy clinic was no place for a see-through blouse, gaudy bracelets and clunky sandals.

Yasmin sighed, her sleep-deprived body suffused with tension. She didn't have children, but she understood the challenges working mothers faced. Balancing career and family was tough. She didn't mind giving her assistant the day off. What bothered her was Niobie's penchant for tight tops, short skirts and fishnet stockings. Yasmin didn't want to fire Niobie, but she was tired of her sashaying into the office dressed like it was happy hour. The single mom was actively searching for Mr.

Right, but A Better Way Counseling Services was no place to make a love connection.

Stealing a glance at herself in the mirror, her thoughts turned to Rashawn. A slow, easy smile graced her lips. Just the thought of him made her heart flutter. She had hoped to see him last week, but her furious schedule had left her with little personal time. Rashawn had attended the Men of Initiative program, and according to the other volunteers, had made a splash with the kids when he gave them free tickets to his upcoming match.

Yasmin hadn't had time to go out during the week, but when Rashawn had said he wanted to see her, she had agreed to meet him at City Bar Tampa for after-work drinks. It would be the first time they had seen each other since their trip to Magic Mountain. They talked every day, but it wasn't the same as being face-to-face. On the phone, he wasn't nearly as playful or flirtatious and she missed seeing him.

Yasmin flicked on her signal and pulled into the left lane. A sleek, black car with tinted windows cut in front of her. Slamming on her brakes, she narrowly missed plowing into the luxury car. Coffee splashed on her, blemishing her crisp white blazer. Annoyed, she smacked the horn, imagining it was the offender's face. The driver gestured in the rearview mirror, infuriating her even more.

The driver sped out of sight, ignorant of the harm he had caused.

When Yasmin reached the parking lot of City Bar Tampa, she turned off the engine and inspected her outfit. Not only did she have coffee marks on her jacket, she had a long line down her skirt. Groaning inwardly, she grabbed some Kleenex and tried to blot out the stains. Her efforts only made it worse. She couldn't go inside the restaurant in stained clothes. She wanted to see Rashawn, but not looking like this.

Yasmin picked up her cell phone and punched in Rashawn's number. He answered on the first ring and the sound of his voice instantly lifted her spirits. "Hey, it's me," she greeted him.

"Where are you?"

"In the parking lot."

"What's the matter?"

Yasmin told him about her near accident and clothing dilemma. "I feel terrible canceling at the last minute, but you understand, don't you?"

"No problem, we'll go to my place instead."

"I'd rather go home and take a long bath. I've had the worst day."

"I'll be right out. Stay put."

The line went dead. Seconds later, Yasmin watched Rashawn stroll confidently out of the restaurant. He glanced around the parking lot, spotted her and smiled. Her heart murmured. The pull of their physical attraction was overpowering. Like two opposing forces joining together. She had never experienced or imagined that this could be real.

He opened the passenger-side door and stepped inside. His scent infused the car and when he leaned over and kissed her, she melted. Pulling away, his eyes slid from her face to her legs. "Doc, the stain's not that bad. I can barely see it."

"Liar!"

"Okay, you look like you had a fight with a coffee machine."

Yasmin laughed. "Thanks a lot. You sure know how to make a girl feel better."

"I'm just playing." He took her hand and kissed her palm. "I'm not letting you get away so what's it going to be, your place or mine?"

"I won't be good company," she confessed, giving him a sad smile. "I have a lot of things on my mind and a million and one things to do between now and Saturday."

"Why don't you go home, relax for a while and meet me at my place in time for dinner?"

Yasmin considered his offer. She didn't have anything to do tonight except fret over all the things that could go wrong at the fund-raiser. Imani was working late, Katherine was going speed dating and her parents were out of town. Why not hang out with Rashawn? They never ran out of things to say and he would help keep her mind off her troubles. "I can't stay long," she told him. "I have an early-morning meeting with the caterer."

"Cool." Rashawn opened the car door. "See you later?"

Feeling playful, Yasmin winked. "Definitely."

Chapter 11

"My feet do not stink!" Yasmin yelled, hurling a cushion at Rashawn. "You wish your toes were as cute as mine!"

Ducking, he dodged the blow and repositioned her legs on his lap. "Don't flatter yourself. Your feet smell like nacho cheese!"

Giggling, she poked him with her toe. If she hadn't eaten two helpings of the shrimp calamari he'd ordered, she would get up and give him the beating he deserved. But after a plate of food and two glasses of wine, Yasmin couldn't move. And the skillful way he was massaging her calves was making her feel drowsy.

Rashawn worked his hands from her legs to her heels. "Do you have time to go shopping on Saturday? I was hoping we could check out some of the furniture stores."

"I can't. Not only am I organizing the fund-raiser, I'm on the decorating committee, as well. I'll probably be at the hall most of the day."

"Do you need more volunteers?"

"Of course. It would be great if you could come by."

"If you need me, I'm there. But what about my place? As you can see, it still needs a lot of work."

When Rashawn had said he wanted help decorating, Yasmin had thought it was a ploy to get her inside his house. But after a brief tour, she had realized he didn't have anything but a couch and some chairs. There were no rugs, no blinds, no lamps. Rashawn didn't have any furniture, but he had a sixty-three-inch TV, a PlayStation 3 and CD stands that held thousands of movies.

Surprised at how bare it was, Yasmin had dug into her wallet, pulled out Essence Gilbert-Clark's business card and encouraged him to call. Rashawn had rejected the idea, insisting they could decorate together. Yasmin wasn't an interior designer, but she loved fabrics and accessories and she knew what looked good. Conflicted about what to do, she'd considered everything Rashawn had done for her since they met. He had filled in at the Men of Initiative program, had scored Pro Bowl tickets for the silent auction and agreed to emcee the fund-raiser. Since he had given so much of himself, the least she could do was give him some decorating tips. "Why don't we go on Sunday?"

"Cool. I'll work out in the morning, then come scoop you."

Yasmin murmured in response. She felt herself slipping away. The last six weeks had taken their toll. Working ten-hour days and then spending her evenings at the center was exhausting. But the soothing touch of his hands and the quiet sounds drifting in through the window quieted her body and soul.

"Can I get you anything? Another glass of wine maybe?"

"No," slipped out of her mouth in a dreamy whisper. Tucking a hand behind the pillow, she leaned back against the cushions and closed her eyes. His touch was sweet. As his hands worked their magic, she reflected on all of the good things happening in her life.

A Better Way Counseling Services was thriving, the renovations at the community center would begin at the end of the month and she'd met Rashawn. A thoughtful, considerate man who made her smile. He was attentive, generous and charismatic. So much so, it was hard for her not to gravitate toward him. He was completely hooked into her wants and needs, and when they were together Yasmin had never felt so sexy. Or desirable. It was a heady feeling, one she had never known.

"This couch is too small for us," he told her, squirting massage oil onto his open palms. "We should go into the bedroom."

He was right, but Yasmin would rather lay on the couch than on his king-size bed. Two glasses of Merlot, soft sheets and his sensual voice were a sensual combination. There was no telling what would happen. "I don't mind. Besides, I'm too full to move."

Rashawn drenched his hands with oil and rubbed her legs. Her mink-brown skin was smooth and silky. She was an impressive five feet eight inches, and proud of her regal height. Tonight, she was flaunting her legs in a thigh-grazing sundress. When he'd opened the front door and seen her standing there, he'd taken her into his arms and kissed her until he'd gratified his desire. Then and only then did he let her go and invite her inside. To him, she was perfection. An incredibly desirable woman with a strong sense of self. Sexy in every imaginable way.

He thought back to the night they had met. From the moment he had spotted her, he had known he had to meet her. She stood out from everyone else in the room and for good reason. Her beauty was evident in her smile, the glow of her skin and the way she carried herself. They had only known each other for a couple of months, but they had developed something special in a short space of time. More memories came to mind. The day he had showed up at her office and caught her doing an impromptu duet with Anthony Hamilton. And the time they'd spent at Food Fest sampling chocolate fondue. But it was the image of her playing soccer that brought a grin to his mouth. Trustworthy, intellectual and sophisticated, Yasmin Ohaji was everything he wanted in a woman and more.

Rashawn worked his hands across her shoulders blades, down her arms, then up to her neck. Her face was the picture of peace. Eyes closed, hands folded, legs crossed at the ankles. Driven by desire, he bent down and kissed her softly on the lips. He was happy to keep things on a casual level for now, but it was just a matter of time until they would become lovers. And when they did, he would make sure to cherish her.

A sigh escaped her lips and he unraveled. He was a slave to his body and it was calling out for more. With massage-oiled palms, he rubbed his hands down the length of her thighs to her legs. Yasmin tilted her head to the right, exposing her collarbone. Before he could stop himself, he was raining kisses along her neck. Rashawn felt her arms around him, drawing him closer. Using his tongue to draw light circles along her ear, he slipped a hand up her dress and caressed her inner thigh. Addicted to the taste of her lips, he kissed her again. They kissed long and hard, the intensity of their attraction rocking them both. His body yearned for her, desired her, needed her. The only thing standing between them making love was an appropriate amount of fear. When she put a hand under his T-shirt and stroked his chest, he groaned. It was time, he decided, slipping a finger into her panties. The setting couldn't be more right. Intimate conversation, a hot-oil massage, soft music. But as he stretched out on top of her, he saw the trepidation in her eyes. This wasn't right. He had to stop. Yasmin wasn't ready for their relationship to become sexual, but that didn't stop him from wanting her.

Nestling his face in her hair, he said, "I didn't mean to wake you."

"You didn't think I was actually sleeping, did you?" Yasmin pulled back so she could see his face. "Trust me, the best way to enjoy a massage is with your eyes closed."

"Well, how did I do?"

"On the massage—" Yasmin lifted a brow "—or the extra services?"

Chuckling, he kissed the tips of her fingers. "Both."

"You're a ten."

The doorbell chimed. But instead of getting up, he traced a finger up the slope of her inner thigh. "Where were we?"

"You're not going to answer the door?"

"Nope."

"It could be an emergency."

"Then they should call nine-one-one."

Giggling, she playfully pushed him off of her. "I'm going to the bathroom," she announced, adjusting her dress. "Get the door, Rashawn. It could be important." Ignoring the wounded expression on his face, she stood and sashayed out of the room.

His eyes trailed her down the hall. As long as he'd lived, he'd never meet anyone as captivating as Yasmin Ohaji. She was the most authentic woman he had ever met. Her confidence, her attitude, her playfulness; he desired her in ways he couldn't explain. They were that much closer to being a couple and just the thought of her being his woman inflated his heart with pride. Grinning, he got off the couch and strolled into the foyer. His smile couldn't get any bigger, but when he opened his front door, it fizzled like smoke. Surprise gave way to annoyance as he folded his arms across his chest. "What are you doing here?"

Armondo sneered. "Is that any way to greet your baby brother?"

Yasmin stuck her hands under the faucet. Peering into the mirror, she scrutinized her look. Her makeup was flawless, her lips were glossy and every hair was in place. Smiling back at her reflection, she shut off the water and searched for something to dry her hands. There were no cloths, no paper towels and no Kleenex. Rashawn wasn't kidding when he said he didn't have anything in the apartment.

Opening the closet, she found a pile of face towels. As she wiped her hands, she caught sight of several miniature vials along the back shelf. Yasmin wasn't one to snoop, but she hadn't rummaged around looking for them. They were in plain view. Having justified her thoughts, she reached in and turned one of the bottles around to the label. "Jintropin—Human Growth Hormone for Injection," she read aloud.

Yasmin blinked. She couldn't believe what she was seeing. This had to be a mistake. Rashawn was using performance-enhancement drugs? Backing away from the closet, she steadied a hand to her chest. It felt like her heart was beating twice as fast. Her mind raced as her thoughts turned to Quintrel Durant.

Years ago, when she had been working at the public health

clinic, she had counseled the amateur bodybuilder. Addicted to steroids and desperate to qualify for Mr. USA, the nineteen-year-old had upped his dosage and ultimately damaged his kidneys. After a ninety-day stint at an Orlando treatment center, he had quit using drugs and cleaned up his life.

Her lips tightened, her face an angry mask. Rashawn Bishop was a liar, a cheat, a fraud. He was preaching health and fitness to the boys in the Men of Initiative program, but was using illegal drugs. He pretended to be honest, sincere and genuine, but he was none of those things. Integrity was a dying trait in the twenty-first century, but she would rather be alone than with a man who lied to her. Yasmin couldn't believe she had been fooled. How could she have been so wrong about him? Flattered by his attention, she'd allowed herself to be swept up in his games of deceit.

Hands shaking, she slowly opened the bathroom door. In the living room, Rashawn was talking to a teenager with oily skin and shifty eyes. In a black Kangol pulled down past his eyebrows, an extra-large football jersey that skimmed his knees and jeans so wide they could double as a parachute, the boy reminded her of the thugs Rashawn had chased off at the Laurdel Lounge.

"You're back. You were gone so long, I was gonna come check on you," Rashawn teased. He motioned to the kid. "This is my brother Armondo."

Her shoulders tensed when Rashawn slipped his hand around her waist. Fighting the urge to smack his arm away, she said, "It's nice meeting you."

Armondo tore his gaze away from the TV. "Yeah, same here." Propping his feet up on the table, he resumed flipping channels with the remote control.

"He stopped by for a quick visit, but he's leaving now. Get up, Armondo." Rashawn spoke in a loud, booming voice. "It's time to bounce."

Yasmin moved out of his arms. "That's not necessary. Visit with your brother. I have to go." Before Rashawn could protest, she had her purse and was marching briskly down the hallway.

Rashawn caught up with her in the foyer. Capturing her around the waist, he begged, "Doc, don't run off. I want you to stay."

Ten minutes ago, Yasmin would have melted into his embrace. Now she wanted to get as far away from him as possible. Untangling herself from his arms, she backed up against the door. "I have to go."

"I understand. I guess I can survive not seeing you for a couple of days. What time do you need me at the center on Saturday?"

"Forget I mentioned it. I think we'll have enough volunteers."

"Are you sure? I don't mind."

"Positive." Yasmin blinked back tears, the sudden demise of their relationship weighing heavily on her. "I can't go shopping with you on Sunday. I just remembered I'm having brunch at my parents' house."

"All day?"

"Pretty much. My mom throws a huge get-together once a month and my entire family will be there. It'll be hard for me to get away."

His eyebrows merged. Rashawn couldn't understand the drastic change in her. They'd had a passionate evening, filled with kisses, caresses and a sensual massage, and now she was cold. Was she upset because Armondo stopped by? Confused, he propped a hand on the wall, preventing her from opening the front door. "Are you mad because my brother's here? You want me to get rid of him so we can finish our date?"

"This isn't about your brother."

"Then, what is it about?"

Yasmin was anxious to leave, but she couldn't go without telling Rashawn how she felt. "Call me when you're ready to get help. I know some of the best addiction specialists in the country." With that, she flung open the door and escaped into the night.

Stupefied, Rashawn watched her climb into her SUV. What the hell was she talking about? He didn't have an addiction.

Aside from a beer or two when he was out with the guys, he didn't touch alcohol. She'd been the one to drink wine at dinner, not him. Averse to taking medication of any kind, he didn't even use over-the-counter drugs. Lost in his thoughts, he ambled back into the living room and slumped onto the couch.

"What's up, bro?" Armondo clamped a hand on his back. "She bust your chops when you went in for a goodnight kiss?"

"I don't know what just happened. We had a good time together, a damn good time. Everything was cool until she came back from the bathroom."

"Maybe she found your secret stash of *Playboy* magazines."

"Shut up, Armondo. This is serious."

"Are you shittin' me? You really diggin' that girl?"

Rashawn's lips curled, his eyes narrowing dangerously. "Is that a problem?"

"Well, no, but she's African."

"And?"

"Don't get me wrong. She's cute and all, but you guys make an odd couple."

"Really? How so?" he challenged, fighting the urge to heave his younger brother out the front door.

"Well, for starters she's real dark and you're superlight. She's professional and you're from the 'hood. See where I'm going?" Ignorant of the disgusted expression on Rashawn's face, he resumed flipping channels with the remote control. "Whatever happened to that sexy Hispanic chick from Long Beach?"

"You mean the gold digger who asked me to pay her rent on the first date?"

Armondo snapped his fingers, his eyes alive with recollection. "Yeah, her! She was fine as hell."

"I'm tired of dating girls like that. I want a woman with substance and women like Evalisse Jimenez are about as common as a lap dance in a strip club." Smoothing a hand over his goatee, his thoughts returned to Yasmin. Something was up. He didn't know why she was mad at him, but he was about to find out.

Rashawn leapt off the couch and Armondo stalked behind

him. "Can we talk about the loan now? All I need is ten grand, bro. You know I'm good for it. I'll have it back to you before you even notice it's gone."

"Not now, Armondo."

"I need the money to cut my demo. Mom would give it to me if she had it, but she doesn't. My rap career's finally taking off, bro. If you don't believe me, check me out next week at the Bamboo Club."

"Things are tight right now," he told him. "I paid cash for this place, remember?"

"But you made three hundred grand on your last fight!"

"Like I told you before, most of my money is tied up in investments, long-term-saving plans and stock options. I'm not going to end up like Mike Tyson—penniless, broke and wondering where my earnings went."

"So, you *do* have money?"

Tuning out his brother, Rashawn threw open the bathroom door and smacked on the light switch. His gaze swept the room. Nothing. Figuring she might have peeked inside the medicine cabinet, he marched over to the sink and opened it. Everything was in place. Had she gone into the master bedroom? There was nothing incriminating in his room, but it wouldn't hurt to look around. Determined to find what had scared off Yasmin, he brushed past his brother who had followed him into the bathroom, and went into the hall.

"Hold up. I think I got something." Chuckling, Armondo poked his head out the bathroom door. "Your girl's a narc, bro."

"What?"

"Looks like she was diggin' around in the closet."

"What are you talking about?" Rashawn snapped, irritated. Glancing over his shoulder, he said, "There's nothing in—" When he spotted the miniature vial of human growth hormone in Armondo's hand, his heart sank to his knees.

Chapter 12

"Did you get my messages?"

Yasmin turned at the slumberous sound of Rashawn's voice, but didn't stop folding napkins. "Yeah, all fourteen of them."

"And?"

"And what?"

"Don't you think we should talk?" Annoyed that she wouldn't stop what she was doing and look at him, he jammed his hands into his pockets. "Let's go somewhere we can be alone."

"I can't. I still have a hundred or so of these to do."

"Then, we'll do it together." Rolling up his sleeves, he watched her tuck the utensils inside the napkin and smooth a hand over the bulge. Rashawn didn't know why she was going to all the trouble of making it look fancy when no one would appreciate it, but he didn't voice his opinion. He was on her bad side and he didn't want to aggravate her any further. Compliments yes, criticism no.

"Did you get home okay last night?" he asked, struggling to fold the napkin in the intricate way she was doing it. Either his hands were too big or he was creatively challenged. "I was going to swing by, but—"

"If you want to make yourself useful, why don't you go help the guys finish unfolding the chairs? Or set up the tables," she snapped. "The fund-raiser starts at seven and we're way behind schedule."

"We need to talk and what I have to say just can't wait."

Annoyed, she shot him a baleful look. "Well, that's too bad, because now's not a good time. If you really cared about the kids like you say you do, you'd push aside what *you* want and get to work."

Rashawn threw up his hands. "Fine, have it your way. I won't stay where I'm not welcome. Since you'd rather write me off than give me a chance to explain, there's nothing left to say. I'm outta here."

The turbulence of her feelings prevented her from going after him. He'd been calling her cell phone for hours, but she hadn't answered any of his calls. She felt bad about giving him a hard time, but what was she supposed to do? Rashawn was a silver-tongued manipulator and if she wasn't careful she'd be conned again. Obliterating all thoughts of Rashawn from her mind, she opened a new pack of napkins and focused on her task at hand.

For the rest of the afternoon, Rashawn served as errand boy, moving man and taskmaster. Dog tired, he flopped down on one of the plastic chairs. He'd gotten up at the crack of dawn, and after a quick shower and a protein shake, headed to the gym. An hour into his workout, he'd been bothered by a headache and cut his training session short. He had come to the community center in hopes of talking to Yasmin, only to be dismissed as a nuisance.

After Yasmin blew him off, he'd gone into the basement, organized the boys into groups and helped carry the remaining tables upstairs. Convinced the cafeteria could be transformed into a rich, elegant space, Melba had ordered him to buff the floors with a high-powered cleaning machine. Rashawn had initially been skeptical. The room needed more than expensive decorations and frilly napkins to make it look good. But he had underestimated Yasmin. She showed religious attention to detail and perfection, but was open to suggestions. She oversaw the decorating, met with the teens who had been hired to serve the guests and took phone calls in between. Rashawn didn't know how she did it. There was a growing list of things to be done, but she was on top of everything.

Yasmin had worked her magic and in the space of a few hours the cafeteria resembled the grand ballroom of a five-star hotel. Round tables were fashioned with apple-red tablecloths, gold place settings and elaborate flower arrangements. Silk seat covers were sure to impress guests, and the crystal chandeliers emitted a warm, natural light. Desiring a cheerful look, Yasmin had volunteers hang oversize paintings on the walls. Children as young as five had captured what the community center meant to them. The paintings contradicted their age and proved that talent could be fostered through time, dedication and commitment. At the end of the night, the artists would be summoned to the stage and presented with thousand-dollar scholarships to Tampa's School of Art.

Searching the room, he found Yasmin beside the window, talking with a casually-dressed man. Rashawn could tell by the stranger's mannerisms that he came from money. A man who probably owned million-dollar properties, sipped cognac and smoked Cuban cigars. He had impeccable posture and there was an air of pride about him. Rashawn was curious who the man was, but he couldn't take his eyes off Yasmin. Her pink hooded-jacket had been matched with black pants and sneakers and her hair was in a loose ponytail. Aside from lip gloss, her face was free of make-up. She was sexy in a simple, unprofessed way and he wanted her more than ever before.

"Lunch is ready!" Melba announced, exiting the kitchen. "Stop what you're doing and come eat." She placed trays of sandwiches, fruit and boxes of juice on a long wooden table. "There's roast beef, salami, vegetarian…"

Around the room, work stopped. Teenagers raced toward the table, only to have Melba stop them and order them to form a single line. Within minutes, people were spread out, eating, talking and laughing. Rashawn glanced at Yasmin and was relieved to see that she was alone. He grabbed a couple of tomato and lettuce sandwiches and two juice boxes and headed across the room. Yasmin was bent over a chair, retying a loose bow.

"Thought you might be hungry." He extended his right hand.

"No, thanks."

"You've been working like a madwoman all afternoon. Come eat."

"I had coffee. That's enough to keep me going."

"Let's go outside. It's a beautiful day and we've been cooped up for hours."

Standing, she reached for her clipboard. "I can't. There's too much to do."

"Don't make me throw you over my shoulder and drag you out of here," he warned, adopting a stern facial expression. "Don't test me, Doc, 'cause you know I will."

Yasmin bit down on her bottom lip.

"I think I see the makings of a smile."

"You're too much."

"That's why you like me."

He was right. She did like him. It was hard not to. Time he could have spent training, he had willingly donated to the center. Yasmin felt her resolve weaken, but hardened her heart. Using illegal drugs was something she couldn't condone, no matter how she felt about him. "Rashawn, leave me alone. I don't have anything to say to you."

"You're important to me Doc, and I care what you think of me." He took a fleeting look around the room. "Can we go somewhere private?"

"I don't associate with people who do drugs." The doctor in her said, "Do you know steroid use has been linked to serious health issues like cancer and strokes?"

"The vials you saw in the cabinet aren't mine."

"Right," she muttered, rolling her eyes.

"It's the truth."

"You don't do drugs, but you have steroids hidden in your bathroom. That doesn't make sense, Rashawn."

"You think I'm lying?"

"If the shoe fits…"

Exasperated, he released a deep sigh. "A boxer at my gym was having problems with his girl, so I let him stay with me for a while. When I found out about his drug problem, I kicked him out."

"Right."

"I'm serious. I have a reputation to protect and I won't have my name tarnished because one of my friends messed up."

Regarding him critically, she considered his words. "You expect me to believe you've never, *ever* used steroids. Not even once?"

"Not even once." His denial was met with skepticism and, when she rolled her eyes, he took her by the arm and led her out a side door. Outside, the janitor mowed an overgrown field. Youngsters picked up garbage and a full-figured Mexican woman pulled up weeds.

"I don't have time for this," she told him, glancing down at her watch. "The banquet starts in two hours and I have to check in with the caterer, give final instructions to the servers and see to it that—"

"Don't you care about what I have to say?"

"No," she lied, refusing to meet his gaze. "I hardly know you. If you want to jeopardize your health for fifteen minutes of fame, who am I to stop you?"

Anger threatened to overtake him, but he censored his mouth. Rashawn could accept the fact that she was mad at him, but he wasn't prepared to end their relationship. It felt good, damn good, being with a strong, intellectual woman capable of taking care of herself. Yasmin didn't have any ulterior motives. She didn't want anything from him and she didn't expect him to take care of her financially. "I may be a lot of things, but I'm not a liar. I've been straight up with you since day one. I'm undefeated because I train hard, and I do not use steroids."

"If you say so." Yasmin stared at the flower garden. Peach-colored tulips waved in the wind and the air smelled sweet. "Are we finished?"

Rashawn stared at her, unsure of what more to say. He had to prove to her that he was telling the truth. "I haven't been a Boy Scout, Doc. I did a lot of messed-up things when I was a kid. I ran with a bad crowd, skipped school and picked fights. I smoked weed with my boys, but I never, *ever* used steroids. Once I started boxing, I got my shit together and focused on my future." Rashawn had fought boxers with lightning-quick speed and Herculean strength, but nothing was more stressful than arguing with Yasmin. Searching for the right words to convince her he was a changed man, he smoothed a hand over his goatee. "Drugs may have been a part of my past, but they're not a part of my present. Or my future."

Yasmin scoffed, her eyes shooting daggers at him. The Blind Boys of Alabama could see that he was lying. Only a fool would believe that he had come by his success honorably. These days, you couldn't turn on the TV without a professional athlete being investigated for illegal drug use. Everyone from baseball players to cyclists to track stars were bending the rules to gain an upper hand. They risked their lives in the pursuit of riches and fame, never once weighing the potential consequences of their actions. As she watched him, she finally saw him for who he was: a lying cheat. Tired of hearing his lies, she said, "Great, now that we've straightened *that* out, I can get back to work."

"I don't want this to change things between us. Not when we're starting to…"

Turning away from him, she refused to listen to another word of his argument. Unconscionably a charmer, he swayed people with his larger-than-life persona and slippery speech. He always knew what to say and when to say it. That bothered her. It was as if he had anticipated her questions and rehearsed his answers.

Marching inside, Yasmin ignored the niggling thought at the back of her mind. It didn't matter that his explanation was believable or that he came off as being sincere or that he looked contrite. Men like Rashawn tailored the truth to suit their needs. He had everyone at the center charmed. Too bad he was a wolf in sheep's clothing.

Eradicating their conversation from her mind, Yasmin swiped her clipboard off the table and continued her swift, soldierlike walk through the cafeteria. She had a growing list of things to do and no time to waste. And thinking about Rashawn Bishop was definitely a waste of time.

Chapter 13

"Good evening and welcome to Parkland Community Center's sixth annual charity fund-raiser!" The human resource director leveled a hand over his tie. "I want to thank each and every one of you for coming out. You're in for a real treat tonight. Coming to the stage, with an impressive record of thirty-seven wins, all by way of knockout, is Tampa's very own Rashawn 'The Glove' Bishop!"

The well-dressed crowed hooted, hollered and cheered.

From the back of the room, Yasmin watched Rashawn emerge from behind a velvet curtain. Momentarily paralyzed by the sight of him, a sigh of longing escaped her lips. Rashawn may have been one of a hundred men wearing a suit, but he was anything but average. She couldn't keep her tongue from lagging out of her mouth when he strolled confidently onto the stage.

Clothed in a tailored caramel-brown suit, with a heart-stopping smile, Rashawn took his rightful place behind the podium. Her eyes gulped up his rugged good looks and muscular body. It didn't matter if he were in a restaurant or walking down the street, he made his presence felt wherever he went. People were drawn to him like moths to a flame.

Acutely aware that any minute she may start to drool all over her gown, Yasmin tore her gaze away from the stage and examined the crowd. Women in formal gowns and men in dinner jackets socialized, drank and sampled hors d'oeuvres. Local celebrities and even the former mayor and his aides were in attendance. For the first time ever, the fund-raiser was sold out and more tables had been added to accommodate additional guests.

"You didn't tell me The Glove was emceeing," Eli said, an awestruck expression on his face. "I would have brought my digital camera if I'd known he'd be here. You know how much I could make selling his picture on eBay?"

Yasmin shook her head. "That's why I didn't tell you. I didn't want you showing up with boxing gloves and other memorabilia for him to sign."

"Help me out! I'm a struggling college student just trying to make ends meet."

Imani smirked. "That's a lie if I've ever heard one."

Mr. and Mrs. Ohaji, who were seated across from their three children, laughed. "Quit being so hard on your brother," Silas Ohaji ordered, draping an arm around his wife's chair. "As I recall, he wasn't the only one who needed a helping hand in college."

Eli nodded. "Thanks, Pops. I knew you'd understand. It's tough juggling school, my friends, the ladies and being the big man on campus."

"I don't think that's the point your father was trying to make, Eli." Zadie tasted her cocktail, her gaze fixed on her son. "Just because we help you out here and there doesn't give you license to blow your money on parties and whatnot. It's time you faced your studies, concentrated on your grades and—"

"Mom, relax." Eli planted a kiss on her cheek. "Don't get yourself worked up over nothing. Besides, that kind of talk is bad for me *and* your blood pressure."

Everyone around the table laughed.

Rashawn directed his gaze to the back of the room. He tried to catch Yasmin's eye, but she was talking to Katherine. One way or another, he had to find a way to make amends. Not only because he cared about her, but because when she'd entered the room on the arm of a tall, preppy-looking man, he'd felt a stab of jealousy. He'd expected to see her in a long, regal gown, not a short, flirty one. Rashawn glanced down at the notes Yasmin had prepared for him. He had never been one to follow a script and he wasn't about to start now.

"Before we go any further, I'd like to acknowledge all of the people who made tonight possible." One by one, Rashawn had administrators, the board of directors, the organizing committee and the set-up crew stand to receive well-deserved applause. "Last but not least, I want to honor the woman whose vision was the driving force behind this event. A woman whose dedication and tireless commitment has been improving the lives of inner-city children for the last six years. Please put your hands together for my gorgeous cohost, Dr. Yasmin Ohaji!"

Yasmin's head snapped up. *Did he just call my name?* And if that wasn't shocking enough, Rashawn hopped off the stage and strode through the crowd. His delighted smile beckoned her and teased her. Microphone in hand, he said, "For the rest of the night, Dr. Ohaji is going to be by my side. Nothing like an attractive woman to keep a guy on his toes, right, fellas?"

Guests chuckled.

Yasmin was as hot as fire. She had planned the program, and nowhere on it was she listed as a cohost. Before she could collect her thoughts, Rashawn was at her table, wearing a mischievous grin.

"Dr. Ohaji?" he prompted, graciously extending his right hand.

Yasmin remained seated. Fingering her chandelier earrings, she glanced around the room. Just as she suspected. Everyone was watching her. Uncrossing her legs, she took a moment to consider her options. There weren't any. It was a charity event. How would it look if she rebuffed the celebrity emcee? Not to mention, she was sitting with her parents and they would be mortified if she were to cause a scene.

"You're not going to disappoint all these people, are you, Dr. Ohaji?"

Polite laughter, followed by more applause.

Yasmin felt a hand on her back, pushing her to her feet. Hiding her feelings behind the veil of her smile, she gripped his forearm and ordered her legs to move. The faces of her friends, family and colleagues swarmed around her, smiling, laughing, waving. "What are you doing?" she whispered. "We never planned this."

Lowering the microphone, he said, "I know. Just shaking things up a bit. Anything for the center, right, Doc?"

Rashawn was working her nerves to the bone. If everyone hadn't been watching them, Yasmin would have smacked the grin off his face. Digging her fingernails into his flesh made her feel better, but didn't draw blood. In her line of work, she had to be a quick thinker and although she had been caught off guard by his sudden announcement, it was nothing she couldn't handle. Once they reached the podium, she took the microphone from his hands and faced the mostly female crowd. "Isn't our emcee handsome, ladies?"

Women shrieked and applauded.

"Not only has Mr. Bishop graciously donated his time to this event, he's also agreed to be auctioned off!"

Rashawn's face crumpled in embarrassment. He coughed, fear flashing in his eyes. His cool demeanor slid away under the bright lights. Smiling ruefully, he pleaded silently for forgiveness. Yasmin felt a pang of guilt, but that didn't stop her from saying, "I know some of you guys were hoping to bid, but this offer is *strictly* for the ladies."

Groans and cheers mingled.

Yasmin subdued her laughter. No one messed with her and got away with it! *Why didn't I think of this sooner?* she thought. Rashawn did everything with a smoothness that heightened his appeal, and tonight his celebrity would benefit the community center.

Shifting his weight, Rashawn tugged impatiently at his silver cuff links. Yasmin took great delight in watching him squirm. She would get rid of him once and for all and make a pile of money for the center. It was a win-win situation for everybody. Well, everyone except Rashawn.

Feeling jovial, she rested a hand on his back and led him to the middle of the wide, open stage. "For those of you who don't know much about boxing, let me tell you about Rashawn 'The Glove' Bishop. He's single, he's never been married and he has no children that he's aware of."

Laughter rang out.

"Only women serious about dating this star athlete are invited to bid. The package includes—" she paused, imagining the perfect date "—his and her massages at the Aqua Beauty Spa, followed by dinner and dancing at the Grand Hyatt. At midnight, you'll be whisked away for a romantic carriage ride to…"

One by one, women abandoned their seats and gathered in front of the stage. Jockeying for position, they stared up at Rashawn as if he were a four-carat diamond in the Tiffany store window.

Yasmin examined Rashawn's admirers. Swathed in furs, gold and designer gowns, they waved their checkbooks in the air. A few hundred dollars? From the looks of things, they were set to make thousands. "Keep in mind, ladies, that this is for a good cause. Parkland Community Center has been an integral part of this neighborhood for over thirty years and we have to expand the facility. To do that, we need to raise a substantial amount of money tonight." Pleased that the audience was nodding in agreement, she extended a hand toward Rashawn. "Now, on with the auction! We're going to start the bidding at five hundred dollars…"

"Looks like I'm going to have to introduce myself."

Goose bumps shot up Yasmin's arm. What was Rashawn doing at her table and why was he shaking hands with her parents? Turning away as if she hadn't heard him speak, she asked Julius if he was enjoying his meal. It took some effort, but she managed to split her attention between her date and the conversation Rashawn was having with her mom and dad.

"Mr. and Mrs. Ohaji. It's an honor to finally meet you." He shifted his gaze to Yasmin. "I've been dying to meet the couple who raised such a remarkable woman."

Zadie smiled politely. "I wish I could say the same, Rashawn but it seems our daughter has been keeping you under wraps."

Silas's laugh was a throaty chuckle. "Don't mind my wife son. She's a former district attorney and likes to use her training to interrogate the kids. But I know all about you. I've been following your career for years. I'm a huge fan and I think you have what it takes to be the next WBC champion."

"You think so?" he asked, taking the empty seat beside the dark-skinned man.

"You remind me of young Joe Frazier. You're light on your feet, you can bob and weave with the best of them and you have a lethal right hook."

"I'm working hard to get to the next level, but it hasn't been easy."

"Just hang in there, son," Silas said, wearing a hearty smile. "They say luck is the residue of design, so keep doing what you're doing and you'll reap the rewards."

"Thanks, Mr. Ohaji."

"Call me Silas. Any friend of my daughter is a friend of mine."

Rashawn winked at Yasmin; she rolled her eyes.

Sweeping her gaze around the room, she searched the crowd for the rest of her family. Eli had excused himself to answer his cell phone and was nowhere to be found; Imani and Niobie were chatting with Cecil Manning, and Katherine was flirting with a guy who looked a decade younger.

The sound of Rashawn's voice made her snap to attention.

"You didn't tell me your father was a fan."

"It must have slipped my mind."

Drawing eye-level with her, he smiled sagaciously. "I wonder what other secrets you've been keeping."

Yasmin wished Rashawn would go back to his table. He was spending too much time with her parents. Her father chuckled at his jokes and even her mother, who had a quiet, refined laugh, had burst out laughing a few times.

Yasmin kept her eyes on Julius, but she was secretly listening to Rashawn. He spoke with reverence as he shared memories of his trip to South Africa. His infinite knowledge of her beloved homeland was sure to impress her parents.

"I have plans to go back next year. I'd love to take my family, especially my nieces and nephews. They've never been outside of Florida and I think they're at the age where they can fully appreciate the experience. I'd like them to have a tour of the shanty-towns and maybe arrange for them to help serve meals at an orphanage."

"Rashawn, you're absolutely right. It's never too early to show children the power of service, sacrifice and giving." Punctuating her words with a smile, Yasmin's mother regarded him carefully. "If you don't mind me asking, where are your parents from?"

He told her, then said, "My family's here. Maybe you can meet them later."

Silas nodded enthusiastically. "That would be great. I would love to meet the woman who raised the next heavyweight champion of the world!"

The trio laughed.

"I don't mean to interrupt," Rashawn said, turning to Yasmin, "but it's time to announce the winners of the silent auction."

Yasmin swallowed the food in her mouth. They were going where? It wasn't easy keeping up with two very different conversations. "Pardon me?"

"It's time to return to the stage."

"It is?"

A quick glance at her watch confirmed it was eight o'clock. Despite her impromptu raffle, the program was running smoothly and she had made up for the time she had lost during the bidding by shortening the mayor's speech. "I didn't realize it was so late," she said, standing. "Thanks for reminding me."

They walked toward the stage, pausing to meet guests and

shake hands with Rashawn's supporters. As they neared the podium, he gently took her arm and steered her to the right. Instead of pulling away, Yasmin shot him a scathing look. He had been calling the shots all night and she was sick of it. And auctioning him off to the highest bidder hadn't been the payback she had imagined it would be. She had hoped to raise money for the center and pawn off the boxer on some rich, lonely spinster.

The former had been accomplished to the tune of ten thousand dollars, but his date, Cheyenne Whitmore, was a leggy TV news anchor with an energetic personality. The Princeton graduate had the highest-rated entertainment program in the state. Cheyenne was the exact replica of Teagan, except she was taller. Rashawn was obviously attracted to thin, Barbie-doll types with curly hair, so why was he pursuing her? Yasmin pretended not to care, but deep down she hated seeing Rashawn with Cheyenne. And when the news reporter wrapped her arms around him and insisted they pose for pictures, Yasmin wanted to push her off the stage. Instead, she smiled and thanked her for supporting the community center.

"My mom wants to meet you," Rashawn said. "I hope that's okay."

As they crossed the room, Yasmin noticed that everyone at table nine was watching them. Unnerved by the attention, she focused her gaze on the forty-something woman with the round, pleasant face. Rashawn's mom. They shared the same intense eyes, thin nose and rich smile. Even from a distance, she radiated warmth. Her evening gown accentuated the rose in her cheeks and her dark hair was done in an elegant bun.

Johanna stood and gave Rashawn a brief, motherly kiss. "Hijo, I'm so proud of you! You're a natural onstage! Maybe you should talk to that Cheyenne woman about being on her TV show."

Calm and confidant, Yasmin waited patiently to be introduced. They weren't a couple and this meeting had no bearing on their future, but Yasmin wanted his mom to accept her just as her parents had accepted him. Accepted? Hell, her father had welcomed him into the family with open arms.

"Ma, this is the woman I was telling you about, Dr. Yasmin Ohaji."

"Yasmin, what a pretty name."

"Thank you."

"You've made quite the impression on my son," Johanna confessed, reaching out and squeezing her hand. "Last week he told me you're a modern-day Mother Teresa, but with long legs and a pretty smile."

Yasmin laughed. "I don't know about that, but I do love working with the kids. They give far more than I ever could."

"That's good to hear. I hope you raise a lot of money tonight."

"I do, too."

"You have to meet everyone else." Rashawn went around the table, introducing his brothers and their significant others. The chatty, fresh-faced women greeted her warmly, but the men wore plastic smiles.

Out of the corner of her eye, she noticed the servers exiting the kitchen. Chaz and Marquise, the youngest of the waiters, had loose ties, untucked shirts and saggy pants. The seventh-graders wore hostile expressions on their faces, but they were just another pair of headstrong teens. They had protested about wearing formal attire and only agreed to work after Rashawn had spoken to them privately. "If you'll excuse me," Yasmin said, smiling at Ms. Bishop, "there's something I have to do before the program resumes."

Rashawn took her hand. "I'll come with you."

"There's no need. Why don't we meet backstage in ten minutes?"

"Deal."

Johanna sat down.

"What do you think, Ma?" he asked, watching Yasmin disappear behind the kitchen doors. "Think she'd make a nice addition to the family?"

Johanna scowled, angry creases deepening her face. "Don't tease me, Hijo. You know how desperate I am for more grandbabies."

"All in good time, Ma. I'm young. I'll get married when I'm old and gray and not a second sooner."

"Spoken like a true Bishop man."

Chuckling, he gave her a one-arm hug. "Ma, you know you're my number-one girl. What would I do without you?"

"Only God knows," she answered, patting his cheek. "Why don't you invite Yasmin over next Saturday? Your father is coming and we'll have more time to get to know each other."

"I'll ask her but she probably won't come. She's mad at me."

"What did you do, Hijo? I didn't raise you to mistreat women and…"

Rashawn spotted Yasmin backstage. "Ma, I gotta go. We'll talk later, okay?"

As he turned away, Armondo seized his arm. "I want those Pro Bowl tickets, bro. Do whatever you gotta do. I'm counting on you."

"I'll see what I can do," he mumbled, stalking away.

Chapter 14

Yasmin dusted the flour off her hands, her gaze drifting to the open window. Her uncles were in the backyard playing horse-shoes, her cousins were sitting on the picnic table chatting and a group of kids were kicking around a soccer ball. Most of the women were in the house, putting the finishing touches on dinner.

Once a month, the Ohaji clan crammed into Silas and Zadie's home for a traditional South African meal. It had been a family practice for as long as Yasmin could remember. She had fond memories of her childhood. Sitting by the fire, perched on her grandfather's lap, listening to tales about her ancestors. Dressing in tribal outfits and posing for pictures. Her family kept her grounded and she credited her parents for making her the woman she was today.

Yasmin tugged the husk off the corn and dumped it into the pot of boiling water. Thoughts of Rashawn—his smile, his lips, his kiss—flooded her mind. They hadn't spoken in a couple of weeks, but he was never far from her thoughts. Voices swirled around the kitchen and mingled with the sounds floating in through the window. Her head spun like a plate when she heard a loud, booming laugh. Had she imagined it? Yasmin pulled back the curtains. No, she wasn't dreaming. Strolling into the backyard, dressed in a baseball cap, T-shirt and shorts, was Rashawn. And following close behind him were her dad and brother. It staggered her to see him here, at her parents' house, shaking hands with her uncles, laughing at their stale jokes.

Imani stood beside Yasmin. "Great, they're here. Now we can eat."

"Did you know Rashawn was coming?"

"No, why?"

"Just wondering."

"Have you guys spoken since the fund-raiser?"

Shaking her head, Yasmin untied her apron and dropped it on the kitchen counter. "Melba said her niece had a great time on their date. According to Cheyenne, he was worth every penny."

"I'm not surprised. Ten grand is chump change for a TV news anchor."

"I wouldn't spend that kind of money."

"You don't need to. Rashawn likes you."

"Too bad I'm not interested."

"God, Yassie. You can be so bullheaded sometimes! You and I both know Rashawn doesn't do drugs. He's strong and healthy and there's nothing artificial about him. Look at him," she ordered, motioning with her head. "Does he look like someone who does drugs?"

"Well, no, but I've counseled people who—"

"Please, don't compare him to one of your drug-addicted clients. He's a cool guy with good taste. He likes you, right?" Winking mischievously, she bumped Yasmin with her hips. "Give the brother a chance."

Imani made a valid argument. He had a natural, open manner and didn't fit the profile of a drug addict. Could she have been wrong about him? Had her stubbornness blinded her to the truth? Inching past her Aunt Fayola, who was bent over taking casserole dishes out of the oven, she shook her twists free from their ponytail.

"Where are you going?" Imani asked, dipping a corn fritter into the frying pan. "I thought you were going to help me make the lemon tarts."

"I can't. I have to go freshen up."

"Why? I thought you didn't care about him?"

Yasmin shrugged. "I don't, but that doesn't mean I shouldn't look my best." With that, she pushed open the kitchen door and escaped down the hall.

Hours later, Yasmin opened the fridge, grabbed two wine coolers and slipped out the back door. She had spent the afternoon in the kitchen and wasn't in the mood to scrub pots. Besides, she wanted to talk to Rashawn before he left.

Spotting him leaning against the fence, she headed across the lawn. Like the teens at the community center, her dad and brother had given Rashawn the star treatment. He had sat in her father's spot at the head of the table, had the last helping of tomato stew and, in honor of his arrival, a vintage bottle of Shiraz, an expensive South African wine, had been opened. Yasmin didn't know what all the fuss was about. Rashawn didn't deserve special attention. And if her parents knew he used steroids, their smiles would dry up faster than water in the Sahara.

Yasmin was going to rise above her feelings and do what was right. She owed Rashawn her heartfelt thanks. He had helped raise thousands of dollars for the center and she suspected he was behind a very large anonymous donation.

The scent of her floral perfume carried on the warm, moist summer air. Rashawn recognized the fragrance, but didn't see Yasmin until she was a step away.

"I thought you might be thirsty."

Rashawn straightened and looked at her, open-mouthed. Her presence threw him off. After a terse greeting, she had disappeared into the kitchen and didn't surface until it had been time to eat. They'd sat on opposite ends of the room, but that hadn't stopped him from watching her during dinner. He hadn't expected to see her for the rest of the night and now she was standing in front of him, smiling. Collecting himself, he took the bottle she offered and unscrewed the top. "Thanks."

"I was, ah, hoping we could go for a walk."

It seemed like minutes, but it was probably only seconds before he said, "Sure, that's cool. Lead the way."

They exited the yard and strolled up the block. It was a picture-perfect night and Arbor Lake Lane was alive with activity. Teenage boys whizzed by on skateboards, girls played double Dutch in the street and a band of silver-haired women reclined on a porch, sipping a sweet-smelling tea.

"I wanted to thank you again for hosting the fund-raiser. You did an amazing job, and I've been fielding calls from other organizations who could use your support."

"No problem, partner." Rashawn stuck out his hand and they clinked bottles. "We make a good team, don't we?"

"I'd say so. Between ticket sales, the silent auction and the raffle we raised almost fifty thousand dollars!"

"That's crazy."

Yasmin tasted her cooler. In the silence that followed, she couldn't help wondering if he was dating Cheyenne now. It had only been a couple of weeks since the fund-raiser, but anything was possible. "I, ah, heard you and Cheyenne had fun on your date. Melba said she has stars in her eyes and has been talking about you nonstop."

"Cheyenne's a cool girl. Smart, down-to-earth, funny."

"That's nice."

"She's not you though." Rashawn smiled. "I thought about you all night."

"You did?"

He reached for her hand, stopping her. "The score is simple, Doc. Of all the women I could've chosen, I picked you. Not Teagan. Not Cheyenne. But you."

Grinning, he dropped his voice to a devilish whisper. "Come here."

Yasmin obliged.

"Let's start over," he suggested, taking her in his arms. "I'm Rashawn and you my Nubian queen are?"

Her lips spread into a smile. "Has anyone ever told you you're crazy?"

"Nope."

"Well, you are."

"I'm crazy about you. And *only* you."

Silence came and with it clarity. Yasmin looked at him and felt a connection she had never felt before. "I should have believed you when you told me the steroids weren't yours. I assumed you used drugs because—"

Rashawn yanked her to his chest before she finished her sentence. "Enough talk," he told her, lowering his mouth to her lips. Surprised, yet filled with joy, Yasmin curled her body into his. She reveled in the feel of being back in his arms. Focusing on the here and now, she pushed all thoughts of their fight out of her mind and welcomed his kiss. He kissed her with finesse, with confidence, with sensuality. His tongue eased its way inside her mouth, inviting her to return his gentle, amorous kiss. Nothing was more important than this moment. She had chosen to forgive him, chosen to trust him and from now on she would believe in him. Rashawn wasn't like other superstar athletes. He was a stand-up guy who put the needs of his family, his friends and his community above his own.

Standing in the middle of the street, kissing Rashawn, under a curtain of stars, was an incredible feeling. Yasmin couldn't remember the last time she had felt such freedom. Such liberation. The easy familiarity she had with Rashawn was more than just shared interests; it was deeper than that. They were kindred souls, brought together to heal past hurts and disappointments.

As he stroked her hair, she finally recognized her feelings for what they were. She couldn't see the future, and didn't want to, but she was falling in love with him. He listened to her, admonished her to live in the moment and acknowledged her inner beauty. He genuinely cared about her and the feeling was mutual.

"We better quit before we get arrested for disturbing the peace," he joked, when he broke off the kiss. Nuzzling his chin against her ear, he slipped a hand under her tank top, stroking the delicate slope of her back. "How do you feel about going to Miami?"

Caught off guard by the question, she forced her mind to focus. It was hard concentrating when he was touching her in such an intimate way. "When?"

"The twenty-third."

"I wish I could, but I have to work."

"You nine-to-fivers don't know how to have fun," he teased, nibbling on her earlobe. "What's the point of having your own business if you can't take time off when the mood strikes?"

Yasmin purred. "W-what's going on in Miami?" she asked, between nibbles.

"My match has been moved to another venue."

"That's good, right?"

"That's real good. A bigger venue means a larger audience and a lot more money. Now, we're the undercard of the Roy Jones Jr. fight. Most people are coming to see him, but it's my pay-per-view debut. Will you come if I cover your expenses?"

"Trust me, you don't want me there. I'd probably embarrass you. I know nothing about boxing and even less about—"

"I don't care. I want you by my side. I can't show up to my victory party without a date." Grinning, he added, "And, you, Dr. Ohaji, are sure to turn heads."

"Oh, I get it, you want me to be eye candy for you and your friends?"

"Absolutely."

"I didn't spend five years doing post-graduate studies to become a groupie," she told him, her tone rich with humor. "Forget it. I'm not going."

"But you're not just another groupie," Rashawn said, in the smoothest of voices. "You're *my* groupie."

Yasmin laughed. "You're too much."

"So, what's up? Are you gonna come?"

"I'll think about it and get back to you. I'm speaking at a conference in Fort Lauderdale that week, so maybe I can come and spend a couple extra days. "

"Cool." Interlocking hands with her, he leaned forward until their heads were touching. He kissed her with such intensity every nerve ending in her body came to life. Yasmin felt like a rebellious teenager in the backseat of a car. Only this time they were outside, in her old neighborhood, kissing on the very street where she had first learned to ride her bike.

Chapter 15

Niobie balanced the appointment book in one hand and pushed open her boss's door with the other. "Sorry I'm late, but Miles was throwing up all night. It's been one of those mornings, but I'm here now and ready to review the day's agenda," she finished, short of breath.

Yasmin slipped off her eyeglasses and rested them on the desk. Reviewing the Kolodenko file would have to wait. "Niobie, this is the second time you've been late this week. The tenth time this month."

Niobie lowered herself onto a chair. "I'm sorry. I tried to make it here on time, but Miles was too sick to go to school so I had to take him to my mom's house. I thought of calling, but my cell phone died on the way over."

Glancing at the clock, she shook her head. Niobie had more excuses than Bobby Brown before a family court judge. And the more she lied, the angrier Yasmin got. "Was traffic to blame when you were an hour late last Friday?"

"No, I couldn't find my car keys, remember?"

Yasmin couldn't believe her assistant had the gall to answer, especially when they both knew her tardiness had nothing to do with her son and everything to do with her new boyfriend. The sanitation worker called several times a day, stopped by the office and brought Niobie greasy cheeseburgers. Niobie had been a model employee before he came along. Sure, she dressed like a backup dancer for Lil' Kim, but her work was faultless. These days, Yasmin spent so much time double-checking her reports, she didn't have time to eat lunch.

"You've always been a dedicated employee, but the last month you've been disorganized, late and your work's been sloppy."

"I'm sorry you feel that way."   .

Frustrated by her response, Yasmin said, "Niobie, no one's going to give you a free ride. Not only do you need the education and skills to do the job, you have to look the part, too." Standing, she educated the single mother about the business world. "People judge you not by what you say, but by what you do. Be on time. Do your best. Take pride in your appearance…"

Niobie wasn't a stranger to hard work, but she'd rather focus her energy on more important things, like finding a husband. A shrewd businesswoman, her boss worked around the clock and foolishly expected her to, too. "I can't stay past five, Dr. Ohaji. My mom works long hours at the nursing home and I don't feel comfortable leaving Miles with just anybody."

"This is not just about your performance, Niobie, it's about your attire, as well." Not only was she twenty-five minutes late, she was wearing a short, shimmery dress that looked like it was strangling her. "This isn't working out. A Better Way Counseling Services obviously isn't the right environment for you anymore."

Licking her plump lips, Niobie shifted uncomfortably in her seat. She didn't appreciate her boss's tone. It was cold, brisk, unfriendly. What was her problem? Bougie, career-minded women had no idea what it was like to be a single parent.

At seventeen, she'd dropped out of high school and moved into a halfway house for teenage mothers. She'd been taking care of herself and Miles since he was born. No child support. No financial aid. No help whatsoever. So what if she was a few minutes late? If Dr. Ohaji thought she was going to forsake her social life to keep her job, she was sadly mistaken. But instead of speaking her mind, she said, "I promise to do better from now on."

"It pains me to say this, Niobie, but I have to let you go."

Niobie squeezed out a tear. If she was going to convince Dr. Ohaji not to fire her, she was going to have to pull out all the stops: tears, trembling and wailing. "I know I've messed up in the past, but I can change. I *need* this job. I have rent to pay, groceries to buy and Miles needs…braces. Where am I going to find another job with full benefits?" Willing herself to cry, she dissolved into tears.

Yasmin came around her desk and rubbed Niobie's shoulder. This was unanticipated; she hadn't expected her to cry. This wasn't the first time she had reprimanded Niobie. The single mother had promised to change before, but instead of improving, things had gotten worse. Niobie wasn't happy at A Better Way Counseling Services, so why was she begging to keep a job she disliked? "I think you'd be a lot happier working as a telemarketer or—"

"No! I want to work here, with you." Burying her face in her hands, she begged for a second chance. "Please, please don't fire me. I need this job."

Yasmin made a mental list of all the pros and cons of keeping Niobie around. The cons far exceeded the pros, but she was willing to give her another chance. A last chance. When she told her the news, Niobie leapt from her chair and threw her arms around her.

"I'm going to make you proud, Dr. Ohaji. You just wait and see."

"That's what I like to hear."

"I'll have the assessment reports typed up within the hour." Cleaning her face, Niobie collected the appointment book and exited the room before her boss had a change of heart. Back at her desk, she took her seat in front of her computer. That was a close one, she thought, typing in her password. If she hadn't invented the story of Miles needing braces and broken down in tears, Dr. Ohaji would have fired her for sure. Niobie couldn't let that happen. She had dreams of a better life, but until she found a multimillionaire to take care of her, she was stuck working at A Better Way Counseling Services.

Niobie checked her e-mail. She had ten messages and all of them were from Lonnie. In the last month, she had started dating Lonnie Boland, a thirty-five-year-old sanitation worker she'd met online. Niobie wasn't attracted to him, but he was liberal with his money and Miles liked him. He wasn't her Prince Charming, but he'd do until someone better came along.

Fixated on the computer screen, Niobie didn't hear the front door open and close. For several seconds, Daquan Maxwell stood with his clipboard to his chest, watching her. Her breasts were obviously her favorite part of her body, because every time he saw her they were on display. Like today. It didn't bother him, though. He liked sisters who flaunted their physical assets and the shapely receptionist had a lot going for her. "Lookin' good this mornin', Niobie."

Disregarding the courier's praise, she stuck out her hand, waiting expectantly for the day's mail. Every time the UPS deliveryman came by the office, he complimented her look and followed it up by asking her out. Today Niobie wasn't having it. He was a decent guy, always polite and complimentary, but what could a minimum wage–earning courier do for her? She needed someone with a 401(k) plan, someone who could buy her cars, jewelry and furs. Lonnie wasn't that man and neither was Daquan the courier.

"Seeing you is the highlight of my day," he told her.

"I don't know why." Niobie scrawled her name on the dotted line.

He handed her a stack of mail. "Not only are you smart, you're pretty, too."

"Thanks. Bye. Have a nice day."

"I have two tickets to the Jamie Foxx concert. What do you think of that?"

Her face warmed. Now, Jamie Foxx was someone she could

get with. The Oscar-award winner was her ideal man. He knew how to work a crowd, had a commanding voice and made enough money to finance her dreams. Despite her modest lifestyle, Niobie liked to be surrounded by beautiful things. It would take some scheming on her part, but if she could find a way to get backstage, she would be one step closer to having that mansion in the hills.

Sorting through the mail, she considered Daquan's offer. The courier wasn't her type. He wasn't rich, he wasn't athletic and he wasn't gorgeous. Niobie would never date him, but she did want to see Jamie Foxx. A package bearing Rashawn's name caught her eye. Dr. Ohaji would fire her on the spot if she saw her opening the package, but Niobie didn't care. Besides, she had been doing it for months and as long as she glued it back together carefully the good doctor would never know. Using a staple remover, she carefully opened the envelope and emptied the contents onto her desk.

Inside, were two first-class plane tickets, a hotel confirmation slip and a short handwritten note. Niobie read it, her shoulders sinking under the weight of the discovery. "Looking forward to seeing you in Miami," it said.

Envious thoughts crowded her mind. Dr. Ohaji didn't need the tickets. She did! Her boss had money; she could afford to pay her way. Thanks to the boxer's generosity, Dr. Ohaji would be attending his match and spending three nights at the lavish Concord Miami Hotel in South Beach. Niobie's face drained of color. Had they been sneaking around all this time? She had been intercepting his calls, chatted with him in length at the charity fund-raiser and had even dragged Miles to the Boxing Institute of Champions a few times. How had she missed this?

"Jamie Foxx's bad on that piano, huh? He does a ten-minute tribute to Ray Charles and everything. I finish work late tomorrow, but I—"

"No, thanks." Niobie didn't have time for idle chitchat. She had been hanging out with Lonnie, instead of seducing Rashawn, and her boss had swiped him right from under her nose! The boxer wasn't a multimillionaire yet, but he was a hell of a lot better than an illiterate sanitation worker. Niobie had been wasting precious time with Lonnie. What she needed to do was concentrate on getting close to Rashawn. They had made a connection; she was sure of it. He hadn't come right out and said anything, but she could tell he liked her.

The telephone buzzed. Niobie pressed the talk button. "Yes, Dr. Ohaji?"

"Have you finished the progress reports?"

"I'm working on it. I'm just sorting through the mail."

"Please hurry. I'm waiting on them."

"I'm on it."

Her boss ended the call.

"God, what's her problem?" Niobie mumbled, glancing at the files piled to her left. "I'd get through this crap a lot faster if *she* came out here and gave me a hand." Grumbling to herself, she stuffed the plane tickets back into the envelope to give to her boss. Maybe she'd finish her work quicker if Dr. Ohaji wasn't checking up on her every ten seconds. Noting Daquan's presence, she snapped, "Why are you still here? Don't you have packages to deliver or something?"

"Nothing's more important than being with you, boo." Daquan stared at her, his eyes wet with lust. "Are you free next Saturday? We could go for dinner or have drinks."

"And why would I want to do that?" she snapped, irritated by his persistence. "I need someone who can take care of me, not a lowly delivery guy who makes eight-fifty an hour. Can you pay my rent? What about my cable bill?" When he didn't answer, she sneered. "I didn't think so, courier boy."

"I—I—I should go," he stammered, backing away from the desk.

"You do that."

Head down, he trudged out the front door.

Niobie had a week's worth of paperwork to do, but instead of tackling the evaluation reports, she settled comfortably onto her chair, kicked off her sandals and signed on to

Blackstuds.com. After clicking on more than a dozen profiles, a handsome businessman with the screen name "Mr. Determined" popped up. Niobie bolted up in her seat. "Now, I'll be damned!" she said to herself. She recognized him from the charity fund-raiser. He was average height, but his refined, almost dignified mannerisms made him seem much taller. Playing a hunch, she composed a short, scintillating message sure to send the bachelor's libido into overdrive.

Eyes narrowed in concentration she bit down on a long, acrylic nail. "I was thinking too small," she decided, visions of five-star restauraunts and shopping Rodeo Drive dancing in her head. "Forget Rashawn and his meager boxing career. I could be a mayor's wife." A smirk crossed her lips. "Or…a well-kept mistress." And with that, she added her cell phone number to the end of the e-mail and hit Send.

Chapter 16

"Frilly hand towels? Purple potpourri? Scented candles? Oh, hell no!" Shaking his head, Rashawn stuffed the items back into the plastic bag and chucked it against the living-room wall. "Can't do it, Doc. Sorry."

"It's not purple, it's lilac. And what's wrong with buying things to make the bathroom smell nice?"

"I appreciate the thought, really I do, but I can't have all that feminine crap in here. What will my boys think?"

"That you have great taste?" she asked, smirking.

"No, they'll label me a punk and enroll me in charm school!"

Yasmin erupted into laughter.

"Don't laugh. You know it's true."

She patted his chest. "Okay, okay, no potpourri. Any other requests?"

"Spend the night."

"What?"

"You heard me."

Yasmin averted her gaze. How could she say no without

hurting his feelings? The afternoon had been filled with laughs, tender moments and, even after spending the entire day together, she wasn't ready to go home. But that didn't mean she was ready to sleep over.

After a brunch at a nearby waffle house, they'd driven to her favorite furniture store. Under her watchful eye, Rashawn had selected a four-piece bedroom suite, sectional sofas and couches, Maytag appliances and an assortment of lights, rugs and picture frames for the living room. He paid extra for same-day delivery, but now his house was finally furnished.

To show his appreciation, Rashawn had taken her to a Mediterranean restaurant that specialized in vegetarian cuisine. During dinner, he had entertained her with stories of growing up in the 'hood, running the streets with his boys and his first taste of love at sixteen. Yasmin had learned some interesting facts about him. He was born on St. Patrick's Day, had three tattoos and had boxed in over twenty countries. And when he confessed to liking Harry Potter and sneaking away to read in the bathroom so the other boxers wouldn't find out, Yasmin had laughed. There was an undeniable ease and things happened naturally when they were together. But they hadn't known each other long. Surely three months wasn't enough time for them to become lovers. Or was it? Grappling with her conscience, she glanced over at the mirror hanging above the sectional sofa. Yasmin liked what she saw. Rashawn was a head taller than she was, but they wore the same facial expression and emulated each other's body language.

"Are you thinking, or sleeping with your eyes open?" he teased.

"I don't know if I'm ready for us to become lovers."

"Doc, it's not like that. Get your mind out of the gutter, girl." Rashawn laughed and when she did, too, he said, "We'll kick back on my *new* couch and watch TV. I just want to spend some time with you before I leave for Miami, that's all."

Yasmin relented. "I guess that's okay."

"Have you given any more thought to coming?"

"Looks like I have no choice. Imani saw the tickets on my dresser and screamed so loud I still can't hear properly," she joked, tugging at her earlobe for effect. "When I left this morning, she was packing."

"Cool." His face visibly relaxed. "It means a lot having you there."

"I don't see why. You have your family, your brothers and your team."

"This is different. Black male athletes get a bad rap for being sex-crazed womanizers, but no one talks about the half-naked groupies who sneak into washrooms or show up drunk at three in the morning. With you by my side, I don't have to worry about adding extra security or switching hotel rooms every other night." He winked. "Unless you want me to."

"Are you sure I'm not going to cramp your style?"

"What are you asking?"

Yasmin shrugged, unsure of what to say. She didn't want to sound insecure, but she was. "You'll have a lot of females clamoring for your attention and I don't want to be lost in the crowd."

Talk of love and commitment and the future normally panicked him, but not this time. Instead of breaking out into a cold sweat or changing the subject, he held her tighter. "I want you there. *Only* you."

"It sounds like you're under a lot of pressure."

"You don't know the half of it," he confessed, wanting to share his struggles with her. "I arrive a few days before the fight, but my schedule doesn't leave me much free time. I have interviews and other publicity stuff to do and most days I don't climb into bed until after midnight."

"I'm not trying to add to your stress," she told him. "I don't mind staying here."

Rashawn saw the question in her eyes. He had the double burden of working against the stereotypes that plagued professional athletes and at the same time not making promises he knew he couldn't keep. "The days leading up to a match are always insane. That's why I didn't want you there until Saturday.

The night before the fight, I'll do a short workout, eat a solid meal and turn in early."

"I understand."

He cupped her chin, then kissed her softly. "After I win, I'm all yours, Doc."

"You're pretty confident, aren't you?"

Rashawn lifted his arm and flexed a muscle. "Don't I have reason to be?"

Rashawn turned onto his side. He hugged the pillow to his chest and his eyes shot open. Where was she? Momentarily disoriented, his gaze darted around the bedroom. The house was quiet, the air was still, but her scent lingered. Last night, he'd piled his plate with pizza and had two beers. Brody would kill him if he knew he had cheated on his diet, but he couldn't help himself. The humid weather and the heaviness of the meal had created his languor. Within minutes of eating, his eyes had been heavy and he'd struggled to stay awake. The last thing he remembered was hitting Play on the remote control and curling up beside Yasmin. Had she gone home? The alarm clock said it was midnight, but the city was very much awake. Cars honked, rock music played in the distance and the voices of his neighbors drifted over the fence.

He sat up and patted back a yawn. Relief washed over him when he saw Yasmin's silhouette out on the balcony. She was sitting on the chaise lounge, hugging her knees to her chest. Her beauty was stunning, exquisite, overwhelming. Wide, almond-shaped eyes, loose flowing braids, mink-brown skin glistening under the light of the moon. He wanted to go to her, but something held him back. She was sitting rigidly, quietly, staring up at the sky. He could only see her profile, but he knew she was deep in thought. Why else would she be outside alone in the middle of the night?

Lost in thought, Yasmin didn't hear Rashawn step out onto the balcony.

"How long have I been out?" he asked, scratching his bare chest.

She turned to him, her lips parting in a soft smile. "Not long."

"Everything okay?"

Nodding, she stretched her legs out in front of her. "I'm just thinking."

Rashawn examined her face. Something was troubling her but he decided not to push it. Yasmin would talk when she was ready. Remembering his conversation with his mom yesterday, he said, "Mom wants you to come over next Saturday. It's my dad's birthday and we're having dinner at the house. Think you can make it?"

After a brief pause, she said, "I'd like that."

"A word of warning. If she starts in on you about having my baby, ignore her." He chuckled heartily. "Ma's desperate for more grandchildren, any way she can get 'em."

"Most parents are."

"Are you feeing the pressure, too?"

"No, I, ah, can't have children."

"For real?" Rashawn sat down at the foot of the chaise. "How come?"

Staring down, Yasmin toyed with the buttons on her shirt. She exhaled, gathered her courage and said, "I always knew something was wrong. My first period came late, and lasted for weeks. My gynecologist prescribed birth control pills to regulate my cycle and it was normal for a few months. But by the time I started college, I had night sweats, hot flashes and severe insomnia. Eventually, my gynecologist referred me to an endocrinologist and after a series of blood tests they discovered my levels of follicle-stimulating hormone were elevated."

"What's that?"

"It's the function that regulates the growth and development of eggs. In short, I'm in premature ovarian failure." Her eyes misted over, but the tears didn't fall. "I have a fifteen percent chance of conceiving naturally."

Leaning forward, he held her gaze. "That doesn't mean you won't be a mother. When you're ready to have children, you can always find a surrogate or adopt." He paused. "I'm just sorry you had to go through all that alone."

"That means a lot. And you're right. I can. I've been thinking a lot about it the last few months," she confessed, nodding slowly. "Eric's death reminded me of how short life is and I want to make the most out of the time I have."

"Doc, you make sure the kids at the community center are fed, clean and safe and you keep on top of their grades and assignments. You're phenomenal that way. In my eyes, you're already a mom," he praised, kissing her cheek. "And if you decide not to go the adoption route, I can always ask my brother if you could have Porsha."

Smiling, she shook her head incredulously. "You're terrible."

"What? That girl's a handful!"

"And so is her uncle."

His smile met hers. "Good thing I have you here to keep me in line, huh, Doc?"

Yasmin couldn't resist smoothing a hand over his goatee. She ran her fingers along his jawline, caressing the gentle contours of his face. Rashawn was amazing in every sense of the word. He was a laid-back, easygoing guy who could find the upside of any situation. He had comforted her and, despite the severity of her confession, he'd found a way to make her laugh. He truly, truly accepted her. *All* of her.

The air was charged with desire. Closing her eyes, she bent down and kissed him. It was a soulful kiss, rife with passion and desire. His mouth was sweet, wet, moist. Despite her feelings for him, there was still a part of her, albeit a small one, that was nervous about them becoming lovers. Was it too soon? Would it ruin their friendship? Though they hadn't discussed being exclusive, she knew Rashawn could be trusted with her feelings. Clearing her mind of her worries, she enjoyed the tantalizing mixture of kissing and touching. All her life she had been told she was too tall, too dark, too heavy. It felt good being with someone who desired her, imperfections and all.

Breathing hard and fast, Rashawn stretched out on the lounger and pulled her down on top of him. His tongue made a trail from her ear to the apex of her breasts. Yasmin wrapped her arms around him and swathed her legs around his waist. Unbuttoning her shirt exposed her white push-up bra and thong panties. He bathed her lips with his mouth, then her breasts, neck and stomach, alternating between gentle and rough kisses. When he sucked her navel, she grabbed the back of his head. He pressed light, feathery kisses on her belly button and the inside of her thighs.

Yasmin was planning their first time together to be in Miami, but if she had learned anything in the last two years, it was to live in the beauty of the moment. They were here, together, loving each other, pleasing each other, sheltered from the outside world. During the week, she counseled couples to abandon the rules and make love whenever and wherever.

"You can't plan to be spontaneous," she told them. "When passion strikes, go for it." It was time she took her own advice.

Outlining her lips with his tongue, his hands voyaged down the delicate slope of her hips. Sensitive to his touch, her breathing deepened. Rashawn's body was conditioned to function at the highest level and he was an expert at conveying pleasure with his lips, his tongue, and his hands. His mouth feasted on her nipples, teasing her, tasting her, caressing her. Mumbled words and desires were whispered into the night. The warm summer breeze played over their sweat-drenched bodes, arousing the fire that burned within. After what seemed like hours of torturously hot foreplay, his hands slid down the length of her body, pausing between her legs. It had been months for her. He wanted to make sure what he was doing felt good. Brushing his mouth against her ear, he whispered, "How does that feel?"

A strangled moan was answer enough.

Sucking gently on her bottom lip, his fingers drew light circles on her stomach. He slipped a finger inside her, stroking, touching, massaging her G-spot. Darkness surrounded them, but there was no mistaking the lusty gleam in her deep-brown eyes. He noticed her jagged breathing, the hazy look on her face and the sprinkles of sweat on her brow. It was time. She was ready.

"I'll be right back," he whispered.

Grazing her fingers precariously close to his shaft, she

brushed her mouth against the hollow of his throat. "Where are you going?"

"To get protection."

"But, I'm on the Pill."

"You can never be too safe."

Rashawn raced back into the bedroom as if it was on fire and Yasmin laughed out loud. She'd never seen him move so fast. For a second, she thought of following him back inside, but decided not to ruin the spontaneity of the moment. He returned, sheathed, and she gawked openly at the sight of his naked body. He was a gym rat and had the pecks, abs and biceps to prove it. His erection was large, hard and thick, drawing her wanton gaze south.

Wearing a small, sheepish smile, Rashawn crossed the balcony. His scent was intoxicating. And like first dates and first kisses, the rush if being with him overcame her. Pulling him down on top of her, Yasmin coiled her long legs around his trim waist. Never had she felt so out of control. It was as if she was dreaming, hovering above, watching herself act out her wildest, sexiest fantasy. His touch fueled her desire, and with every kiss, caress and stroke, she fell deeper in love.

Soon, her entire body was a hotbed of nerves. His loving was sweet torture. Soulful, raunchy, intense. The sexual equivalent of an R. Kelly song. And when he parted her legs and slid inside her, she felt a rush of divine pleasure. Every part of her skin was sensitive to his touch. His movements were controlled, gentle and painstakingly slow, but each thrust brought Yasmin closer to euphoria.

Burying himself between her legs, his breathing deep and ragged, Rashawn pushed her knees up against his chest, deepening the penetration. Hands and legs entwined, they moved in a delicious rhythmic motion. It took some effort, but Yasmin forced her eyes open. She wanted to see him, wanted to see the look on his face when he exploded inside her. Rashawn gripped her hips, plunging into her forcefully, and a quick, electrifying sensation ripped through her body. Hugging her possessively to his chest, he gathered her full lustrous hair in his hands. Yasmin was a respectable businesswoman, the most refined and elegant woman he'd ever dated, but she surprised him by digging her nails into his flesh and kissing him so passionately he saw double.

The rest of the night was given to soft and sweet lovemaking, and when the early-morning sunshine fell across the house, Rashawn and Yasmin were just going to bed.

Chapter 17

"What do you think? The teddy or the French maid costume?"

Yasmin stared at her sister through the bathroom mirror. Imani held a piece of lingerie in each hand, a naughty grin on her red-hued lips. Dusting loose powder over the bridge of her nose, she joked, "Neither. You don't have to impress me, roomie."

"Roomie? Girl, please. Dean booked us the honeymoon suite at the Concord and I plan to thank him in *every* room."

"Dean?"

"Yeah, you know, the tall, hard-bodied hunk I've been doing—" her eyes bulged and she cupped her mouth in mock surprise "—I mean, dating for the last year."

Yasmin's smile faded. "I didn't know he was coming."

"I thought I mentioned it."

"No, you didn't." Releasing a deep sigh, she peered into the mirror and applied a second coat of eyeliner. "If I knew Dean was coming, I would have invited Katherine. At least she would have kept me company."

"What's *that* supposed to mean?"

"Nothing."

Imani plunked down on the toilet seat. "No, let's talk abut it. You're obviously upset about something, so speak on it."

"Forget I said anything. I don't want to argue."

"Who's arguing? Say what you have to say. I'm not a kid. I can handle it."

Yasmin didn't want to have this conversation with Imani. If she did, her sister would get angry and they'd ignore each other on the flight. "Why don't we discuss this when we're both in a better frame of mind?"

"Is that therapist talk? Good God. You're a pro when it comes to disguising your feelings," she said, her voice reeking with sarcasm. "I hope your clients don't take your approach to resolving conflict. They'll never get anywhere if they do."

Hurt by the stinging retort, but refusing to lash back, Yasmin outlined the rim of her lips with a lip pencil, then applied a dab of gloss.

"What is it?" Imani pressed, blowing her bangs out of her face.

"It's nothing. I just thought we were hanging out this weekend."

"Why?"

"Because when I invited you, you said you wanted to go Jet Skiing and snorkeling on Saturday morning."

"Yassie, I never expected us to do those things together. This trip isn't a sightseeing excursion or one of our weekend getaways. It's about you supporting your man. And the only reason Dean is coming is to watch the match. When I told him we were going, he called Rashawn and begged for a ticket. You're lucky Eli has an exam to study for and Dad has to work because they wanted to tag along, too."

"I didn't realize so many people wanted to see the fight."

"Yeah, girl, your man is a superstar!" Chuckling, Imani eyed her sister sympathetically. "Is there anything else?"

Yasmin didn't answer. Libras were loveable but selfish and Yasmin had learned a long time ago that when it came to Imani, she had to take the good with the bad. It was still hard for her to believe her sister had found yet another man who was willing to

put up with her me-me-me attitude, but she had, and an excep-
tional one at that.

Yasmin would rather be miserable than stir the pot. Listening
to couples bicker on a daily basis was emotionally draining and she
didn't want the same atmosphere at home. But if she kept quiet,
her resentment would grow and that wasn't healthy for anybody.
"We bought this place because we wanted to live together, but
you're hardly here. You spend weekends at Dean's and the few
times you're here, you're working in the office or on the phone with
him."

"Is it my fault the brother can't get enough of me?" Imani's
attempt to make her sister laugh failed.

Silence gripped the room.

"You're not here for me anymore and sometimes it feels like I've
lost my best friend…" Yasmin's voice cracked, forcing her to stop.

Imani jumped to her feet. "Are you serious? That's crazy.
We're sisters! Nobody can come between us!"

"You forget about me every time you start dating somebody
new. Then, when you break up, you expect me to drop everything and console you."

"You make me sound like a self-centered bitch. Am I really
that bad?"

A pause, then, "Sometimes."

"I never knew you felt that way," she confessed, pausing re-
flectively. "Okay, from now on I'm going to make more time for
us. You have my word." Feeling sentimental, she kissed Yasmin's
cheek. Hoping to alleviate the mood, Imani pitched an arm
around her shoulder and said, "Are you packed and ready to go?"

"Yeah, I just have to toss my toiletries in my carry-on."

"Let's go to your room. I want to see what you're taking."

"Why?"

"I can't have you walking around the beach in that repulsive
one-piece bathing suit you bought at Sears ages ago. Miami's a
sexy city. The more skin the better."

Laughing, the sisters exited the bathroom and stepped into
Yasmin's room.

Spotting the suitcase next to the dresser, Imani unzipped it and examined the contents inside. "Did Mom give you the carrying case I asked for? You know, the Versace one with the gold buckle."

Puzzled, she shot her sister a look. "I haven't seen Mom all week."

"But you didn't come home last night. If you weren't at Mom and Dad's, then where were you?"

"I, ah, stayed at Rashawn's."

"Stayed over or *slept* over?" she asked, raising her brows suggestively.

Yasmin wore a smirk. "What do you think?"

"No you didn't!"

"I did."

"No way!" Imani shrieked, bopping around the room like she was on a pogo stick. "Was it good? Does he move in bed the way he does in the ring? Did you finally have a frickin' orgasm?"

"Yes, yes and yes!" Yasmin squealed, giving in to her laughter. "One minute we were talking and the next thing I know we're going at it on the lounge chair!"

"I don't believe you! You're lying!"

"It's true."

"Shut up!"

"Keep it down, Imani. I don't want our neighbors to hear you."

"I'm just…I can't believe it!"

"I know. I still have goose bumps."

"You filthy harlot!" Imani teased, her eyes alight with mischief. "How long has *this* been going on?"

"Last night was our first time."

"And?"

"It was everything I thought it would be," Yasmin gushed, unable to wipe the dreamy smile off her face. "He was sweet and sensitive and—"

"No, wait. Don't say another word," Imani ordered, grabbing her sister's hand and dragging her through the bedroom door. "We need to have this conversation over a bottle of wine and some of those tasty cheese rolls."

"I can't spend the rest of the morning on the patio. I have to go into the office."

"What for? We leave for Miami in a few hours."

"I know, but I'm not done preparing for my Mind and Body Seminar. The psychotherapy convention is on Tuesday and I still have a ton of work to do."

Imani stopped abruptly. "Okay, give me ten minutes to change."

"You want to come with me to the office?"

"Hell, yeah! Yassie, this is bigger than big news! You slept with that fine-ass boxer and if I believe your body language—" she flicked her index finger up and down "—which I do, he *literally* rocked your world."

Yasmin stared at the computer screen. For the last twenty minutes, she'd been sitting in her first-class seat, racking her brain for a titillating introduction to her seminar. Her laptop was on, but instead of creating an outline for the workshop, she was thinking about Rashawn. Hours had passed since he'd kissed her good-bye, but she still couldn't wrap her mind around what had happened last night, or rather, that morning. How had an innocent conversation led them to making love? And even more shocking, now she couldn't concentrate long enough to finish her work!

Yasmin glanced around the cabin. Most of the passengers were sleeping, a few read and others chatted with their seatmates. Imani sat beside her, flipping through a stack of *Property Investor* magazines. She had been reading since they'd arrived at the airport and would likely continue until the plane landed. Yasmin wasn't surprised. Everything about her sister centered on work. Sure, she was enamored with Dean, but the Web designer couldn't compete with her career.

Imani had been a real estate developer for six years and at twenty-nine was on the fast track to becoming president of J&M Properties. Smart and personable, she made friends easily. She studied the ebb and flow of the real estate market religiously but it was her celebrity clients who had put her name on the map.

Outside the window, wispy clouds sailed by. The sky was a fiery shade of red and orange. The flight had been delayed a half hour, resulting in irritable passengers and a ten o'clock arrival time in Miami. Because of the delay, Rashawn wouldn't be able to pick them up, but promised to have a limousine waiting. After some shameless flirting and a discussion about foreplay that made Yasmin blush, he had wished her a safe flight and promised to take them for breakfast in the morning.

Needing a distraction, Yasmin minimized her file and typed Rashawn's full name into the Google address bar. His image filled the screen. A smile lit the corners of her mouth. He was bare-chested, in shorts, runners and gloves, flaunting his washboard stomach and wide shoulders. Sitting up, she slowly licked her lips. Rashawn stood in a boxer's stance, hands up, chin down, a primal expression on his face. Smoothing a hand over her collarbone, the very spot he had plied with buttery-soft kisses, educed a visual slide show of last night. They had been so aroused, so consumed with gratifying their desires they hadn't even made it to the bedroom. On the lounger, under the glow of the moon and the radiant backdrop of the stars, they had given themselves to each other.

Exhausted, they'd stumbled back inside and crawled into bed. Sleep called, but they'd cuddled and kissed, relishing the excitement of their newfound love. Clueless about the boxing world, but wanting to know more, Yasmin had asked him about the nature of the sport. He had spoken openly about the challenges he faced and his struggle to remain grounded when everyone around him had changed. Pressure mounted from every side. Relatives, friends and acquaintances posed new deals, suggested possible fight matchups and lined up business meetings without his knowledge. Yasmin was surprised to hear about his rocky relationships with his brothers, mainly Armondo and his constant demands for money. Yasmin listened quietly. It wasn't another therapy session and he wasn't her client. They were a couple now and she didn't want to drive him away by analyzing everything he said.

"Ms. Ohaji?"

Transfixed by his image on the screen, Yasmin didn't hear the flight attendant call her name. Imani jabbed her in the ribs and she slid her gaze to the stewardess with the cottonlike hair.

"Ms. Ohaji?"

"Yes?" she replied, closing her laptop and returning it to the carrying case.

"This is for you." The flight attendant handed her an enormous basket wrapped in cellophane. "You'll find the card inside."

Before Yasmin could respond, the lady turned and marched briskly up the aisle.

Her eyebrows climbed. "Do they deliver gifts on airplanes nowadays?"

Imani shrugged. "I guess so." She tore the wrapping paper, grabbed the card and opened it. "Girl, you must have put it on him *fierce*. Listen to this. 'It's not chocolate fondue, but I hope it satisfies your sweet tooth until I see you later.' Hot damn!"

"I can't believe he'd do something like this." Yasmin took the card and read it for herself. Giggling, she tucked it into her purse.

"What's so funny?"

"Nothing."

"Nothing, my ass," Imani scoffed. "You've fallen for him, hook, line and sinker, but you don't want to admit it."

Yasmin organized her thoughts. She'd been in love before, but not like this. This was something every woman dreamed of. Being romanced by a loving and sensitive man was an intoxicating drug. Rashawn made her feel special, valued, respected and there was no greater feeling than knowing there was someone out there who thought the world of her. "We're just dating. I care about him but it's not as serious as you're making it sound. We—"

"You want me to believe this thing with you and Rashawn is just a fling? A one-time thing? Come on, Sis, you're talking to me. If you're rolling between the sheets with him, it must be serious because you're not a casual-fling type of girl. You dated boring Eric for a year before you gave him a taste, but you let

Rashawn dip his spoon into your chocolate after only a few months!"

"This has nothing to do with sex, Imani. It's not like that."

"Then, what's it like, Yassie?"

To signal the end of the conversation, Yasmin tucked the wrapping paper into the seat pocket and poked her nose into the basket. It was a dizzying array of sweet-smelling scents. Juicy, succulent fruits—plums, strawberries, grapes—and her favorite snacks—cinnamon-roasted cashews, mint chocolate and a jumbo box of gummy bears—lined the basket. Nestled next to a bottle of pinot blanc was a book titled *Bedtime Stories for Lovers* and a box of flavored condoms.

Imani swiped the condoms and sniffed the box. "A box of fifty, huh? You've been holding out on me, Sis." Smirking, she wagged her finger in her sister's face. "You naughty girl. I can only imagine what he has in store for you tonight!"

Chapter 18

Dazzling lights shone down on the chic crowd at the Seminole Hard Rock Hotel & Casino. Women in spray-on dresses and men in suits placed last-minute bets, hunted for seats and ordered drinks. The scent of cologne, perfume and cigar smoke mingled, creating a sweet-musky fragrance. Rap music pulsed in the background, distracting Yasmin from her thoughts. Her throat was tight, her palms were damp and her legs were trembling. The fight hadn't even started yet and she was a nervous wreck.

"Yassie, don't look so scared." Imani patted her hand. "Try to relax."

"What if he gets hit really hard? What if he gets hurt?"

"Rashawn will be fine."

"How do *you* know?" she snapped, annoyed.

Imani nudged Dean. "Tell her Rashawn will be fine," she ordered, taking a sip of her cocktail.

Dean leaned forward, so he could be heard above the chatter of the high-energy crowd. "There's nothing to worry about, Yasmin. He's talented, he's fast and he hardly ever gets hit. I've been following his career for years and he's never been knocked out."

"Really?"

"Lipenski's old. A one-time champ just trying to make some money to pay his kid's tuition. His last match was a year and a half ago and, according to published reports, he was so banged up he couldn't move for a week."

"Are you sure Rashawn will be okay?"

Dean nodded, then returned his eyes to the ring.

A tuxedoed man with a microphone took center stage. His stentorian voice sliced through the cheers, whistles and applause. The atmosphere in the arena was one of excitement and anticipation. And when Russian music filled the air, the male-dominated crowd roared. After counseling Sophie Kolodenko for months, Yasmin had picked up a modicum of Russian words and understood the chorus of the song. "I'm a man, a soldier, a fighter. No one will conquer me." When Yasmin saw Luis "AK-47" Lipenski, fear zipped up her spine and clogged her throat. The veteran boxer was built like a bulldozer and had the face to match. He was a large, broad-shouldered man with remarkably big hands and dark, cold eyes.

By the time Lipenski reached the ring, the audience was on their feet, chanting his name. He jogged around the ring, smacking his gloves together, glowering at no one in particular. He was powerful and mighty, like Goliath, and though Dean had labeled him a washed-up fighter, he didn't look much older than Rashawn. Lipenski tossed his robe into the third row of spectators, rousing the crowd's fervor.

When the ring announcer started talking again, Yasmin stood. She didn't want to miss Rashawn's entrance. She didn't recognize the song playing, but she liked the strong, contagious beat. Around her, people bobbed their heads, swayed to the music and sang the lyrics. His handlers—a Caucasian man with stringy hair, his brothers Vincente, Fenton and Armondo, and three beefy men she didn't recognize—surrounded him. His name was splashed across the back of his shiny blue robe with the Puerto Rican flag below. Rashawn entered the ring quietly, confidently. His cornrows had been rebraided and his goatee was trimmed. It had only been two days since they had seen each other, but to Yasmin it felt like weeks. His gaze combed the audience and when their eyes met, his face broke out into a smile. Comforted by his smile, Yasmin waved. He winked in response, then fixed his eyes back on Lipenski.

After the referee advised the fighters of the rules and they knocked gloves, they were whisked back to their respective corners.

Yasmin shifted in her seat. Cleaning the sweat from her hands, she tucked her feet under her chair. This was nerve-racking. Feelings of foreboding surfaced, but Yasmin pushed them away. Nothing bad was going to happen to Rashawn. He was undefeated. He was the younger, healthier fighter. He had thirty-nine knockouts under his belt. But when the bell rang and Lipenski came charging out of his corner like Mike Tyson on Prozac, Yasmin cupped a hand over her mouth to stifle a scream.

Lipenski tried to take Rashawn's head off with the first punch. The one-time champion threw wild, out-of-control punches, pushed Rashawn into the ropes and used his elbows and forearms to inflict pain. Yasmin watched, mortified. Why wasn't Rashawn hitting him back? She couldn't understand why he wasn't throwing as many punches as Lipenski. Was this part of his strategy or was he hurt? The three-minute round seemed to last an hour.

Yasmin reached across Imani and gripped Dean's arm. "Is Rashawn winning?" she asked, when the bell rang. "Does it look like he's favoring his right side?"

"No. Try not to worry. He knows what he's doing."

"If you say so," she mumbled, facing the ring. Yasmin wished Rashawn would look at her or give her a signal to let her know he was all right but he was too busy guzzling Gatorade.

The longer the fight went on, the more scared Yasmin got. Lipenski was an animal—rough, mean, aggressive. He raged, throwing blows like a crazed man. Rashawn moved rapidly, economically, averting hits, but there was nothing he could do to stop Lipenski.

In the fourth round, at the bell, Rashawn cocked his fist and roared out of his corner. He landed a crushing left hook to the veteran's jaw, sending him reeling back into the ropes. Sensing the shift in power, the crowd stood, yelling, chanting. And with the noise building, Rashawn threw a flurry of jabs, hooks and uppercuts. Oversized and overmatched, Lipenski couldn't do anything but duck, run and rest against the ropes. Drenched in sweat, Rashawn sent a right hook to the side of the veteran's head. Lipenski's face blinked in pain and his knees buckled. Fans shouted for him to stay up, to keep fighting, to persevere.

While Lipenski was slow, listless and disoriented, Rashawn was balanced, coordinated and focused. Yasmin loved how he moved. Fluid, insouciant steps; loose arms, swift footwork. He was poetry in motion. He moved with speed and quickness, drawing words of encouragement from his team. Rashawn pounded Lipenski for three more rounds, blasting punches off his head, his chest and ribs. The one-time champion had a fat eye, a cut lip and blood oozed out of his nose, but he didn't drop. At the end of the eighth round, the veteran staggered over to his corner and slumped down like a sack of potatoes.

Confident that he would be victorious, Yasmin leapt to her feet and began chanting Rashawn's name along with the crowd. Ten seconds into the tenth round, he shot a powerful blow off the side of Lipenski's head. His opponent stumbled forward before falling facedown onto the mat. Lipenski rolled onto his side and didn't move. When the referee reached the count of five, Rashawn threw his hands up in the air and his brothers hoisted him onto their shoulders. Seconds later, the large overhead screen showed the summary of the match, eliciting cheers and, from Lipenski's supporters, mumbles of frustration. Yasmin's heart overflowed with relief. It was over. The referee declared Rashawn the winner and only then did she release her breath.

"You were amazing!" Yasmin praised, throwing her arms around Rashawn's neck. Fans and supporters were celebrating his win at

Heat Wave, the hottest new bar in South Beach. Music blared, champagne flowed and the air was perfumed with smoke. The club was packed, but a steady stream of people continued arriving. With all of the people crammed inside, it was hard to steal a moment alone, but they'd found a secluded spot on the terrace.

The still night and bountiful stars set the mood for romance. Sheltered by the overgrown palm trees waving in the wind, Rashawn snaked an arm around her waist. Yasmin had no idea what she was doing to him. A simple flick of hair, her effervescent laugh and her smile knocked him sideways every time he saw her. Trading in his player card wasn't an issue; if she asked he'd gladly burn it.

"I've never seen you look more beautiful than you do tonight," he confessed, his voice infected with lust.

She was stunning, a vision of beauty in a vibrant mustard-colored dress that complimented every slope of her full figure. Her twists tumbled around her shoulders, a diamond chain graced her neck and bracelets hung from her wrist. She struck the perfect balance between sexiness and elegance. Staggered by her beauty and the subtle shimmer of her mink-brown skin, he bent down and kissed her. She tasted like honey, smooth and sweet. "Finally," he announced, when they parted. "I've been waiting for my victory kiss all night."

"All you had to do was ask."

"I'll remember that next time. Did you enjoy the match?"

"Oddly enough, I did. It was terrifying, exhilarating and exciting. I've never seen anything like it. You were incredible out there!"

"You think so?"

"Definitely," she affirmed, lovingly caressing his cheek. He had a small gash above his left eye and his face was slightly swollen. Despite his battle wounds, he was the most attractive man in the club. His linen dress shirt and slacks hung loosely, casually. "How are you feeling? Any soreness? Are you hurt?"

Rashawn took his time answering. A boxer never conceded to pain. Pain was the enemy, the sickness that exploited an athlete's weaknesses and limitations. Aside from some swelling, there was no visible evidence of Lipenski's rage. "I'm good," he told her, ignoring the angry throbbing in his head. "You're here with me on the biggest night of my life, what more could I want?"

Yasmin's eyes were laced with awe. "I don't know how you did it. Lipenski's so big and strong. He's fearless."

"What's that supposed to mean?"

"Nothing, never mind, that didn't come out right." Yasmin gave him a peck on the lips. "Were you scared?"

Rashawn answered with confidence. "Fear is a quality every good boxer needs. It's what makes you alert, what makes you aware, what pushes you to keep fighting when you're ready to throw in the towel. It's a rush of adrenaline more potent than any street drug."

"Well, I'm just glad you're okay. Don't *ever* put me through that again."

"I won't. Next time I'll knock him out in the first round, okay?"

Yasmin laughed. "I'm serious, Rashawn. Now I understand why your mom doesn't come to your matches. It's a little too intense for me. I've never experienced that many emotions in the space of an hour."

"Are we going to talk about the fight or about us?"

"I like us."

"Me, too." He lovingly brushed a strand of hair out of her face. "Did you get the basket I sent?"

"Yeah, I finished all of the candy on the plane!"

Rashawn chuckled. "I figured you would. Do you like your suite?"

"I love it."

"How much?" he asked, trailing the border of her dress with his finger.

He was daring her to make the first move, so she did. Pressing up against him, she locked her hands around his neck. Moved by the intensity and ferocity of her feelings for him, she held his gaze. "I'm glad I'm here, Rashawn. Thanks for inviting me. Now that I've seen this side of you, I think I understand you better."

Closing her eyes, she parted her lips and invited his kiss. Yasmin felt his arms circling her waist, pulling her, urging her closer. She caressed his shoulders and grew aroused by the strength and definition of his upper body. His chest was layered in muscle, firm and hard. Yasmin stroked his neck, his arms, his back. Her mouth strayed from his lips. Burying her head in his neck, she pressed her lips against his collarbone. The world around them ceased to exist. They weren't in a packed nightclub, surrounded by friends and family, they were alone, oblivious to the activity swirling around them. But when Rashawn snaked a hand up her dress and tugged at her panties, she sobered quickly. "Not…here. Someone…might see us," she panted. Bracing her hands against his chest, she forced him to look at her. "Slow down, honey. You're moving too fast."

Despite the darkness, she could see the apologetic look on his face. "My bad. I'm always amped up after a fight," he explained, feeding her a smile. Brushing his fingers across her cheek, he buried his face in her sweet-smelling hair. His hands swept over her arms, then stroked her back. Tilting her head to the right, he gently coaxed her tongue out of her mouth.

"Bro, what you doin' out here?"

Yasmin broke off the kiss, but Rashawn wouldn't relinquish his hold.

"Oh, I see. Gettin' a little action before the party takes off?" Armondo took a swig from his Heineken bottle. Glancing over his shoulder, his wanton eyes roved over the cluster of scantily dressed women at the bar. "I like how you think, bro. I'm gonna find myself a piece of ass, too."

Rashawn's eyes caught fire. "Don't ever disrespect Yasmin like that. You hear me?" he demanded, his voice caked in anger.

"Yeah, all right, bro. Take it easy."

Clapping his brother on the shoulder, he pointed him in the direction of the lounge. "Now, go inside and don't come back, got it?"

Wincing in pain, he rolled his tongue over his teeth. "Got it."

Armondo left and Brody entered. "There's the man of the

hour!" his trainer announced, marching over. "Champ, I've been lookin' all over for you."

Groaning inwardly but concealing his frustration, Rashawn said, "Hey, Brody. What's up? Yasmin and I were just talking."

Brody squinted. "You're the therapist lady, right?"

"Guilty as charged," Yasmin said, smiling.

He raised his champagne flute in the air. "My boy thinks mighty highly of you and, now that I've met you for myself, I can see why."

"That's very kind of you."

"Do you mind if I steal the champ away for a moment? We have some important business to discuss."

"Not a problem." Yasmin squeezed Rashawn's hand. "I'm going to look for Imani and Dean. Come find me when you're done."

"Don't go far!" he called, as she sailed through the terrace doors. Rashawn didn't want her to go, but he couldn't blow off his manager. His career was bigger than just him. And as much as she was his woman, he needed the freedom and space to hang out with his friends, and tonight they wanted to drink the night away. Beating Lipenski had been the proudest moment of his ten-year career. It had been a hard-fought match and though he'd never admit it to anyone, there was a point in the fifth round when he'd thought he wouldn't win. But he'd dug deep and in the end his perseverance had paid off.

"There's someone I want you to meet, champ." Brody beckoned over a bearded man wearing a pinstripe suit. "This is the Las Vegas promoter I've been telling you about. Let's hear him out. He's itching to make a deal, but don't agree to anything."

"Mancinii's the name, boxing's my game," the stranger announced, with a hearty laugh. "You looked good out there tonight, kid. Like a heavyweight contender."

"Thanks. I put my heart into that fight."

"I believe you. By the end of the match even the diehard Lipenski fans were rooting for you. If you let me, I could make you a major force in boxing. Like Hearns, Lennox and Oscar. They were nobodys until I got ahold of them."

"Really?" Rashawn said, his face lined with skepticism.

"I've been a promoter for over three decades and I can spot a superstar a mile away. You're the complete package, kid. You have talent, charm, charisma and a smile that will make the ladies cream." Sneering, he smoothed a hand over his cleft chin. "Think you could go twelve rounds with Vito 'Terminator' Garcia and make it interesting?"

Rashawn brushed off his competition. "It's not a matter of could I, it's a matter of will I. I'll fight anybody, if the conditions are right."

"December first, the MGM Grand, a million-dollar purse."

"We'll take it," Brody said, nodding vigorously.

Rashawn shook his head. "It's too soon. I can't get ready for a title match in four months," he admitted. It was a tempting offer, but he wasn't going to be enticed by dollar signs. Vito 'Terminator' Garcia had a stellar record and trained with the biggest names in boxing. If Rashawn was going to beat the Spanish phenom, he needed adequate time to prepare. "Make it March and we're on."

"Sorry, kid, it's a nonnegotiable deal. A one-time offer. Take it or leave it."

Brody pulled Rashawn aside, his face alive with excitement. "Did you hear the man? You could be among the greatest of the greats. Think about what that money could do for your future, your family, the team. It's a short turnaround between fights, but I believe in you, champ. We all do."

His trainer was right. This was his chance, his break, the fight that would catapult him into the international spotlight. Squelching his doubts, he gave Brody a terse nod.

"We'll take it," Brody said, pumping Mancinii's hand. "I'll call you next week to finalize the details."

The promoter grinned. "Let's toast to our new partnership!"

As Rashawn followed the two men inside, he couldn't help thinking he'd just made a deal with the devil.

Chapter 19

"You ready, Doc?" Rashawn glanced at his watch. Every time he went upstairs to check on Yasmin she said she needed five more minutes. Thirty minutes later and she still wasn't dressed. "Come on, we're gonna be late."

"I'll be right down."

Deciding there was no use getting angry over something he couldn't control, he went into the kitchen, poured himself a glass of juice and climbed the staircase. The scent of cinnamon assailed his nostrils and enticed his stomach. He'd had a big dinner, but these days he had the appetite of three men. Training six hours, seven days a week could do that to someone.

Rashawn poked his head into the bathroom. "You've gotta hurry or we'll miss the show." Grinning, he smacked her bottom. "If you're not ready in the next ten minutes I'm tossing you over my shoulder and carrying you out of here."

"Is that a promise?"

"Don't taunt me, Yasmin. You know I'll do it."

"Bring it on, boxer boy!"

Chuckling, he shook his head. "I don't understand what the holdup is. Just throw some clothes on and let's get out of here."

"You want me to look my best, don't you?" she asked, applying a coat of eye shadow. "I'm almost finished. Go watch TV until I'm done."

Shrugging his shoulders, he strolled into the bedroom and stretched out on the bed. It felt good putting his feet up. These days, he had all sorts of aches and pains. Since returning from Miami, his days and nights had been consumed with training. And when he wasn't at the gym, he was at home, watching tapes of Garcia. The Mexican-born fighter had patterned his game after Sugar Ray Leonard. Unlike Lipenski, he had power, agility and speed. Garcia fought in a very calculated way, punishing his opponents before knocking them out in the later rounds. Supporters labeled him the Top Dollar because he gave fans what they wanted to see: an entertaining, twelve-round fight. Rashawn had never boxed twelve rounds, but he wasn't worried about going the distance. Sparring, running and weight training gave him the stamina he needed to defeat Garcia.

Swiping the remote control off the side table, he pointed it at the TV screen and hit the power button. He flipped channels and struck gold when he landed on a Miami Heat preseason basketball game.

In the bathroom, Yasmin examined her outfit. Her look was simple but sexy. A tube-top dress, flirty accessories and heels. Peering into the mirror and noting the circles under her eyes, she added a thin layer of concealer. After another demanding week at the office, the only thing Yasmin wanted to do was relax at home. She would much rather cuddle on the couch with her man than go watch Armondo and his band perform at the Bamboo Club, but Rashawn insisted they go. His brothers and cousins would be there and it would look bad if he didn't show up.

Smiling at her reflection, she considered their relationship. Yasmin had never dated someone as affectionate as Rashawn. He couldn't keep his hands off of her. It didn't matter if they were visiting family, working out at the gym or driving in the car, he was always touching her, kissing her and whispering in her ear.

Eric had been nothing like that. Her boyfriend was thrilling, exciting and wonderfully naughty. He had elevated flirting to an art form and knew precisely what to say and do to get her in the mood. Their hearts and minds were connected and she felt safe in his love. Rashawn didn't have a doctorate degree, he didn't come from money and she never would have imagined herself with a boxer, but he was good for her. Like hazelnut coffee. Chocolate fondue. And massages. They'd only been dating for six months but Yasmin couldn't picture her life without him. Rashawn had an incredible capacity to love and he didn't shy away from expressing his feelings. Yasmin knew exactly where she stood. No guessing, no wondering, no insecurities. Rashawn spoiled her and there was no question in her mind how he felt about her. He loved her deeply, fully, completely.

That morning they had slept in, had lunch and then driven to Clearwater Beach. Teens stopped Rashawn for his autograph, seniors chatted him up about the Lipenski fight and bikini-clad women boldly ogled him. They had strolled along the shore, arm in arm, talking about everything and nothing.

Yasmin shut off the lights and closed the door. Rashawn was lounging on the bed, yelling at Dwayne Wade to pass the ball to Shaquille O' Neal. Grinning, she propped her hands on her hips and sauntered confidently into the room. "Well, what do you think? Was I worth the wait?"

"You look hot."

Her forehead creased. "Rashawn, you didn't even look at me."

"I don't have to. You're gorgeous," he praised, stealing a quick glance. "You'd look good in a Halloween costume."

Laughing, she swiped her clutch purse off the bed. "I'm dressed and ready to go whenever you are."

"Cool. Hang tight. There's only two minutes left in the game."

Yasmin stared down at Rashawn. He was the picture of calm. Head back, hands folded, legs crossed. Ten minutes ago he was barking at her to hurry up, and now he was so caught up in the game he didn't want to leave. As she watched him, something stirred within her. She wanted to touch him, to taste him, to feel his heat. He loved when she took control in the bedroom, so why not give him his heart's desire? Seduction in mind, she sashayed over to the bed. Yasmin lifted her dress high enough for him to see her thong, then sat down on his lap. Obscuring his line of vision, she placed soft kisses on the side of his exposed neck.

"I know…what you're up to…but…it's not going to work," he choked out as she flicked her tongue against his ear.

"I'm not up to anything," she lied, donning a look of pure innocence.

"Oh, yes you are…you're tying to seduce me into some freaky-type mess."

Smiling seductively, she zigzagged a finger down his chest. "And why would I do that?" Yasmin pressed her lips to his and pulled back before he could savor the feel of her mouth. "Want more?" When he nodded, she gazed at him through her extra-long fake lashes. "Did you know the body is made up of a series of meridians?" she asked, massaging his shoulders.

"Huh?" his voice was drowsy, weak, like he'd just rolled out of bed.

"According to the principles of Chinese acupressure, meridian points are a series of interconnected communication channels that run throughout the body. For example, the spleen meridian runs from your big toe to your groin to your chest," she told him, licking his bottom lip.

"Ah…go on… I'm, ah, listening…"

"Each channel controls how well a specific system works. If you stimulate the muscles in any given channel, the corresponding body parts will loosen and increase blood flow to that zone." Caressing his chest, she showered long, sensual kisses on his face. His muscles quivered under her touch and his excitement soared when she unzipped his jeans and put a hand inside his boxer briefs. "When the right amount of pressure is applied, it can cause an intense physical reaction."

"Ohhhh, I believe!" he crooned, grabbing her hips and grinding himself into her. Open-mouthed, he watched her unzip her dress. His eyes sparkled, his lips were moist and she could feel him harden between her legs. He wanted this as much as she did. The smile in her heart spread to her lips. Arching her back, Yasmin lifted her hands and undid the clasp on her strapless bra. Her breasts spilled out, enticing him, teasing him, beckoning him. Placing his hands on her breasts, she swiveled her hips with the confidence of a porn star.

The noise of the TV created the perfect background, loud, invigorating, frenzied. Yasmin tugged off his T-shirt, exposing his abs. Voyaging down his neck with her mouth, alternating between soft and wet kisses, she stroked his chest. She moved a hand to his groin and stroked his shaft. Yasmin sucked his nipples, magnifying his desire. She needed more of him. All of him. Helping him out of his jeans, she tossed them onto the carpet. Her eyes raked boldly over his physique. Fingering the fine hairs sprinkling his stomach, she kissed the trail down his chest. Pitching his head back, he dug his fingers into her hair, hollering her name.

Rashawn couldn't take it anymore. The onslaught of pleasure was more than he could stand. He wanted to be inside her; wanted to feel the sweet release only the melding of their bodies could provide. With the sounds from the TV urging him on, he flipped Yasmin onto her back and used his mouth to take off her thong. He sprinkled kisses on the inside of her thighs, the back of her knees and her legs. Careful not to put his full weight on her, he put on a condom then lowered himself between her thighs. Thrusting slowly, patiently, he resisted the urge to go faster until their bodies moved in tune. They kissed, whispering words of love and adoration, as their passion intensified. Yasmin locked her legs around his waist and he increased his movements. His eyes bore down on her, full of promise, hope and love. Riveted by the sight of her naked body, he held her protectively in his arms. Yasmin was a vision of beauty, his own private portrait, a heavenly work of art. Never before had he known a

love so sweet, so pure, so real. She was his Nubian queen and
he would love her for always.

Rashawn plunged deeper inside. She stroked his hair,
rubbed his back, gripped his butt. She never knew lovemaking could be so erotic, so zealous, so damn sexy. Yasmin
wanted to please him and was so overcome with emotion, she
hid her face in his chest so he wouldn't see the tears pooling
in her eyes.

His skin pricked from the heat of her touch. He couldn't
disguise his body's reaction and didn't try to. He was drowning,
falling, losing himself to the splendor of their love. A guttural
moan ripped from his mouth. Clinging to him, she rolled her hips
forward. Yasmin cried out as she reached the height of pleasure,
blanketing her in a thick, sleepy haze. Seconds behind her,
Rashawn shuddered as he released his seed. Laying kisses on her
damp face, he rolled off and gathered her in his arms.

"Guess we won't be going out after all," he said, his voice
cracked and jagged. "Armondo's gonna kill me."

"I'm sorry. I shouldn't have—"

"Don't apologize. I'd gladly do it again." He grinned. "And
we will."

Nestling her face against his chin, she drifted off to sleep, a
smile of sheer contentment on her lips. In her dreams, she was
in an opulent church with a host of stained-glass windows. A
short man stood before them, holding an open Bible. Friends and
family, dressed in expensive suits and gowns, sat in shiny
wooden pews. Rashawn was handsome in a crisp white suit. He
held her gaze, communicating the depth of his love with his eyes.
Yasmin's gown was a combination of modern and traditional
design. Diamonds sprinkled the bodice, the train spilled down
the aisle and the veil kissed her back. Her hair was scooped up
off her shoulders, a bed of loose flowing curls, held in place by
a crystal tiara.

"Do you, Rashawn Bishop, take this woman to have and to
hold, vowing to love her and only her from this day forward until
death do you part?" the minister asked, facing the groom.

A hint of a smile, then "I do. She's all I've ever wanted, all I ever need."

Female guests sighed softly, wishing they could trade places with the bride.

"Yasmin Ohaji, do you take this man as your husband, to have and to hold from this day forward, for better or worse, for richer or poorer, in sickness and health for as long as you both shall live?"

Beaming, she squeezed her fiancé's outstretched hands. Yasmin opened her mouth, but the words didn't come. Silence infected the air. Behind her, Imani urged her to speak. From the front row, her mom sniffled, her dad nodded fervently, and Eli grinned. She commanded her lips to move but the harder she tried to speak, the tighter her throat felt.

Stirring from her sleep, she opened her eyes. Brilliant beams of sunshine bounced around the room, signaling the dawn of another day. The air was perfumed with their love, coaxing memories of the previous night. The bathroom door was closed. Rashawn had probably gotten up early, gone for his jog and was now about to take a shower. Puzzled by her dream, she rolled onto her back. When Yasmin thought of marriage, she didn't think of a Vera Wang gown, a six-tier wedding cake or a thousand-guest reception. She thought of commitment, trust and a lifelong friendship.

A low, murmuring sound shattered the silence. Her eyes shot open. Either she was dreaming or the wine she'd had last night was still having its way with her. She sat up. Maybe she was hearing things. Maybe it was a figment of her imagination. But the sound continued, growing louder, more intense. Yasmin crawled to the foot of the bed.

Rashawn! He was sprawled out on the floor, in nothing but a pair of shorts. Seeing him, unresponsive, she leapt from the bed and scrambled to his side. He was sweating profusely and his breathing was shallow. Fear surged through her. Images of Eric's lifeless body flashed in her eyes and mingled with her tears. "Oh, God! Not again!"

"Rashawn! Wake up! Baby, answer me!" she begged, shaking his shoulders. Praying earnestly, she reached out, swiped the cordless phone from its base and punched in the three numbers that meant the difference between life and death. Returning to his side, she smoothed a hand over his damp face.

"Hello, nine-one-one. What is the nature of your emergency?" a calm, controlled female voice asked. A pause, then, "Hello? This is nine-one-one. Is anyone there?"

Yasmin forced the words from her mouth, "My boyfriend's unconscious."

"Is he breathing?"

"Yes."

"Has he used drugs or alcohol in the last—"

Anticipating the question, she said, "No. Never."

"Is he on any medication, prescribed or otherwise?"

"I—I don't know. I'm not sure," she fumbled, wishing she knew the answer to such an obvious question. "He was fine when we went to bed last night."

"How long has he been out?"

"I don't know. I just woke up."

"Ma'am, what's your address?"

Rashawn's eyes flittered open.

"Oh, my God!" Yasmin dropped the phone, tears of joy coursing down her cheeks. "Honey, what happened? I'm so glad you're okay!"

"I don't know," he croaked, propping himself up on his elbows. "I went for a run, took a shower and was on my way back to bed when I felt my legs slip out from underneath me. The next thing I know you're standing over me, calling my name."

"How do you feel now?"

"Like I went eight rounds with Lipenski," he said, rubbing the back of his neck.

"Don't worry, the paramedics are on the way."

"No!"

"But this could be—"

"I said no." His voice was firm, hard, as strong as steel. "It was nothing. I'll take it easy for the next few—" He broke off when he heard a tinny woman's voice. Spotting the phone in Yasmin's lap, he picked it up.

The operator asked him a series of questions.

"I'm sorry we disturbed you. It was a misunderstanding. Everything's fine." Rashawn clicked off the phone. A crippling pain shot through his ribs as he turned, but he didn't react. Yasmin was watching and he didn't want to scare her.

He'd been on the floor so long his legs had fallen asleep. His fingers ached, but he rubbed the back of his leg to bring back feeling. Aware that she was watching him for the slightest sign of pain, he stood and climbed into bed with ease. "Told you I was fine," he lied, supporting the back of his head with a pillow.

"Let me get you some water." Yasmin tore out of the room and returned seconds later with a glass of water and an ice pack.

"Are you sure you're okay?" she asked, pushing the drink into his hands.

"Positive."

"Has anything like this ever happened before?"

Rashawn opened his mouth, then closed it. Yasmin didn't need to know his mom had found him unconscious a few months back.

It had been over ninety degrees the morning he had gone running. His doctor had said dehydration was likely to blame for the collapse. "Yeah, but it was a long time ago."

"Did you get a second opinion?"

"What for? I trust Dr. Gutierrez with my life. He's been taking care of me since I was seventeen. I wouldn't feel comfortable with anyone else."

"I know, but it's possible he missed something. Doctors make mistakes all the time. What if you have an undiagnosed illness or—"

"Drop it, Yasmin." He slammed the glass on the side table. "I don't want to talk about it anymore. Let it go."

"I'm only trying to help. I don't want anything to happen to you."

"Just because your fiancé died unexpectedly doesn't mean I'm going to." Reassuring her and himself there was no cause for concern, he said, "Doc, I'm in kick-ass shape. If something was wrong, I'd know."

Tears threatened to come, but Yasmin pushed them away. "I care about you and I'd never forgive myself if something happened, Rashawn. Promise me you'll see your doctor first thing Monday morning."

"I'll try."

"You'll try?" she repeated, incredulously. The soft, flattering glow of the sunlight masked the anger in her eyes. "This is your health we're talking about. It could be a matter of life and death!"

"You're overreacting again. It's not that serious."

"It could be. How do you know until you see your doctor and he checks you out?"

"All right, all right, Dr. Phil. Quit badgering me. I'm going." Chuckling, he pulled her down on top of him, momentarily calming her fears. Rashawn slipped a hand under her nightgown, caressing between her legs. "I know what'll help me feel better…"

Yasmin returned his kiss, but it didn't squelch the heaviness in her heart.

Chapter 20

Rashawn smacked the heavy bag. He threw a straight jab, then a combination of uppercuts and right hooks. A million thoughts raced through his mind. The most important of them being his relationship with Yasmin. She had been treating him like a seven-year-old ever since he had collapsed. Finding him unconscious had changed her from a supportive girlfriend to a smothering, on-edge, motherly type. What had made him fall for her was her independence, her confidence, her love. She had always been a dependable source of guidance and understanding. But these days Rashawn felt like he was on around-the-clock surveillance. He'd had no intention of seeing Dr. Gutierrez, but he grew tired of her pestering. Despite the midday appointment, she had accompanied him to the plush downtown clinic and when Dr. Gutierrez asked about the circumstances behind his collapse, she recounted a startling account of what had happened two weeks earlier.

Afterward, he went to the gym. "Champ, get in here!" Brody roared, projecting his voice through the gym.

Rashawn gave the punching bag a final blow. Yanking off his

gloves, he tucked them under his arms and strode down the hall. He entered the office and was surprised to see Dr. Gutierrez Mancinii and his newly acquired attorney, Morgan Duke.

When he had told Yasmin he was looking for representation, she had recommended the lively entertainment lawyer he'd met briefly at the wine-tasting party. Now that he was in the big leagues, he needed someone to negotiate on his behalf. Someone who would protect him and advise him on the most efficient way to build his financial empire.

They must have come in through Brody's private door, because he hadn't seen them in the gym. Or maybe they had arrived when he was in the weight room, talking on his cell phone with Yasmin. She said she had a romantic dinner waiting for him, but he was in the mood for something sweet. He had an itch only she could scratch and, once he was finished with Brody, he was going home to his woman.

"What's up, fellas?" He winked at Morgan. "And lady."

She acknowledged him with a smile. "Nice seeing you again, Rashawn."

"Take a seat, champ." Brody nodded at the empty chair. "We need to talk."

Sitting down, he prepared himself for bad news. The fight was off. That's the only reason why Mancinii would crawl out of his rat-infested hole. Wanting to know who he was doing business with, he had done some digging into the promoter's background. Brody thought the man was a legend, the God of all boxing promoters, but Rashawn had read all about his shady business practices. He had a mile-long list of double-dealings and unpaid debts. Disgruntled boxers who'd been duped had posted their experiences on the Internet and Rashawn had printed them out. When he had showed the postings to Yasmin, she had warned him to be careful and to get everything in writing. Sound advice from a smart, educated woman.

"There's a glitch in our plans," Brody began, scratching his stubbly chin. "December first isn't gonna work out after all."

Rashawn couldn't say he was disappointed. After the exhausting, eight-round match with Lipenski, his body needed sufficient time to heal. Dazzled by dollar signs and Brody's steadfast support, he had agreed to a match he wasn't physically ready for.

Dr. Gutierrez was speaking when Rashawn broke free of his thoughts.

"The results of your MRI are particularly concerning. You suffered a cerebral concussion either during the weeks leading up to the Lipenski fight or during the match itself. I can't say for sure. That explains why you've had double vision, bouts of dizziness and sporadic headaches…"

Rashawn blinked. He was staring at Dr. Gutierrez. He could see the physician's mouth moving, but he couldn't hear anything. The room was spinning, snatching up all his hopes and dreams and tossing them into a pool of despair. "What are you saying?" he demanded, his hands balling into tight, angry fists. "Are you saying I'm sick?"

"You need to rest. If you don't, you could do irreversible damage to your brain. Take a year off and—"

His voice blasted across the room. "Are you crazy? I can't take a year off!"

Morgan patted Rashawn's leg. "Calm down. You're getting worked up over nothing. Let Dr. Gutierrez finish what he—"

"Nothing? Nothing?" he raged, leaping from his chair. He stalked the length of the room, pacing, talking to no one in particular. "This is my career we're talkin' about. I can't take time off! I'll be over if I do."

"You're right, you will. You'll be another washed-up boxer who didn't reach his full potential." Mancinii nodded, a smug expression on his face. "I propose we bump up the fight. How does November third sound?"

"Like suicide," Brody said, resting back in his chair and clasping his hands on his stomach. "My boy can't be ready by then. He still has a lot of work to do."

Mancinii leaned forward in his chair. "Hear me out, kid. Your last physical was a couple months ago and everything looked good, right?"

Rashawn nodded absently.

"We can submit that medical report to the boxing commission, showing a clean bill of health, and change the date of the fight to the third."

Dr. Gutierrez spoke up. "As your physician, I have to inform you of the risks involved with going through with the match. You could collapse in the ring, die from internal bleeding or slip into a coma." He had a worried expression on his face and his fingers drummed restlessly on his thigh. "Rashawn, I've been your doctor for ten years. Your mind and body have suffered significant damage during your career. If you want to reverse the effects, you have to stop fighting. Maybe somewhere down the road you can return to the ring."

Mancinii locked eyes with Rashawn. "What if I guarantee you a million plus a cut of the pay-per-view profits? You're looking at an extra seven hundred thousand. With that kind of money, you'd be set for life."

Everything Rashawn had ever heard or read about Mancinii came back to mind, but he ignored his thoughts. Right now the boxing promoter was on his side, fighting to keep him in the ring, and that was the only place he wanted to be.

Headlights shone through the kitchen window. Whipping off her apron, Yasmin flew down the darkened hallway. Seconds later, she heard keys jingle and Imani's breezy voice. Her shoulders slumped. Where was he? Rashawn should have been here hours ago. Her repeated calls to his cell phone and home phone went unanswered. Concerned, she had phoned his mom. Johanna hadn't heard from him, either, but told her not to worry.

"Hijo probably lost track of the time. He'll be there soon," she assured.

Trudging into the living room, she flopped down onto the couch. Where could he be? An image of Cheyenne and Rashawn at the charity fund-raiser popped into her head, but she shook off the thought. He had been his usual playful self when they spoke earlier in the day. Nothing was amiss. Besides, if he wanted another woman, he would tell her. Rashawn didn't play games and he cared enough about her to be honest. Yasmin trusted him completely. There was no way he was romancing Cheyenne or anyone else. He made her feel safe, he catered to her and he was committed to her.

Questions swirled around her head, deepening her fear. Something was wrong. Why else would he stand her up? Ever since she had found him unconscious, things had been tense between them. He thought she was overreacting; she thought he wasn't taking it seriously enough. Deep down she knew the accident was more than just a case of fatigue, but she had suspended judgment until they had met with his doctor. After speaking to Dr. Gutierrez, her fears had finally been put to rest. "Athletes often faint as a result of fatigue, dehydration or exhaustion," the genteel physician had explained. "But we'll do an MRI just to make sure there's nothing else going on."

Yasmin had left the clinic feeling twenty pounds lighter. And it felt good smiling and joking with Rashawn again. Since the doctor's appointment, she had made a concerted effort not to hassle him and had been rewarded with sweet words, soft touches and tender kisses. Life had returned to normal and that's how she wanted things to stay.

Imani blew into the living room, chatting a mile a minute into her cell phone. Moving the phone away from her mouth, she said, "Yassie, what are you cooking? It smells great in here!"

"Honey-glazed ribs, corn on the cob and garlic mashed potatoes."

Her forehead wrinkled. "When did you start eating meat?"

"It's not for me. It's for Rashawn."

"Aren't you sweet? I'm going to change. Mind if I stay for dinner?"

Yasmin nodded. "Sure, the more the merrier."

"When are we eating?

"As soon as Rashawn gets here."

Two hours later, Yamin cleared the table of the plates and cutlery. The ribs were cold, the salad soggy and the wine tepid. Her romantic, candlelit dinner for two turned out to be a quiet, uneventful meal for one. Imani had eaten but Yasmin wasn't hungry. She was too worried to eat. Covering the leftovers with aluminum foil, she placed the containers in the bottom of the fridge and slammed the door shut.

"Dinner was great, Sis. Keep making meals like that and I'll be here every night," Imani teased, putting her dishes in the sink. She hopped up onto the marble counter. "Do you want to talk about it?"

"I'm fine."

Imani eyed her sister. Yasmin was as far away from fine as a person could be. She wore a sad, worrisome expression and was stomping around the kitchen slamming cupboards and drawers. "Have you tried calling him again?"

"No."

"Don't you want to know where he is?"

"No."

"Do you want me to try?"

Another one-word reply.

"At least send him a text messa—"

"Leave me alone, Imani. I'm fine." Yasmin dropped plates into the dishwasher. "It's Friday night. Why don't you go to Dean's house like you usually do?"

Imani leapt off the counter like it was on fire. "I was only trying to help." Mumbling under her breath, she snatched the bottle of Merlot off the table and stormed out of the room.

Yasmin filled the sink with soapy water and scrubbed the Crock-Pot. The starless evening mirrored the darkness in her heart. Rashawn hadn't returned her calls and worse, she didn't know what she had done to warrant him treating her this way. She was a strong, spirited woman who deserved to be treated with the utmost respect. Isn't that what he was always telling her? If he cared about her, why would he hurt her like this?

The night was still young. She could call Katherine and meet up for drinks at their favorite bar. Yasmin swept away the thought. The only place she wanted to be was with Rashawn. She was desperate to hear his voice and was starving for one of his kisses. He was a ray of sunshine, a light, and seeing him always made the good even better. Unlike her relationship with Eric, she was able to love him without losing herself. She still hung out with her family, spent time at the community center and took regular women-only trips with her girlfriends.

Sighing deeply, she stared out the kitchen window. How would she sleep without him tonight? She had grown accustomed to cuddling with him and looked forward to their nightly ritual of reading to each other. They took turns reading passages from *Bedtime Stories for Lovers* and found it was a powerful aphrodisiac. Sometimes they laughed; other times they were inspired.

The phone rang. Yasmin let it ring. She wasn't in the mood to talk. But what if it was Rashawn? Dropping the pot, she cleaned her hands on her skirt. She stared down at the caller ID box that didn't reveal the identity of the caller. "Hello?"

"It's me. Don't hang up!"

Relief washed over her and mingled with her disappointment. Resisting the urge to yell at him, she exhaled her frustration. "What do you want? I'm busy."

"I'm sorry."

"You should be."

"Are you mad at me?"

Yasmin slid open the patio door and stepped outside. The wind was bouncing the tree branches and the air smelled like barbeque. Her neighbors' bulldogs barked next door, spoiling the peaceful night. "No, I had a lovely evening," she said easily. "Imani and I had dinner together and she *loved* the ribs."

"Oh, okay."

"Where are you?" Her voice softened. "When you didn't show up, I thought maybe you got hurt during your—"

"Quit worrying. Like I told you before, everything's fine. I'm in my car, on the interstate, heading west."

"Where are you going?"

"I don't know."

"Did you get your test results back today?"

Rashawn coughed. "No. It's gonna take a few more weeks."

"Why? Did they find something?"

"What's with all the questions?" His voice was sharp, like a jagged piece of glass. "I told you I didn't get the results. How am I supposed to know what the holdup is?"

Yasmin didn't care that Rashawn was evasive and irritable. She wanted to see him, wanted to touch him, wanted to feel the warmth of his kiss. Her mouth softened into a smile and seeped into her voice. "You can still come over. I'll reheat the ribs and open another bottle of—"

"No, thanks." His reply was like a slap in the face. "I need some time… alone."

Hurt and frustrated, she blinked away tears. If Rashawn didn't want to see her, she didn't want to see him, either. "That's fine. I have a lot of work to do anyways."

"I'll call you later. Okay?"

"There's no pressure," she told him. "Do what you have to do."

"Don't be like that, Doc. We'll hook up tomorrow or—"

In a flare of anger she cut him off. "I wasted my time cooking for you and you didn't even have the decency to call and tell me you weren't coming. You're right, I don't understand. I don't understand how you could be hot one minute and cold the next. Maybe you can explain it to me, Rashawn. Go ahead, I'm listening."

Silence, followed by a rumble of coughs.

"I just called to let you know I'm thinking about you."

"*Whatever.* Enjoy your drive." Fuming, Yasmin hung up the phone and chucked it onto the lounge chair. When it rang seconds later, she didn't answer it.

Chapter 21

Bustling toward her office, Yasmin pulled up the collar on her tweed jacket. Two nights ago, she had sat on the patio reading and now the wind was so fierce she was scared it would blow her away. As she entered A Better Way Counseling Services, her thoughts turned to Rashawn. After a rough couple of weeks, they were back on track. He was more attentive, more affectionate and, aside from the occasional disagreement here and there, they got along fabulously. She felt good about them, their relationship and their love.

Yasmin only wished her relationship with Niobie was as encouraging. Her assistant had been on time every day since their "talk," but her productivity had taken a dive. Tasks that used to take her minutes to do now took hours. It was time to let her go and not a moment too soon.

Yasmin was considering a business partnership with a group of other professional women and for the next few months her time would be split between the clinic and the Health and Wellness Center. Life was full without the added pressure of creating development programs for female parolees, but the opportunity to mix with other like-minded entrepreneurs was too much for her to resist. All she needed now was a new receptionist. Nothing got done unless she was harping on Niobie and she needed an office assistant she could trust.

Yasmin was heading into her office, a steaming mug of hazelnut coffee at her lips, when she caught sight of Niobie through the front window. She was sitting in her Ford Escort, smacking the steering wheel. Puzzled by her odd behavior, she rested her mug on the desk, marched briskly through the lobby and pushed open the door.

"Niobie, what's going on?" she asked, knocking on the driver's-side window.

Cleaning her face with her sleeve, she slipped on her sunglasses and stepped out of the car. "Everything's fine. I'm not feeling good. Stomach flu, I think," she explained, tugging down the hem of her dress.

A gut-wrenching odor hit Yasmin between the eyes. Stepping back, she glanced away and took a mouthful of fresh air. Niobie had sunk to an all-time low. Not only was she wearing the same outfit she had on yesterday, she reeked of vodka.

"I—I think I'm going to be sick," Niobie croaked, clutching her stomach. "I can't work today. I have to go home."

Ripe with anger, Yasmin folded her arms across her chest. Niobie was easier to read than a picture book. She didn't have the stomach flu, as she claimed. She had gone clubbing after work, had too much to drink and woke up so hung over she didn't have the energy to change. A spritz of Chanel No. 5 perfume and she was out the door. Yasmin would rather answer the phones herself than let Niobie work for her another day.

"I'm terminating your contract of employment *immediately*. I'll mail your final paycheck once the keys are handed in and everything at your workstation is accounted for." With that, she turned and strolled calmly back inside. Niobie followed, excuses flying out of her mouth at lightning-fast speed. Tuning her out, Yasmin grabbed her coffee off the front desk and went into her office. Sipping from her mug, she checked the wall clock. It was nine fifteen. If she called now, the job placement agency would send a receptionist over in the next hour. Tired of her assistant's incoherent rambling, she asked her to go home. "You're a mess. I don't want my clients to see you. Please leave and don't ever come back."

"You don't understand. I—I—"

"Grow up," Yasmin snapped, annoyed. "Quit blaming everyone else for your mistakes and take some responsibility for yourself. Instead of spending the nights in seedy bars looking for men, maybe you should concentrate on getting your life together."

"I wasn't looking for trouble…I just wanted to have some fun… I thought he was a nice guy…" Her voice faded in anguish.

"Niobie, I don't want to hear any more of your excuses. Just go."

"But it's not my fault. I didn't do anything!" she yelled, her tone a fevered pitch. "I didn't ask…for any of this to happen…I told him to stop…but he wouldn't…" Sobbing, she collapsed onto the couch.

Yasmin tried to piece together what Niobie was saying, but her assistant wasn't making any sense. Staring at the single mother with fresh eyes, she put down her coffee mug. Blinded by anger, she'd failed to see the bite marks on Niobie's neck and the holes in her nylons. Her hair always looked salon-perfect, but today there were pieces sticking up in the back and specks of fuzz throughout.

"I told him no…I swear I did…but…"

Fearing the worst, she sat down on the couch. She reached out and slipped off Niobie's extralarge sunglasses. Yasmin swallowed a gasp. Niobie looked like she had been in a street brawl. Her eyelashes were clumped with mascara, her bloodshot eyes were puffy and her cheeks were stained with tears. "Who did this to you?" she demanded, anger seeping into her voice. "What's his name?"

Sniffling, she used her fingertips to wipe her tears. Her eyes seemed heavy, almost droopy, as if she was fighting to stay awake. "I met this guy."

"Where?"

Niobie sniffled. "W-we met at the charity fund-raiser. Weeks later when I saw his profile on BlackStuds.com I sent him a message. We've been trading e-mails since then."

"What happened last night?"

"W-we had dinner at the Blue Water Grill. That really expensive seafood restaurant downtown." Her gaze strayed to the window. Remorse flashed in her eyes. "I know you think I'm stupid for meeting a man off the Internet, but I have dreams. I want a husband, a house, stability. It's tough being a single mom and not having someone you can depend on, you know?"

Nodding, Yasmin reached out and squeezed her hands.

"He suggested we go to the Grand Hyatt for drinks. Normally, I wouldn't follow a guy home on the first date, but I felt safe with him, you know? He seemed different," she explained. "He asked me about my job and was interested in what I had to say."

"We've all been there, Niobie. You want what every woman wants. It's not your fault he—"

"Yes it is! If I hadn't gone to his suite…he wouldn't have… have…" fresh tears spilled down her cheeks and splashed onto her crumpled dress.

Yasmin hugged Niobie. A feeling of protectiveness washed over her. Sexual assault cases were rarely prosecuted. In the eyes of the police department, it was a private matter, a case of he said-she said. Thoughts of sending Rashawn over to the perpetrators' house to execute a warrant with his fist circled in and out of Yasmin's mind. Aware of how disastrous split-second decisions could be, but wanting swift justice, she shelved the idea until she could give it more thought.

Minutes passed.

"I wanted to leave, but he kept giving me drinks and telling me how pretty I am." Her hands trembled as she recalled what happened next. "We started kissing and stuff. I wanted him to like me so bad," she confessed, lowering her eyes. "I gave him a…we had oral sex and then he got rough. He was pawing me and jamming his tongue in my mouth." Niobie shuddered at the memory. "It was disgusting. I starting screaming and he slapped me hard across the face. He wedged his knees between my legs…I begged him to stop, but he just laughed in my face. He said I'd been asking for it all night, but I wasn't, I swear!"

Cradling Niobie in her arms, she smoothed a hand over her clumpy hair. Listening intently, Yasmin made a mental note of all the pertinent information she could pass on to the police. Niobie could cry on cue and knew how to appeal to her sensitivities, but Yasmin believed her. There was no disputing the physical evidence. She had a bruised face, bite marks and a ripped dress. "Did he force himself on you?" Yasmin asked, forcing Niobie to look at her. "Did he rape you?"

"Well…no…not exactly. We were in bed and all I had on were my panties."

"What happened when you asked him to stop?" Yasmin questioned gently.

The quiet lasted for seconds.

"He got rough again, but this time I fought him off. Someone must have called the front desk because the hotel manager knocked on the door. While they were talking, I pulled myself together and got the hell out of there. Didn't even stay to talk to the manager, though he kept calling after me."

Yasmin was disgusted. It was hard to believe that in this day and age men were still assaulting and forcing themselves on women. Yasmin was going to see to it that the creep was found and severely punished. Even if it meant hiring a private investigator to find him. Online dating sites were popular because of their confidentiality. A man or woman could log on using a false name and assume a brand-new identity. Criminal records miraculously disappeared, divorces ceased to exist and, with the help of computer graphics and manipulation, Shrek could look like Tyrese. "What's his name?"

"I don't want anyone to know."

"But—"

"People will say I asked for it, that I shouldn't have been in his hotel room to begin with." Rocking back and forth, she hugged her hands to her chest. "I just want to forget this ever happened."

Yasmin grabbed a box of Kleenex off the end table and handed it to Niobie. "It doesn't matter what anyone says. You have to do what's right for you."

"That's why I'm going to keep my mouth shut!" Her voice reverberated around the room. "He said no one would believe me. That I'd shame my friends and family if I went public. I can't do that to my mom. She's the only one who's been there for me and Miles…Miles! Oh, my God, if this got out, the kids at school would… No, I can't."

"Niobie, please reconsider."

"No! He'll label me a slut and ruin my name." Staring blankly at the window, she released a deep, painful sigh. "I've done things in the past, Dr. Ohaji. Things for money. If my mom found out, she'd be so ashamed of me. I won't hurt her again."

"It doesn't matter, Niobie. He has to pay for what he did to you."

Niobie blew into a tissue and balled it up in her hands. "I'm going home. I came straight here because my mom spent the night with Miles and I didn't want them to see me like this."

Yasmin stood. "I'll take you. You're in no condition to drive."

"No. I want to be alone."

"We don't have to talk. I'll drop you off at your apartment and leave. I promise."

Niobie cleared her throat. "About my job—"

"It will be here for you whenever you're ready."

The single mother looked wan and tired, like hadn't slept in weeks, but she managed a thin smile. "Thanks, Dr. Ohaji."

"The most important thing is that you get better. If you need anything or change your mind about going to the police, call me. It doesn't matter the time. Day or night, okay?" Yasmin eyed her thoughtfully. She had underestimated her assistant. Niobie was a fighter. She had the bruises to prove it. "Is it all right if I come by later to check on you?"

Nodding, she slipped on her sunglasses. Niobie straightened her clothes and took faltering steps toward the door.

Something Niobie had said earlier came back to Yasmin. If they had met at the charity fund-raiser, there was a good chance she knew him. At the very least, she would be able to find out who he was. "Niobie, what's his name?"

She paused and turned. "Cecil Manning."

* * *

Exhausted, Yasmin sunk into her armchair. The day hadn't even started yet, but she felt like she could use a nap. After cleaning Niobie up, she had walked her outside, helped her into the Volvo and driven the thirty minutes to her apartment. Since it was too late to cancel her ten o'clock appointment, she had raced back to the office and awaited the arrival of the Kolodenkos.

Yasmin stretched out her aching legs. Now more than ever she needed the smooth, calming voice of Anthony Hamilton. Closing her eyes, she prepared to be comforted by the neosoul balladeer.

The last three hours played over in Yasmin's head. Surely she was dreaming. Driving Niobie home, photographing her injuries and making arrangements for her to begin counseling immediately were not a figment of her imagination. Physically and emotionally drained, Yasmin had her temporary assistant, Ms. O'Grady, cancel her appointments for the remainder of the day.

Talking to Katherine had given her some ideas. Her best friend had suggested she call Morgan to seek some legal advice. The phone had rung three times, then a prerecorded male voice had asked her to leave a message. It might be weeks or even months before she got justice on Niobie's behalf, but Yasmin didn't care what it took. Cecil Manning was going to pay.

The city councilman was clean-cut and always dressed in a suit, but Yasmin had learned a long time ago that looks could be deceiving. Cecil had preyed on the single mother's insecurities and misguided trust. He deserved no less than a long, healthy prison term but because Niobie refused to go to the police, Yasmin had something else in mind for the Boston native. Politicians were petrified of scandal. One whiff of impropriety and he'd be back in his hometown working at a local car wash. It didn't matter if Niobie were naked; she had said no and he was bound by law to honor her decision. By the time she was finished with the dapper city councilman, he'd be begging for mercy.

Line three buzzed. Yasmin lowered the music, took a deep breath and answered the phone. "Dr. Yasmin Ohaji speaking."

"Hey, Doc. Got a minute for me?"

"Always," she replied, a smile overwhelming her mouth. Yasmin could tell by the hitch in Rashawn's voice that he was in a playful mood. "How are you?"

"Better, now that I'm talkin' to my sexy girlfriend."

"Aren't we full of compliments? To what do I owe this praise?"

"Can't a brother tell his woman she's fine without being accused of wanting something?"

"'Fess up, Rashawn. I'm onto you."

He chuckled heartily. "All, right, all right, you got me. I'm starving and there's nothing in my fridge but a block of moldy cheese. Wanna grab a bite to eat?"

Yasmin's forehead creased. "How come you're not at the gym?"

"I had, ah…" The line went quiet. "I decided to take the day off."

"Is everything all right?"

"Perfect. Are you going to let me take you out, or what?"

"Um, okay. Where?"

"Let's go to City Bar Tampa," he suggested. "I could go for one of their double-decker cheeseburgers."

"Is it okay if we meet in an hour? I have some errands to run first."

"It's all good. See you then, Doc."

An hour later, Yasmin was stuck behind a Chrysler minivan in the thick of traffic. Her cell phone hummed. Adjusting her earpiece, she answered the call. "Hello?"

"This is Ms. Duke's office returning your call." The pleasant-sounding man had a slight British accent. "She's available to speak to you now. One moment please."

Seconds later, Morgan's effervescent voice filled the line. "I'm sorry it's taken me so long to get back to you, Yasmin, but I've been in meetings."

"It's no problem. It sounds like you've had a long day."

"Girl, you don't know the half of it! I've represented my fair share of athletes, but this NFL quarterback I just signed is manic-depressive with bipolar tendencies and a hint of good ole crazy thrown in!" Morgan laughed. After a few minutes of idle chitchat, she asked, "What can I do for you?"

Yasmin liked that Morgan was straightforward. She was an entertainment attorney, specializing in celebrity divorces, contract negotiations and the like, but she had a keen legal mind. "It's a personal matter. Something I wish to keep private."

"I can't say I'm surprised. I expected you to call."

"You did?" Yasmin asked, perplexed. She had sworn her friend to secrecy, so how did Morgan know that Cecil had attacked Niobie? "Did you talk to Katherine?"

"I didn't have to. Wives, coaches, girlfriends and long-lost family members call my office on a daily basis pleading with me to talk some sense into their loved ones. I'm going to tell you what I tell them."

"This isn't about—"

Morgan cut in. "I know you want what's best for Rashawn, but it's *his* career, *his* choice. He's been boxing for what, ten years? He knows his body better than any doctor. If he wants to disregard the test results and go through with the fight there's nothing any of us can do to stop him, including you."

Yasmin almost lost her grip on the steering wheel.

"I can't change his mind. Believe me, I've tried. I pulled him aside this morning before he signed the contracts…"

Yasmin's vision blurred. Her head throbbed with horror. Behind her, drivers honked. Her legs were numb but she eased her foot off the brake pedal and onto the gas. The car lurched forward, mirroring the hollow feeling in her stomach.

"The contracts have been signed. It's a done deal. Now, all you can do is support his decision."

"What did the MRI reveal?" she asked, the sound of her own voice sounding foreign in her ears. "Is there inflammation? Is their bleeding in or around the brain?"

"He didn't tell you?" Morgan rushed on. "Try not to worry too much, Yasmin. He'll be fine. Besides, what's the worst that can happen?"

Chapter 22

On Monday nights City Bar Tampa resembled a fraternity house. College students clad in oversize football jerseys gathered in front of the wide-screen TVs, devouring chicken wings and guzzling beer. In the lounge, professional men and women sat in padded armchairs, sipping a slew of colorful cocktails. The room was flanked by pool tables, arcade games and a seventies-style jukebox. Waiters dressed in checkered shirts carried trays, served drinks and squared bills. The dining area brimmed with unruly children and the haggard-looking parents who chased after them.

"Is there anything else I can get you?"

Glancing at the ruddy-faced waiter, Rashawn cleaned his mouth with his napkin. "No, I'm straight." He caught a glimpse of the basketball-themed clock. Hours had passed since he had talked to Yasmin. Normally he wouldn't trip about her being late, but Imani had called looking for her, too. Tired of waiting, he fished his car keys and wallet out of his pocket. "Can I get the bill now? I'm in a hurry."

"What about the vegetarian pizza? Should I put it in a take-out container so you can take it with you?"

Rashawn stared down at the plate of cold food. "Yeah, sure."

"I'll be right back." The waiter cleared the table of the dishes and left.

Yasmin had been late to meet him before, but this was ridiculous. He'd carved time out of his schedule to see her. Why couldn't she do the same? There were only a handful of places she could be. He knew from talking to Imani that she wasn't at home or at her parents' house. That left the office or the community center. Once he settled his tab, he'd swing by the clinic and have a look around.

Rashawn flipped open his cell phone. No missed calls. This wasn't like her. If she were going to be late, she would call. Another scenario came to mind. Had something happened to her as she left the office? Yasmin was savvy, smart, aware of other people and her surroundings. She couldn't have been attacked. The morning's headlines raided his thoughts, confronting him with the shocking reality of their community. Carjackings, drive-bys and kidnappings were a daily occurrence. And inner-city residents were the most helpless, often targeted and rarely reporting the crimes.

"Can you autograph my T-shirt, please?" a voice asked behind him.

Rashawn turned around. A pale boy with ocean-blue eyes was staring at him, waiting expectantly. "Sure, kid. What's your name?"

Ten minutes later, Rashawn had a large, mostly female crowd at his booth. He was so busy scribbling his signature on shirts, he didn't notice Yasmin standing off to the side. When he did, his face broke out into a smile. Mesmerized by the sight of her, he licked his lips. She was wearing her hair the way he liked it, gathered off her shoulders, swept up in a loose ponytail. Her navy business suit was smart, yet soft and elegant. Rashawn lifted his gaze past her legs, over her hips and up her chest. His smile evaporated when their eyes met. One look at her face and he knew she was angry. Her lips were a taut line. She stood motionless, watching him, her eyes passing judgment.

Rashawn swallowed his frustration. She was two hours late

but had the nerve to cop an attitude. "Sorry, guys. That's it," he announced, handing the pen back to the girl in the blue J-Lo sweat suit. "My girlfriend's here and we'd like to be alone."

Groaning in disappointment, the group meandered back to their respective tables.

Yasmin sat down at the table, a poisonous look in her eyes. "You didn't have to send your groupies away on account of me. They look so disappointed, especially the redhead with the fake boobs."

"Is your cell phone dead?" he asked, annoyed by her sarcasm. "No."

"Then why didn't you call?" Rashawn didn't give her time to respond. "I've been sitting here for hours. Where the hell have you been?"

"With Dr. Gutierrez, of course."

Rashawn closed his eyes as if in prayer. He'd bet his wallet his doctor had told her about his test results. This couldn't have happened at a worse time. After spending the day with his team, developing a new training regimen and diet, he didn't have the energy to argue with Yasmin. And that's exactly where the conversation was headed. He sat in a moody silence as she interrogated him. He wanted to defend himself but decided on the wait-and-see approach. He'd listen to what she had to say, then go from there.

"I marched into Dr. Gutierrez's office and asked to see your file. He refused. I understand and respect the importance of the patient-doctor privilege but I wanted answers. I was grilling him when it hit me. He doesn't have to tell me anything. *You're* my boyfriend. *You're* the one who lied to me."

"I didn't tell you about the results because I didn't want you to get on my case. I wanted to decide what to do without you cramming your opinion down my throat."

"I can admit that I was a little overbearing in the weeks following your accident, but I had every reason to be! I found you—"

"Lower your voice," he ordered, snatching a look around the restaurant. The dinner rush had cleared, but he didn't want anyone to overhear them. "My decision to go through with the fight is none of your business. I discussed it with my team and we decided what was best for my career."

"It's none of my business?" she repeated, her eyes narrowed like laser beams. She pointed a finger to her chest. "*I* was the one who held ice packs on your eyes after the Lipenski fight. *I* ran out to get you extra-strength Tylenol when you were moaning in pain and *I* was the one who massaged your blistered feet."

"And I don't do shit for you, right, Yasmin?" His tone was loud, harsh, angry. "Didn't I shell out fourteen hundred dollars for you to come to Miami?"

"I told you I didn't want to go but you insisted." Her voice trembled with feeling. "I didn't ask for any of those things!"

"And I didn't send you to Rite-Aid in the middle of the night, either. You chose to go so don't put that shit on me."

Cheers exploded around the room, pulling his attention to the bar. Uproarious laughter and friendly conversation filled the air. The mood was light and festive but tension hovered above their booth like a thick billow of smoke. They should be at home, relaxing on the couch, not arguing at City Bar. "Let's get out of here."

"I'm not going anywhere until you tell me exactly what Dr. Gutierrez said."

"It's my career, my life. I'll do what I want."

"What about all the plans you have for after boxing? What will happen if you get seriously hurt during the match?"

"Like I said, it's *my* life."

"You know what, Rashawn. You're selfish. You didn't stop for one second and consider how this would affect me."

"This argument is stupid," he mumbled, shaking his head. "Life was so much easier when I was single." The moment the words left his mouth he wished he could suck them back in. Her face crumpled and her eyes watered. "I didn't mean anything by it."

"Don't you dare call me names!"

"I never said you were stupid, I said this argument is stupid." Rashawn wasn't going to debate the issue with her any longer. He was fighting Garcia and that was it.

It killed him inside to see her cry, but he couldn't back out now. People were counting on him. Two million dollars was at stake. He had to do this. "I'm not going to argue with you about my career, Yasmin. It's my sweat, my tears and my sacrifice that got me here. And I'm not going to quit boxing because you have a problem with it."

Yasmin shook her head. "This is crazy. You're willing to risk your life for a belt that doesn't mean anything?"

"It means something to me. I've worked my whole life for this. I've been dreaming about being a heavyweight champion since I picked up my first pair of gloves."

"B-but you could die."

"No one's going to die," he snapped, his eyes piercing her flesh. "God, when did you become so preoccupied with death?"

"When I found you unconscious."

"This is not about me. It's about him."

"Leave Eric out of this."

"He died and now you have it in your head that I'm going to die, too."

"And you will if you disregard your doctor's advice!"

Rashawn exhaled. They weren't getting anywhere. In an attempt to explain away her fears, he took her hands and said, "This is a once-in-a-lifetime opportunity, Doc. I may never have a chance like this again. My team believes in me—they know I'll win."

"Of course they do! They don't care about you—all they care about is their paycheck. They're not thinking about what's best for you in the long term."

"My brothers, my cousins and my parents are behind me."

"I'm sure they are," she scoffed, rolling her eyes. "They're wooed by dollar signs just like everybody else."

He ran his teeth along his bottom lip. "Don't talk about my family."

"What if you get hurt? What if things don't go as planned?"

"None of that matters. Win or lose, I'm guaranteed almost two million dollars. Do you know what that kind of money can do for us?"

Yasmin snatched her hands away. "Us? I don't want anything from you! I've never asked you for anything."

"But you didn't say no when I was spending money on you. You like expensive shit, too. First-class tickets, five-star hotels and champagne cost a grip."

"I won't be a part of this."

"I'm not asking you to be."

Sliding out of the booth, she snatched her purse off the seat and slung it over her shoulder. "I—I guess there's nothing left to say."

"So that's it? You're going to leave me because I won't do what you want?" he asked, standing. "Don't you think you're being dramatic? Lots of athletes fight through injuries. I'm no exception." He waited for her to respond, but she didn't. She had a heart-broken expression on her face and she couldn't meet his gaze. "Let's make a deal. After the Garcia match, I'll take some time off. How's that?"

"What happens when you're offered more money for the next fight? Your team will talk you into it and you'll ignore my feelings again."

"I'm not ignoring you."

"You can't have it both ways, Rashawn. If we're going to be together you have to take my feelings into consideration, too."

He smoothed a hand over his head. Yasmin was right. He wanted the security and companionship of a relationship, but he also enjoyed the freedom of not having to consult anyone about what he wanted to do. She put his needs above her own, pampered him and made him want more than just a sexual relationship, but Rashawn wasn't ready to say good-bye to his independence. "I care about you, Doc, more than anyone I've ever been with, but I'm not going to ask for your permission regarding my career. I'm going to do what I want to do. Period."

"Whatever. It's your life, do what makes you happy. I have to go." Yasmin turned away, but Rashawn yanked her to his chest. Embracing her, he nuzzled his face in her hair. He inhaled the fresh, peachy scent, his thoughts drifting back to the last night they had been together.

Yasmin had ordered him to lie down on the bed and close his eyes. She had run a light, fuzzy item over his shaft and when he had guessed that it was a feather, he had been treated to a sensuous massage. He had gone along with her game, enjoying the waves of pleasure radiating through him every time a silk scarf had skimmed his nipples. His body was a hotbed of erogenous zones and Yasmin knew exactly which buttons to push. By the time they had made love, his head was spinning and he was sweating down to his toes.

Rashawn stared down at her, his heart overcome with love. Having her in his arms like this reminded him how special she was. They had an honest relationship, the sex was off the charts and he trusted her completely. How many men could say they had the love of a good woman? Moved by his feelings, he lifted her chin and bent down until their lips met. Her mouth lacked its usual warmth and her arms hung firmly at her side. "Doc, don't do this to us," he said, when she pulled away. "I need you."

A sad smile touched her lips. "I can't stand by and watch you get hurt. I love you too much." She kissed him softly, tenderly, underlying her feelings for him with her lips. Pulling away abruptly, she turned and walked away.

Rashawn watched her leave. Maybe things were better this way. That afternoon, he'd sat down with his team and they'd opened his eyes to the truth. According to the guys, he'd lost his focus ever since he had started dating her.

"Training is everything. You've gotta respect it," Brody had preached. "Love's made you soft. Get your mind off that therapist woman and back into boxing. Millions are on the line, champ."

The fight was only weeks away. He had to get his mind right if he was going to beat Garcia. He respected Yasmin for being strong-willed and opinionated but he was tired of feeling like everything was a struggle. They weren't on the same page, but it had nothing to do with his boxing career. It had everything to do with her need for control. Rashawn already had a mother; he didn't need another one. He was a grown man. He didn't want

Yasmin babying him or telling him what to do or handing out orders. He wanted her in his life, but he wasn't going to abandon his dreams for anybody. Not even for the woman he loved.

Chapter 23

The carefree days of summer gave way to the shortened, breezy days of autumn. Yasmin loved the sound of leaves crunching under her feet, the invigorating morning air and the vibrancy of the season.

Yasmin arched her back, swung her arms and increased her pace. Nothing like a brisk walk to help clear the mind. Her eyes twinkled in the sunshine and her hair flapped restlessly in the wind. The sky was alight with color, subtle shades of orange, pink and red.

Her chest heaved and sweat trickled down her back, but she felt good. After weeks of finding solace in potato chips and gummy bears she had flabby arms and thunder thighs. Eliminating junk food from her diet would be more challenging than running the Boston Marathon, but it had to be done. Her business suits were tight and when she sat down the skirts rode up her hips. The number on the scale had pushed her to action, but walking was a great stress reliever and gave her some much-needed time alone.

As she thought over the day, she made a mental note to call Niobie. The bruises on her arm and neck had turned black a couple of days after the assault, forcing her to come clean to her mom. Not only had Ms. Slade encouraged her to press charges against her attacker, she had called Yasmin asking for help. Despite the support of her friends and family, Niobie was vehemently against going to the police. Yasmin felt she was making a mistake, but supported her decision. Cecil Manning wouldn't face a judge or a jury of his peers, but once Morgan met with the councilman's attorney, he'd be punished where it hurt the most: his wallet.

In the weeks since the assault, Niobie had attended individual counseling as well as group sessions and had found comfort in speaking with other assault victims. Aware of the single mother's financial situation, Yasmin had arranged for her to take a four-week leave of absence with pay. Her replacement, Ms. O'Grady, was proficient, hard-working and completed tasks on time, but the woman had no personality. She rarely smiled, smelled like Ben-Gay and her unsolicited advice put people off. Yasmin missed Niobie and so did her clients. Everyone from the cleaning staff to the UPS courier asked when she was coming back and gave Yasmin messages to pass on to her. Bothered by the way Niobie dressed and her carefree, life's-a-party attitude, she had never noticed how comfortable she made clients feel or the little things she did to brighten up the office.

A Hispanic man in spandex shorts jogged up the block. "Good morning," he greeted, as he passed by.

Yasmin returned his smile. He was an early riser. Like Rashawn. On cool, breezy mornings like this, Rashawn would forgo his run and bike instead. Sighing deeply, she stared up at the cloudless sky. It was hard not having him around. She occupied her evenings with work but the more hours she put in at the office, the emptier she felt. Her free time should be spent with Rashawn, not poring over old case files and medical journals. He was always invading her thoughts, but what Yasmin missed most was hearing his voice.

Last Thursday when he hadn't shown up for the Men of Initiative program, she had slipped out of the room and called him. He hadn't answered, but that hadn't stopped her from calling again. Every night before bed, she phoned and left a message on his answering machine. Hearing his voice softened the sting of their breakup and made her feel close to him. Yasmin wanted Rashawn to know that she was thinking about him. And she was. In the morning when she ate breakfast, at night when she read *Bedtime Stories for Lovers* and whenever an Anthony Hamilton song came on the radio. Rashawn had been such an integral part of her life that not seeing him made her miserable. Imani and Katherine saw to it that she had things to do, but trips to the mall couldn't replace him. Who was she going to vent to? Who was going to massage her feet at the end of a long day? And most importantly, who would she share her hopes, dream and fears with?

Lifting her arms above her head, she stretched her tight, underworked muscles. Since their breakup, she had dissected every word of their argument, piece by piece. Were his accusations founded? Was she preoccupied with death? But after reviewing the facts, Yasmin realized she had every reason to be afraid.

Rashawn was risking his health, all for the sake of fame and fortune. She didn't care what his team said. He had no business fighting Garcia or anyone else. Extensive research into head injuries had uncovered shocking findings. Internal bleeding wasn't often found in healthy twenty-seven-year-olds, but it was a common occurrence among athletes. And a boxer was five times more likely to suffer a cerebral concussion than any other athlete. Their relationship was over, but that didn't mean Yasmin had stopped worrying about him. In recent weeks, her anger had cooled. Loneliness had set in and despite her efforts to keep it at bay, she couldn't shake the feeling. Friends and family commented on how well she was coping with the breakup, but it was all a façade. Every night she sat by the phone, willing it to ring. And on several occasions, she'd hopped into the car and driven by his house. When she saw his Mustang in the driveway, she sighed with relief; when it wasn't there, thoughts of him being with another woman harassed her mind.

Yasmin rounded the corner. One more block to go. The residents in Hillsborough were ready to start the day. Students stood in line for the bus, stay-at-home moms pushed strollers and canine lovers walked their pets. A bearded man stood at the bus stop kissing with an Asian woman half his age. The couple groped each other like a pair of horny teenagers. Shaking her head, she considered her eight-month relationship with Rashawn. A therapist and a tough-as-steel boxer? Who would have thought? They were an unlikely pair, joined together by past hurts and disappointments. Yasmin wanted to be a partner in his world, his confidante, his sounding board, someone he could go to when everyone else failed. She had a successful practice, a loving family and friends, but life was richer and fuller with Rashawn by her side. He was her lover, her king, her everything. If only he had listened to her. If only he cared enough about her, enough to— Yasmin killed the thought. No more fretting over Rashawn. He had made his choice and she would respect it, no matter how much it hurt.

"Have you put on weight?" Ms. Ohaji queried, as her daughter came in through the back door. "Your skirt is so tight I can see your panty line."

"Hi, Mom. It's good to see you," Yasmin said dryly. She took off her blazer and draped it behind the chair. "Please don't start in on me about my weight. I've had a rough day and the last thing I need is more unsolicited advice."

"Well, someone has to warn you about the dangers of being overweight. What kind of mother would I be if I didn't tell you the truth? Not a very good one."

"I've gained a few pounds, big deal."

"Big deal? Do you know the health risks linked to obesity?"

Sitting down on a stool at the eating bar, she patted back a yawn. "Mom, please don't start. I can't take another one of your lectures."

"I don't know why you struggle with your weight. I weigh less than I did on my wedding day and I've had three kids," she pointed out, a trace of self-satisfaction in her voice. "None of the women in our family are heavy and you shouldn't be either."

Yasmin helped herself to the bowl of almonds. "Well, you'll be happy to know I started a new diet and exercise program last week."

"What you need to do is put down the snacks and pick up some weights." Ms. Ohaji reached out and cupped her daughter's chin. "You have bags under your eyes and your skin is dry. Start taking those multivitamins I bought you. They'll help bring your color back."

"Mom, I'm fine and so is my color."

"No it's not. You look sick." Her face wrinkled with concern. "Maybe you're coming down with the flu or something. You should stop in the walk-in clinic on your way home."

Yawning, she stretched her hands lazily over her head. "No need. I have a doctor's appointment on Friday."

"You need to get more sleep," Ms. Ohaji advised in a stern voice. "That's the third time you've yawned since you sat down and you just got here!"

"Mom, you worry too much." Anxious to change the subject, she said, "Where's Dad? Is he working late again?"

"The last time I saw your father he was sprawled out on the couch watching the Fight Network." Ms. Ohaji examined her daughter. "Speaking of sports, have you spoken to Rashawn?"

"No, and I don't plan to."

"I think you should give that young man another chance."

Yasmin's mouth sagged. "You do?"

"Did he cheat on you?"

"No."

"Did he ever push you around or call you names?"

"Never."

Ms. Ohaji wore a triumphant smile. "Then your relationship is salvageable!"

"No, it's not."

"In case you haven't noticed, your generation is experiencing a man shortage. Everyone's talking about it. *Ebony, Essence* and *Upscale* magazines all did articles on the subject, and Oprah devoted an entire show to the matter. Single, career-oriented women are having a terrible time finding suitable mates."

Feigning surprise, Yasmin smacked her cheeks. "Say it ain't so! Poor ole me. What will I do without a man to take care of me?"

Scowling, Ms. Ohaji eyeballed her eldest daughter. "You won't be laughing when you're forty-five and everyone around you is happily married. It's a very serious issue, Yasmin. One you shouldn't take lightly." Her tone softened. "Give some thought to what I said. You don't want to wake up one morning and realize you let a second chance at true love pass you by."

Ms. Ohaji turned to the stove, leaving Yasmin alone with her thoughts. Her mother was right. She had thought about marrying Rashawn and even dreamt about it, too. The idea of spending the rest of her life living with him and loving him was an exciting prospect. They embraced the same family values and spiritual beliefs, shared common interests and loved each other completely. But Yasmin couldn't sit back and watch him get hurt, year after year, fight after fight. It wasn't fair to her, and he wasn't prepared to leave boxing. It was his dream, his passion, his life. How could she ask him to give up doing what he loved? Yasmin understood her mother's concern, but she didn't share her opinion. If she couldn't have Rashawn, she didn't want anybody.

Eli ambled into the kitchen. "I'm starving," he announced, sticking his hand into the pot and plucking out a chicken breast. "How are the baked beans coming along?" he asked, biting into the meat.

"Get out of here and don't come back!" Ms. Ohaji ordered, shielding the pot with her hands. "That's your third piece. By the time you're finished sampling, there will be nothing left."

Chuckling, he wiped his mouth with the back of his hand. "Hey, Sis. What's up?"

"Nothing much. I just stopped by to see what you guys are up to. How's school?"

Eli groaned. "Insane. I have more assignments than I can handle."

Yasmin laughed. "Welcome to the real world, little brother."

"It's not all bad." He finished the meat and tossed the bone into the garbage. "I've decided to join Pi Kappa Sigma. They're the hottest frat on campus and they really know how to get down."

"Fraternities were founded to enrich the community, strengthen the brotherhood and develop leadership qualities, not to host weekly parties. And if I'm not mistaken, academic achievement is a top priority."

"Yeah, whatever." Eli plopped down on the stool beside her. "I need a favor."

"You can't crash at my place, you can't borrow my car and I don't have any money to lend you."

"That's cold, Sis." He lobbed an arm around her shoulder. "Can you ask Rashawn for some tickets to his match? If I can hook up my frat brothers with front-row seats, they might take it easy on me during pledge week."

"Why don't you call him yourself?"

"I did. We spoke last week. He asked about you."

Yasmin stared at her brother. "He did?"

"I don't know why you guys broke up, but I know he still cares about you. Why else would he be asking about you every two minutes?"

It took all Yasmin had not to interrogate Eli. Her face remained expressionless when she asked, "What did he say?"

"He wanted to know what you were up to, wanted to know if you were seeing anybody, asked if you were still mad at him." Eyeing his mom, he dropped his voice to a conspiratorial whisper. "I invited him to Mom and Dad's anniversary party. He said he'd try to be there."

Her smile was slow to form. It felt good knowing Rashawn was thinking about her. She wasn't the only one lamenting their breakup. Apparently he was, too. "Why didn't you ask for tickets when you talked to him last week?"

"Because the idea just came to me a few days ago. I've tried calling, but I haven't been able to get ahold of him. But if you call, he'll answer."

Eli's words circled her head. Rashawn was coming to her parents' party? It had been a month since they'd broken up and the prospect of seeing him again excited her. Glancing down at her suit, she wondered what Rashawn would think of her loose midsection and flabby thighs. Just because they weren't together anymore didn't mean she could let herself go. Yasmin slid off the stool. "I've got to go."

Covering the pot, Ms. Ohaji glanced over her shoulder. "I thought you were staying for dinner?"

The sweet-smelling aroma of cornmeal soup filled the kitchen. Yasmin's mouth watered and her stomach rumbled. Ignoring her hunger, she grabbed her jacket, tossed her purse over her shoulder and pushed open the back door. If she hurried, she could make the seven o'clock step-aerobic class at Bally's Gym.

Chapter 24

Yasmin leafed through her second issue of *Women's Health* magazine. After spending an hour in the lab and waiting another twenty minutes before the nurse had called her, she was hungry, tired and anxious to go home.

Yasmin heard the clack of high heels and then there was a sharp knock on the door. It opened and Dr. Fitz-Simmons swept into the room, her white coat flapping restlessly behind her. She was a slender, fifty-something woman with a short Afro. "Yasmin," she greeted brightly. "It's been awhile. How are you doing?"

"I'm okay, and you?"

"Great. It's good to see you." Dr. Fitz-Simmons sat down on the stool. "It looks like congratulations are in order," she said, smiling. "I must admit I was shocked when I saw your test results."

"I—I—I don't understand."

The doctor's smile fell away. "I thought you knew."

"Knew what?"

"You're pregnant!"

Her purse slipped off her lap and crashed onto the floor. "I'm what?"

"Pregnant. Based on the level of HCG in your blood, I'd guess you were about eight weeks, but we'll know for sure once I examine you."

For a moment, Yasmin thought she was joking. But when Dr. Fitz-Simmons patted her hands sympathetically, she knew the doctor was as serious as the IRS.

"M-m-my blood work must have been mixed up with someone else's," she stammered, her heart pounding in her ears like steel drums.

Dr. Fitz-Simmons opened the file on her desk. She scanned the documents inside. "Everything matches up. The pregnancy hormone was detected in both your blood and urine, but if it makes you feel better we can run the tests again."

"Yes, please do. It's wrong." Bending down, she stuffed her wallet, compact and cell phone back into her purse. "I can't possibly be pregnant. I've been in premature ovarian failure for years."

"They might be failing, but they're still working. And they're obviously functioning better than expected, because you got pregnant without even trying."

"Can you please stop saying that," Yasmin ordered, bolting upright. "I'm not pregnant."

"When was your last period?"

Squinting, she racked her brain for the answer. Confused thoughts and fears flooded her mind, increasing her anxiety. "I—I can't remember. I've never had a normal menstrual cycle so it's hard for me to say. But I *know* I'm not pregnant."

"Maybe it will help if I explain. Human chorionic gonadotropin, or HCG, is released into the body by the placenta when you conceive. This hormone is also responsible for causing some of the initial symptoms of pregnancy, such as fatigue, exhaustion and breast tenderness."

"But I'm fine. I've been feeling a little queasy but..." Her voice drifted into silence as she thought back over the last month. She woke up feeling lethargic, her clothes were snug and she often fell asleep after dinner. But that didn't mean she was pregnant. She had the flu. At this time of year, everyone was sniffling, coughing and wheezing. It was the change of the season and nothing more. Yasmin burrowed her arms defiantly across her chest. "I have the flu."

Dr. Fitz-Simmons wore a knowing smile. "Flu-like symptoms are similar to the early signs of pregnancy. Women often complain of feeling run-down and nauseated during the first trimester. It's perfectly normal."

"I'm not pregnant," she protested, swiping the magazine up off the floor and stuffing it back into her purse. She made a point of adding, "I'd know if I was pregnant. I'm a doctor, too, you know."

"And I've been a gynecologist for almost thirty years. I know what I'm doing, Yasmin. You're pregnant."

Rocked by the news, she sat in stunned silence. On the outside, she was composed, but inside she was trembling with fear. She was trying to keep it together. Trying to remain strong. How would it look if she threw herself down on the ground and started bawling? No, that's not how a therapist behaved. Besides, if the test results were accurate, there would be plenty of time for crying later. After several seconds, she found her voice. "H-How could something like this happen?"

Dr. Fitz-Simmons chuckled. "I should be the one asking *you* that question."

"B-B-But I'm on the pill. I've been on it for years. I've never missed a dose. And I used condoms."

"You and I both know abstinence is the only form of birth control that is a hundred percent effective. And alcohol, stress and weight gain can reduce the efficiency of the pill. And condoms can break."

Yasmin pressed her eyes shut and massaged her temples. "This can't be happening. This can't be happening," she repeated, rubbing her fingertips in a circular motion. "The test is wrong. The test is wrong."

"You'll be fine, dear. Women give birth every day. It's a glorious and wonderful part of a woman's life. You can do it. You're a lot stronger than you think."

"I can't have a baby!" Yasmin poured out all of her fears. "I have a clinic to run, I just started a new project at the women's center and…and Rashawn and I broke up. If I was married it wouldn't be so bad, but I'm not. I can't be an unwed mother! What will people say?"

"Yasmin, I've known you and your family for years. Once you get over your shock, you'll realize just how fortunate you are. Not everyone can get pregnant, you know. Some couples struggle with infertility for years before they conceive. And others never do." Dr. Fitz-Simmons punctuated her sentence with a smile. "You beat the odds. That's something to be grateful for."

"None of this feels real… It's like I'm dreaming or something."

"It's real all right. Just be thankful you don't have morning sickness."

A bolt of panic flashed in Yasmin eyes.

"My daughter's in her twenties now but I remember my pregnancy like it was yesterday." Sighing wistfully, she said, "The first time you feel the baby move, you'll never be the same. It's an incredible feeling, a mixture of awe, joy and love."

Dr. Fitz-Simmons was right; if she was pregnant, she'd be changed forever.

"Before I send you back to the lab, why don't I examine you?"

Yasmin slid onto the examining table and lay down. She lifted up her shirt, embarrassed at the softness of her once firm stomach.

Dr. Fitz-Simmons's hands were warm. She pressed gently on top of Yasmin's abdomen, before making her way down to the pelvic bone. Digging into her coat pocket, she produced a tape measure and stretched it vertically. "Just as I suspected, you're measuring almost eight weeks. It's too soon to detect the baby's heartbeat, but you'll be able to hear it when I see you next month." Dr. Fitz-Simmons gripped Yasmin's elbow and helped her up. "Start taking prenatal vitamins immediately and make an appointment to see me in a few weeks."

"Dr. Fitz-Simmons, are you sure? There's an actual baby inside of me?"

The doctor laughed. "I'm positive. But don't hesitate to call if you have any other questions or concerns. I like to make myself as accessible as possible to my patients, especially the pregnant ones."

Yasmin was quiet. She remained on the examining table, too scared to move, too scared to speak. Shaking her head, she stared down at her stomach. *I'm pregnant?* The thought was too overwhelming to comprehend. Feelings of uncertainty, fear and regret swarmed her mind. "I had a glass of wine last week. I didn't know I was…is my baby going to be okay?"

"Don't worry. One glass of wine won't harm the fetus but no more alcohol from now on." Dr. Fitz-Simmons smiled. "Try to get some rest while you still can. You're going to need it."

Hours later, the full impact of Dr. Fitz-Simmons's words still played in Yasmin's mind. *You're pregnant…I'm pregnant, pregnant, pregnant…* The words echoed in her head, challenging her, taunting her, reinforcing their truth. What would her friends and family say? The smile in her heart spread to her lips. Her parents would be overjoyed. Their first grandchild. Her mom would proclaim the pregnancy a miracle and call South Africa to share the good news with their extended family. The Ohaji clan would be walking on air for the next seven months. But how would Rashawn feel?

He was single. A carefree, laid-back bachelor not ready to start a family. Most twenty-seven-year-old guys were thinking about what clubs to go to, not changing diapers and burping a crying baby. Would he be angry? Would he resent her? Yasmin would have to make him understand. She hadn't planned this.

Yasmin locked the front door, wandered into the living room and plopped down on the couch. She pressed her eyes shut and took a deep, cleansing breath. In the darkness of her mind, she saw Rashawn. Memories of the afternoon they had spent at Clearwater Beach brought a smile to her face. They had strolled along the shore, splashed in the pure blue water and fed each other fresh fruit. Happy thoughts were replaced with guarded ones. What if he rejected her and the baby? What if he didn't want to be a father? What-ifs plagued her mind, intensifying her doubts. Shaking off feelings of despair, she hung her head and stretched her hands across her stomach. There was a living, moving being inside of her. A child who would one day call her Mom. Her eyes pooled with water and a lone tear trickled down her cheek. It had been months since she had prayed, but Yasmin needed guidance now more than ever.

"God, please take care of my baby. I know children are a gift from you and I am thankful and deeply honored you chose me to be a mother. Help me, God. I'm scared. And God, please help my baby to grow strong and healthy in my womb."

Someone cleared their throat.

Yasmin's eyes shot open. For a minute, she and Imani stared at each other, communicating silently with their eyes. Then, her sister's face broke out into a radiant smile. "You're pregnant?"

The words touched the deepest place in Yasmin's heart. Overcome with a sudden sting of emotion, she nodded. "My doctor confirmed it this afternoon."

Imani screamed. "Oh. My. God. I can't believe it!" She chucked her jacket on the armchair and rushed to her sister's side. "Have you told Mom and Dad? What did Rashawn say? Are you guys back together now? Oh, my God, I'm going to be an auntie!"

Yasmin laughed. She had never seen Imani so excited.

"This is amazing! You never thought you'd have children and now…now you're pregnant. How in the world did this happen?"

Tears filled Yasmin's eyes, clogging her throat. Coughing, she rubbed a hand over her belly. "I know. I'm still in shock myself."

Imani bent down until her mouth was just inches away from Yasmin's stomach. "Hi, Peanut. It's your Auntie Imani. We're going to be very close. I'm going to sneak you money and toys and candy when your mom's not looking." Her light, breezy tone grew serious. "I can't wait to meet you, Peanut. Your mom used to push me around when I was a kid, so give her a nice, hard kick for me, okay? Bye, baby. I love you."

Yasmin smiled through her tears. "That was beautiful, Imani. Well, except for the part about him kicking me!"

The sisters laughed.

Linking arms with Yasmin, Imani pulled her legs up onto the couch and tucked her feet under her bottom. "I bet Rashawn fainted when you told him! I could only imagine—"

"He doesn't know. No one knows, except for you. Not even Mom and Dad."

"What are you waiting for?" she pressed.

"The right time. I just found out, Imani. I need to figure out how I'm going to break the news to him."

"Rashawn should have been the first to know. I know you guys haven't spoken in a while, but you're carrying *his* child."

"So, I should call him up and say, 'Hi, how are you? Oh, by the way, I'm eight weeks pregnant.'" Yasmin laughed dryly. "This is not the kind of thing you discuss over the phone."

Rolling her eyes, Imani nudged her sister with her elbow. "I never said you should tell him over the phone. You know where he is. Go see him."

"I'll tell him when the time is right."

"When will that be?"

"After my sixteen-week checkup."

Imani gasped. "Sixteen weeks!"

"The possibility of having a miscarriage drops significantly in the second trimester. I don't want to tell him about the baby until I'm sure everything's okay."

"Why?"

Yasmin answered without hesitation. "Early in my career, I counseled a couple struggling with infertility. It was causing a great deal of strain in their marriage and they were considering getting a divorce. But finally, after years of trying, they conceived with the help of in vitro fertilization. You could imagine how excited they were when they discovered they were having twins. They told all their friends and family and the husband took out a full-page ad in the newspaper announcing the pregnancy. At ten weeks, the wife miscarried. She was devastated.

And her grief was compounded because she felt like the whole world knew."

"Peanut will be just fine. And even if something were to happen, wouldn't you want Rashawn to lean on? Wouldn't you want to know he cared and loved the baby just as much as you do?"

Yasmin sighed deeply, the veracity of her sister's words softening her heart. She hadn't considered his feelings in all of this. It had never occurred to her that Rashawn might actually want the baby. He was a natural with kids and there was no doubt in her mind that he would be a terrific father. "You're right. I should tell him."

"Hopefully, the baby will help you guys find your way back to each other."

She paused, drawing a short breath. "I doubt it. As long as he's boxing, I won't be a part of his life."

"I think he's starting to come around."

"How do you know?"

"Dean and I had drinks with him last week."

Yasmin's mouth fell open. "You did? Why didn't you tell me?"

"Slipped my mind?"

"Try again, Imani."

"I knew you'd get mad, so I didn't say anything." Her lips shaped into an apologetic smile. "You've been real moody ever since the breakup and I didn't want to upset you. See, I was being considerate."

"Thanks a lot. Thanks for taking his side."

"Hey, I'm not the only one hanging out with him. Mom and Dad had him over for dinner on Saturday and Eli goes to the gym a couple times a week."

"Are you serious? You guys have been seeing him behind my back?"

Imani chuckled. "You sound like a whiny teenage girl."

"I'm not whining," she said, pouting. "I have every right to feel betrayed. You've been keeping secrets from me."

"It's your fault. You picked a great guy who we all fell in love with."

"Whatever." Then, "Did he say anything about me?"

"Did he ever! He spent the whole night talking about you. On and on and on," she explained, rolling her eyes in mock annoyance. "After two hours of his babble, Dean and I had enough and called it a night."

"How is he doing? Is he okay?"

"Why don't you come with us to his place on Friday. Then you could see how he's doing for yourself."

"You're going to keep seeing him even though I don't like it?"

"Just because you're not dating him anymore doesn't mean the rest of the family should kick him to the curb." Smirking, she reached out and rubbed Yasmin's stomach. "I hate to break it to you, Sis, but now that you're pregnant with his baby, he's in the family to stay!"

And deep down Yasmin knew she was right.

Chapter 25

"Jab! Jab! Uppercut!" Brody hollered, pounding the mat with his fist. "Attack! Attack! Attack! Go in for the kill, champ!"

Rashawn threw a left hook. His sparring partner stumbled back against the ropes. They traded punches, but the round belonged to Rashawn. He was stronger, faster and every punch hit its intended mark. Terrell bent his shoulders, hit Rashawn between the legs and when he fell to his knees, lifted his arms in victory. "Take that, bitch." Terrell smirked, swaggering over to his corner. "I own this ring!"

Incensed, Rashawn leapt to his feet. When Terrell spun around, Rashawn punched him in the face. Blood oozed out of his nose, staining his white muscle shirt.

"What's with the sucker punch?" Terrell yelled, touching his fingers to his nose. "What, you can't take the heat?"

Brody stepped between the two fighters. "That's enough for today, guys. I can't have you killing each other days before a title match. It's bad for business," he joked.

Rashawn took out his mouthpiece. "I should kick your ass for that little stunt you pulled. Try it again and the medics will be carrying you outta here."

"Bring it on, tough guy." Terrell beckoned with his blood-stained hands. "These punk fighters might be scared of you, but I'm not. I'm from Harlem, son. We eat pieces of shit like you for breakfast!"

"I don't make threats. I let my record speak for me," Rashawn said, bending down and stepping through the ropes. "I'm out of here, Brody."

Minutes later, Rashawn was strolling out of the front doors. Storm clouds sailed across the deep-blue sky but the air was warm.

"Champ, what was that about?" Brody demanded, following him outside. "You guys have sparred before. Why'd you let him get to you today?"

"Terrell's dirty but he's always crying foul."

"Don't sweat it." He patted Rashawn's back, a proud smile on his face. "You were looking good in there, champ. You ready for Garcia?"

"I was born ready."

"You've got this. All you need to do is keep your eyes on the prize."

"I'm straight."

"You're about to move into the big leagues, champ! This is gonna be the biggest payday of your career. "

Rashawn pitched an eyebrow. "It's never been about the money, Brody. The first time I ever put on a pair of gloves I made a promise to myself. I was going to be the world champion no matter the cost." He shrugged. "That's what I've been working for all these years. What I've sacrificed for. The money's a bonus."

"I hear you, champ. I hear you."

Kori poked her head out the door. "Pops, the phone."

"Don't you see I'm talkin'? Who is it?"

"Mancinii. Said he has something to run by you."

Brody had stars in his eyes. "Keep him on the line! I'll be right there," he gushed, his words rolled into one long sentence. "I gotta take this call. Come back inside when you've cooled down."

"Naw, I'm done."

"Done? But we still have weight training to do and—"

"I'm going home." Rashawn pulled his car keys out of his pocket. "I'll be in early tomorrow. I can work on my conditioning then."

His face brightened. "That's what I like to hear! All right. Take it easy."

Forty-five minutes later, Rashawn pulled into the parking lot of A Better Way Counseling Services. He found an empty space behind a suburban truck. It eclipsed his Mustang but not his line of vision. He cut the engine and waited.

Any minute now Yasmin would emerge from the clinic, looking as gorgeous as ever. It didn't matter where he was, every day at six o'clock, he drove over to her office to catch a glimpse of her. Seeing her lifted his spirits and reminded him of all the good times they had. The boat cruise. Feeding each other chocolate fondue. Making love on the balcony.

Rashawn rubbed a hand over his face. He had a very vivid picture in his mind of the night they had met. Yasmin had been a vision, positively stunning, a Nubian queen. And these days, he couldn't close his eyes without seeing her face. It didn't matter if he was lifting weights, shooting pool or at a club with the guys, she was there. Having her in his life had made him a more thoughtful, more loving man, and he'd finally discovered the power of true love. But as quickly as it came, it was gone.

His gaze fell on the clock. Yasmin was late, but he didn't mind. She was worth the wait. The night she'd seduced him brought a lazy grin to his mouth. An image of her straddling him flashed in his head. Visions of her, wet, naked and aroused, tortured him. The memory would stay with him forever. Sucking on her nipples, using his fingers to stir her need, undressing her with his mouth. They had made slow, easy love that night. Swept up in the beauty of the moment, they had satisfied their desire for each other until sunrise. Rashawn knew he was a good lover, but it was Yasmin who had taught him the art of lovemaking. It wasn't about duration or technique as he once had foolishly thought, it was about giving. The unselfish giving of yourself and not asking for anything in return.

He imagined himself at home, lying in bed with her, caressing her long legs. She would kiss him gently, then hungrily. They'd tear off each other's clothes, their desire mounting with each kiss, each stroke, each touch. Before his thoughts could carry him away, he changed the channel in his mind. He was losing it. And that wasn't cool.

Rashawn glanced around the parking lot and noticed that Yasmin's SUV wasn't parked in its usual place. In the eight months they had dated, she had never missed a day of work. Not even when he'd tried to bribe her with back rubs, foot massages and bubble baths. Where was she? The only way to find out was to go inside. He slid out of the car and stalked toward the clinic, his mind racing a thousand miles an hour.

He pushed open the door. His mouth gaped open when the woman behind the desk waved. Gone was the outrageous weave, heavy makeup and tight miniskirt. Niobie's hair had been cut, she was wearing a conservative but stylish blazer and her face was free of the thick eyeliner and bold-red lipstick. Her transformation had shaved years off her appearance. "Niobie?"

"Hey, Rashawn. It's been a long time. How have you been?"

"Obviously not as good as you! For a minute there, I didn't recognize you."

She smiled. "Thanks. I've been getting that a lot lately."

"I bet. What happened? You finally marry an old sugar daddy?" he teased.

"No, nothing as scandalous as that." It was, but Niobie wasn't going to share the torrid details. It didn't matter how many times her counselor told her it wasn't her fault, she knew deep down it was. And according to Cecil Manning, she had been a willing participant that night. If Ms. Duke hadn't produced pictures of her injuries and eyewitness reports from Dr. Ohaji and the night clerk at the hotel, he would have gotten off scot-free. But thanks to Ms. Duke, Cecil had made a large donation to a women's shelter, promised to undergo counseling and had to compensate for her pain and suffering. It wasn't enough to buy the mansion in the hills Niobie had always dreamed of, but it helped to change her life. One day she would have her palatial home with the Lexus out front, but she'd buy it herself.

The sound of Rashawn's voice nudged her from her thoughts. "Come on, Niobie. Don't keep me in suspense."

"I had an awakening of sorts," she explained. The memories of that night made her eyes water, but she swallowed her tears. "I, ah, came into some money and with the help of Dr. Ohaji, I got my act together. I enrolled in night school, paid off my debts and moved into a better neighborhood. And this is just the beginning. I'm going to be somebody one day, you just wait and see!"

"Go on, Niobie. I'm scared of you!"

They shared a laugh.

"Where's the boss?" he asked, his gaze sliding to Yasmin's office door. "I was in the neighborhood and figured I'd stop by to say hello."

Now it was Niobie's turn to make jokes. "In the neighborhood, huh? Well, *neighbor,* if you must know, Dr. Ohaji took the afternoon off."

He tugged at his baseball cap. "How's she been?"

"You mean besides missing you?"

"Yasmin misses me?" he asked, his voice lit with surprise. "I mean, that's cool. We had some good times, you know?"

"You should give her a call."

"You think so?"

"I know so."

"I'll think about it. I have a big fight coming up. I gotta stay focused."

"I hear you, but you should try and hook up with her before you leave for Vegas. Dr. Ohaji would like that."

He considered Niobie's advice. Regular visits with her family made him feel close to her, but it wasn't the same as being with her, talking with her, laughing with her. He missed watching her get dressed in the mornings, missed kissing her, missed the way she wrapped her arms around him while he was sleeping. Rashawn spoke with a smile. "I guess I could make some time for us to have lunch or something."

"Now you're talking!" Niobie sighed wistfully "I hope I have a relationship like you guys' one day. You two were made for each other. You were as close as Bonnie and Clyde, but without all the guns. It's too bad things didn't work out, huh?"

Her words hung in the air, prompting him to say, "Yasmin is an incredible woman and I was damn lucky to have her."

"Then why did you let her go?"

The question echoed in his mind, teasing him, taunting him, mocking him. Pride had been the downfall of many men and he was no exception. Instead of listening to his doctor and the woman he loved, he had set out to prove them wrong. He was a fighter, a warrior, a champion. He would fight through his injury and come out on top, victorious, right? He'd have it all. Money, fame, stardom. And once he was the WBC champion, he'd get Yasmin back.

"What's her schedule like tomorrow? Maybe I'll stop by with lunch or—"

The phone rang, interrupting him. "Hold that thought," Niobie said, reaching for the receiver and putting it to her ear. "A Better Way Counseling Services. Niobie Slade speaking. How may I be of assistance?" A pause, then the formality in her voice fell away. "Hey, boss. Yeah, everything's fine." Laughing, she glanced up at Rashawn. "I was just talking about you. You'll never guess who stopped by."

Rashawn waved his hands, hoping Niobie would conceal his identity. "Don't tell her I'm here," he mouthed, stepping away from the desk.

Niobie cupped a hand over the phone. "Stop trippin', Rashawn. You know you want to talk to her, or you wouldn't have driven all the way over here. Go in her office and I'll transfer the call there."

"I gotta go."

"Not before you talk to her." Niobie motioned with her head to her boss's office. "Now hurry up before I tell her you're stalling."

Shaking his head, he pushed open the door and went inside. A flower arrangement sat on her desk, perfuming the air and arousing his curiosity. Who were the flowers from? Pushing aside the thought, Rashawn picked up the phone. "Hey, Yasmin. What's up?"

"Rashawn?"

His mood improved as soon as he heard her voice. "Yeah, it's me."

"What are you doing at my office?"

"I was in the neighborhood and I thought I'd stop by to say hello." The explanation sounded cornier every time he said it, but it was all he had. Sitting down on the edge of her desk, he asked, "How've you been?"

"I'm good. And you?"

When did talking to him make her sound *this* uncomfortable? Why couldn't they laugh and joke and flirt like they used to? He hated the tension crackling over the line. It reminded him that they were no longer lovers, no longer friends. Gone were the days when they laughed for no reason, read the other's mind and finished each other's sentences. "I'm straight, hangin' in there."

Silence came.

"How is training going? Are you ready for the fight?"

"I've got this. That belt is mine."

"You sound pretty confident."

"Have you ever known me to be anything but?"

Yasmin laughed. "It's good to see you haven't lost your sense of humor."

"I've been thinking about you."

"Same here," she confessed, her voice a whisper.

His heart soared but doubt tempered his joy. Did she mean it? Or was she just toying with his feelings? Rashawn struck down the thought. Of course she meant it. Playing games was beneath her. And Yasmin didn't say what she didn't mean.

"Do you have plans tonight?"

His eyes widened. Did he hear right? "Tonight?" he repeated, wishing he didn't sound so eager. Calming his nerves, he wiped the enthusiasm from his voice and said, "No plans. What are you up to?"

"I was hoping we could talk." She added, "That is, if you're not too busy."

"I'm never too busy for you, Doc. You should know that by now." Rashawn wanted to say more, but stopped before he embarrassed himself. He treasured her, loved her, needed her like air. And just the thought of seeing her made his heart quicken with desire. "Where do you want to meet?" he asked anxiously.

"You could come here for dinner. I just turned off the linguine and I have some of that Italian bread you like so much."

After a brief pause, he decided to take Yasmin up on her offer. Standing, he pulled his car keys from his pocket. "Give me an hour," he said, before she could change her mind. Then, he hung up the phone and strode out of her office.

Chapter 26

Yasmin exhaled. For the last half hour, she'd been peering out the living-room window, hoping to catch a glimpse of Rashawn's late-model Mustang. To occupy her time, she'd turned on the television and watched a documentary on A&E. Entering a world of espionage had taken her mind off Rashawn, but now that he was on the other side of the door, her fear was back with a vengeance.

Her heart was muddled with apprehension, despair and hope, but she refused to buckle under the pressure. She could do this. No, she *had* to do this. Chasing away her anxiety and embracing inner peace, she opened the front door.

"Good God," she sharply drew in her breath. They had dated for eight months; she knew him intimately, deeply, but that didn't stop her from practically drooling. He looked just as handsome in a white ribbed shirt and jeans as he did in a designer suit. His cornrows were neatly braided, his diamond twinkled and his smile almost knocked her over.

Yasmin had never swooned over a man, but she felt light-headed and her vision was hazy. It had nothing to do with the baby growing inside her and everything to do with Rashawn Bishop. There was something just so darn sexy about him. And as she watched him exit his car, images of the last time they had made love came to mind. The music, the wine, the crescent moon showering their naked bodies with light. Was that the night they had conceived? Or the following morning when he had surprised her in the shower? Shelving her thoughts, she raised a hand in greeting. "Hi."

Rashawn stepped inside, his eyes wandering past her face, down her chest and over her hips. "You're lookin' as fine as ever."

"Thanks, so do you." Self-conscious about her stomach, she had selected a loose shirt and slim pants. Only ten days had passed since she had learned of the baby, but Yasmin felt different. She didn't know what was happening in her head and her heart, but she felt softer, wiser, more focused. Like life finally had meaning. It would be weeks before she started showing and months until she felt the baby move, but she knew instinctively that this was a defining moment in her life. Earning her doctorate had given her a great sense of accomplishment, but it paled in comparison to being pregnant. She had never known joy like this and it was only the beginning.

"Can I get you something to drink?" she asked, closing the door and turning the lock. "Water? Orange juice? A cold beer, maybe?"

"No, thanks. I'm straight."

"Are you sure?"

"Positive. But I'll let you know if I need anything."

Yasmin licked her lips. The expression on his face made her heart flutter. He was flirting with her, teasing her, just like that afternoon he'd showed up at her office posing as a client. "Why don't we go in the kitchen?"

"Or, we could stay here."

Her heart skipped a beat. Why was he staring at her like that?

"This is nice. Me and you together, like old times." Never shy about his feelings, he confessed, "I'm glad you invited me over. Like I said on the phone, I've been thinking a lot about you."

She couldn't hold back her smile.

"Do you know what I've been thinking?"

Yasmin gulped. When had he shortened the distance between them? "No, what?"

"That I was a fool to let you go."

"Really?" she asked, hopeful. Yasmin had imagined those words coming out of his mouth, had dreamed it, prayed it and hoped beyond hope he would come back to her.

He folded his hands around her. "I'm for real, Doc. Who else is going to put up with my moods, rub me down when I'm sore and read me dirty stories in bed?" he joked.

"And don't forget run out in the middle of the night to get you aspirin," Yasmin added. She breathed him in, his scent, his voice, his touch.

"I haven't been the same since you left." His breath caressed her face. "I miss being with you, miss being around you, inside of you…"

Desire seized her mouth, leaving her mute. Her eyes zoomed in on his lips. She recalled the thrill of their lovemaking. The soft pleading of his kiss, the gentle prodding of his tongue, the urgent caress of his hands. Swallowing, she pushed past her lustful thoughts and said, "It's been hard for me, too."

"I need you," he whispered. Just the thought of her legs around his waist caused him to stifle a moan. Rashawn wanted her in the worst way. Wanted to rip off her clothes and worship her with his lips. Love her like she had never been loved before. He wanted to brand her with his mouth and cement them together with his hands. "I can't take it anymore. I want you, Doc."

"Well, I'd like a diamond ring but we can't all get what we want, right?"

The light in his eyes dimmed. "Come on. Don't make me beg."

"I want you, too, but—"

"But what?" he asked, trailing a finger along her arm. "We're good together, Doc. You and I both know the sex is off the charts."

"Is that what this is about? Sex?"

"No, but I'm hungry for you. Have been since the day you left."

Yasmin had never wanted Rashawn as much as she wanted him now. She didn't know if it was the tenderness in his eyes, the sweetness of his touch or the knowledge that she was carrying his child.

"Do you forgive me for being such an ass?"

"That depends on what you're going to do to make it up to me," she teased, enjoying their sexy banter. "You know I'm a sucker for—"

Tired of talking, he kissed her. Pressing her against the door, he cradled her face in his palms. His hands were relentless, his lips punishing, his words mesmerizing. "Everything about being with you just feels right."

"It does?"

He nipped her earlobe. "You're my princess, my Nubian queen, my soul mate."

"Rashawn, you've given me hope," she confessed, holding his gaze and stroking the back of his head. "I didn't think I'd ever find love again…then I met you and—"

The rest of her sentence was stolen by his kiss.

Lifting her in the air, he grabbed a handful of her braids and kissed her arched neck. He desired her in ways he couldn't explain and would be hard-pressed to say what he loved most about her. "You're gorgeous, Doc."

Inclining her head to the right, she welcomed his tongue into her mouth and his hands inside her blouse. Yasmin pushed his shirt up off his shoulders and dropped it on the floor. She caressed his neck, his shoulders, his nipples. Kissing him, she slipped her arms around his waist. Being apart had made her more appreciative of what they had. How many women could say they had the love, support and understanding of the men in their lives? Most of her female clients told painful stories of betrayal, neglect and abuse. Having Rashawn in her life was living proof that she had been given a second chance at love. He was her soul mate, sent to heal her broken heart. And as he swept her into his arms, Yasmin felt complete for the first time in her life.

* * *

"I'm pregnant."

Rashawn chuckled. "I know I'm good, Doc, but I'm not *that* good," he teased, the soft light of the beside lamp illuminating his smirk. Dropping a kiss on her bare shoulder, he swung his feet out in front of him. "I'm starving. I could really use a snack. Want something from the—"

"Rashawn, I'm not joking. I'm serious. I'm pregnant."

His grin dissolved. "You're bullshitting me, right?"

"No, I'm not."

The expression on his face changed from amusement to shock. "I—I thought you couldn't have kids," he said, his tone thick with accusation. "That's what you told me."

"That's what I thought." Her words gushed out of her mouth like water from a dam. "I didn't mean for any of this to happen. If I had known I could get pregnant, I would have been more careful."

"Are you sure? Those home pregnancy tests can be wrong. Maybe it was a false positive or something."

Yasmin told him about her appointment with Dr. Fitz-Simmons. "I insisted the tests be repeated, but after she examined me there was no point."

His eyes passed over her face, trying to make sense of her words. "B-But you look the same. Just how pregnant are you?"

"Almost three months. I know you're surprised. I was too, but—"

"I bet you were." Shaking his head, he mumbled, "I could be the poster boy for safe sex. What happened?"

She pleaded her case. "I didn't know I could get pregnant. I swear. I guess the condom broke."

"Shit!" He ran a hand over his head, his gaze darting aimlessly around the room. "This couldn't have happened at a worse time."

Yasmin flinched. Is that how he felt? Nothing was more important than winning his match, not even the news that she was carrying his child? Instead of labeling him an insensitive jerk, she took a moment to collect her thoughts. "I know this is going to take some getting used to, but what's done is done. We're going to have a baby and the sooner you get on board the better."

"Get on board? What's that supposed to mean?"

"We have some important decisions to make."

"About what?" His mouth a hard, firm line he swiped his jeans off the floor and yanked them on. "I can't deal with this now. I can't let anything sidetrack me from beating Garcia. The match is in two weeks, did you forget?" He stuffed his feet into his sneakers. "How the hell am I supposed to win with all these distractions?"

She watched him, her mouth agape. The darkness of the night concealed the tears in her eyes. "Is that what I am to you? A distraction? Is that why you came over tonight?" Clutching a pillow to her chest, she swallowed the other questions too painful to ask. "Inviting you over here was a big mistake."

"You're right. It was."

His shoulders were squared away like he was plotting his escape. "This is messed up. I've worked hard to keep my reputation clean and now…now I'm going to be another statistic. Another black man making babies out of wedlock. What a trip!"

His words cut her to the bone, but Yasmin didn't crumble, she fought back. "Don't put this on me, Rashawn. I didn't get pregnant by myself. We are *both* equally responsible for what happened."

"I'm not blaming you. I just don't understand how you couldn't know."

"All I know is what the endocrinologist told me. I'm just as surprised by all this as you are, but I'm not going to cry about it for the next six months. I'm going to deal with it and move on. I suggest you do the same."

"Do you expect me to be happy?" he asked, the ferocity of his tone intensifying her pain. "I'm not going to pretend to be excited about this, because I'm not. Too many of our kids are growing up without fathers. I told you what it was like without my pops. He'd come over, spend the night with my mom, then split. Life was damn hard and I wouldn't want that for my son."

Yasmin slipped out of bed. Covering herself with her robe,

she went to him. "It doesn't have to be that way, Rashawn. We could make a great life for our child."

"What are you saying?"

"I was shocked when I found out about the baby, too, but now I feel incredibly blessed. I'm going to be a mom and I wouldn't trade that for the world." She took his hands and put them around her, snuggling into his chest. "We can do this, together," she said, emphasizing each word. "We can raise our child in a loving, two-parent home."

His hands dropped from her waist. "You don't want to get married, do you?"

Yasmin's eyes hardened. He was asking because he thought it was the right thing to do, not because he wanted to. An hour ago, they had been in bed, making love, and now they were acting like strangers. "No, of course not," she lied, burying her childhood dreams of having a husband and child. "I'm fully capable of taking care of myself and the baby. I don't need your help."

He dipped his chin and smoothed a hand over the back of his neck. "I can't deal with this right now. I gotta go."

Yasmin put a hand on her stomach, as if to shield the baby from his rejection. "I won't have you playing mind games with our child. If you're not going to be a loving, committed father don't bother coming around at all. The baby and I will have more than enough support from my family and friends."

Rashawn started toward the door, then stopped. "I'm not walking out on you, Yasmin. I'd never disrespect you like that. I just need some time to think, to get my mind right, okay?"

"Take as much time as you need."

"I'll call you."

Yasmin nodded, knowing it might be weeks or months before she heard from him again. He was trying to let her down easily and she was trying fruitlessly to preserve her dignity. Toying with the belt on her satin robe, she allowed the tears to fall. She wanted to throw herself into his arms, wanted to beg him to stay, wanted him to know how much she loved him and their baby.

But she did none of these things. "Take care of yourself," she said, for lack of anything else to say.

Rashawn tossed a final look over his shoulder, then stalked out the bedroom door.

Chapter 27

Yasmin kicked off her high heels. Whoever said pregnancy was a glorious time had obviously never been pregnant, she decided, stretching her weary legs out in front of her. Her back ached, her feet hurt and she couldn't keep her eyes open long enough to get anything done. Overwhelmed by sudden bursts of exhaustion, she eagerly anticipated that burst of energy often associated with the second trimester.

A light breeze drifted in through the open window. It was another cool autumn day. The sky was free of clouds, the midday sun dazzled. Closing her eyes, she rested back in her chair. All she needed was ten minutes of peace and quiet, then she could tackle the pile of progress reports cluttering her desk. These days, she could barely finish her work before Niobie was bringing her more. Not only had her assistant updated her look, she had buckled down at the office, too. She arrived early, had coffee brewing by the time Yasmin walked through the door and, since finding out about the baby, stocked the cupboards with gummy bears and chocolate bars for when Yasmin was craving sweets.

As she rubbed a hand over her stomach, her thoughts turned to Rashawn. A month had passed since she had told him about the baby. Four long, painful weeks. No visits, no phone calls, not even a measly text message. Sighing, she rubbed the tenderness out of her lower back. What she wouldn't do for one of Rashawn's massages. He had the strong, skilled hands of a masseur and knew when and where to apply pressure. As she kneaded the knot in her neck, she wondered how he was doing, and if he had thought about her and the baby during his thirty-day absence.

Last Saturday, she had crawled into bed with the intention of watching his match, but ten minutes into the fight, she was sleeping. The following morning, she had caught the highlights on ESPN. Everyone from the newscaster to the local sports columnist said Rashawn had been robbed of the belt but that didn't change the facts. Two out of three judges scored the fight for Garcia and the Mexican phenom was still the WBC champion.

Her office door creaked open.

Groaning in mock disgust, Yasmin slid down lower in her leather chair. "Niobie, quit bringing me work!" she joked, rubbing her heavy eyes. "Don't you remember how tired you were when you were pregnant with Miles?"

Someone chuckled. "I'm having déjà vu, except you're not butchering an Anthony Hamilton song."

Her eyes flipped open. "Rashawn?"

"Don't look so surprised. It hasn't been that long since we saw each other."

"No, no, that's not it."

"It's the bruises, right?" He touched a hand to his swollen cheek. "It'll heal."

She hastened to explain, "No, that's not it. You look great. You always do."

"I should be the one handing out compliments. I couldn't imagine you ever looking more beautiful, but you do. You're glowing, Doc."

"It's a good thing you can't see me from behind," she said, her voice rich with humor. "These days, everything I eat goes straight to my hips."

Rashawn wore a lopsided grin. "How's our baby?"

Her mouth shaped into a smile. "The baby is just fine. I had my first ultrasound on Monday. I was trying to figure out the gender, but baby wouldn't cooperate. The little one was wiggling and squirming all over the place. The technician said it's much too soon to tell the sex anyway."

"Why didn't you tell me about the appointment?" He was quick to add, "I would've liked to see the baby, too."

"Oh, I didn't know. I assumed you wouldn't be interested… next time," she said, standing. "I'll have another one at twenty-four weeks. I'll make sure to give you a call."

His smile returned. "Cool." His gaze passed over her lips, then slid down her chest. Rashawn fought the overwhelming desire to be close to her. Instead of reaching out and twisting one of her braids around his finger, he reached into his back pocket. "I came here to give you this."

Yasmin stared down at the small gold envelope in his outstretched hand. She took it, careful not to touch his fingers. There was no telling what would happen if she did. The last time they'd been in kissing distance, they'd had explosive, mind-numbing sex. As much as she desired him, she wasn't going to make a habit of falling into bed with him. No matter how good it was. "What's this?"

"Open it and you'll see."

She did. "Join me on Saturday, December First, at the Laurdel Lounge." Yasmin felt the sting of tears as she finished reading.

"What's wrong?" he asked, watching her. "Is it the baby?"

Shaking her head, she smiled softly. "No. It's just that…my birthday's on Saturday." Her voice was a whisper. "You forgot, didn't you?"

"My bad." His smile was apologetic. "I'll make it up to you. I swear."

"No need," she said, feeling silly for getting emotional. Back when they were dating, he'd promised to take her to Paris to celebrate and now her birthday meant nothing to him. There was a time when he drew her bathwater, massaged her feet and cuddled her in his arms. Now, those occasions were a distant memory, shrouded in regret. To alleviate the mood, she joked, "These days my hormones are so out of whack, I cry during Hallmark commercials."

"What are your plans?"

"Katherine and I are going to dinner. Then, we might check out that new dessert café that opened beside the civic center."

"Cool. Swing by my party before you go."

"What's the occasion?" she asked, flipping over the card over to the back.

"I didn't win the Garcia fight, but I have a lot to be thankful for. I want you there, Doc. You and the baby."

"Really? Why the sudden change of heart? I haven't heard from you since the night we…since I told you about the baby." Giving voice to her frustration, she told him what a distressful time the last four weeks of her pregnancy had been. "While you were in Las Vegas living it up with your friends, I was here, alone, battling severe morning sickness."

He saw the hurt in her eyes and searched his mind for the right words. "I'm sorry the baby's been giving you such a hard time."

"Sure you are. That's why you haven't been around the past month."

Angry at himself for neglecting her and the physical barrier between them, he came around the desk and placed his hands lovingly around her waist. "I'm here, now, Yasmin, and I'm not going anywhere."

His breath tickled her ear and for a moment she forgot what they were talking about. Rashawn stared down at her, a lazy grin between his scrumptious lips. His smile brightened the entire office and the scent of his aftershave induced thoughts of the last time thay'd made love. It wasn't his touch, his kiss or the delicious warmth of his body that she missed, it was what happened after. Lying in each other's arms, swapping stories, laughing until the sun peeked over the horizon. That was what she missed most.

"Doc, you're right, I should have been here. I wanted to come to see you sooner, but I didn't think you wanted to see me."

Turning away, Yasmin focused her gaze on one of the clown-fish in the aquarium. After a beat, she returned her eyes to his face. Rashawn seemed to be deep in thought. Time lapsed. In the silence, she chastised herself for coming down so hard on him. It wasn't his fault her back hurt. Boxing was his dream, his life, his livelihood and she had no right to make him feel guilty for doing what he loved. Even if it had taken him away from her. "I'm sorry I snapped at you. I've had nothing to eat but soup and soda crackers the past few days and I'm kind of crabby," she confessed.

"No problem. From what my brothers' girlfriends tell me, pregnancy isn't nearly as glamorous as celebrities make it look."

"I couldn't agree more."

Rashawn chyckled. "So, does that mean you'll come?"

"I'll think about it."

"Aw, come on. You can do better than that." Touching a hand to her warm cheek, he bent down so close his mouth grazed her ear. "You're not going to make me beg, are you, Doc?"

Yasmin laughed. "I can't say no to my baby's daddy, now can I? If you want us there, then we'll be there."

"That's all I am to you? Your baby's daddy?"

It was a trick question. If she said no, he'd think she wanted more from him and if she said yeas, she'd be denying her true feelings. Yasmin never imagined that expression would come out of her mouth, but until he stepped up to the plate, that's all he was: her baby's daddy. "It's not for me to decide who you are—it's for you to decide," she said, her eyes challenging him to disagree with her.

"Fair enough."

"Do you mind if I invite—"

"It's already been taken care of. I sent out invitations to your family, your friends and everyone at the community center."

"That's very generous of you."

He winked. "That's just the kind of guy I am." Before Yasmin could protest, Rashawn bent down and kissed her. Instinctively, she arched toward him. The kiss did more than heat her body; it touched the deepest, most intimate part of her soul. Angling her head to the right, she returned his fervor a hundred-fold, gently stroking the back of his head. Wishing they could stay like this forever, she snuggled comfortably against his hard chest. But before Yasmin had her fill of him, he ended the kiss. Hiding her disappointment, she stared up at him, a small, rueful smile on her lips.

"You taste even better than I remember," he whispered, pressing his lips against her forehead. "I'll see you—" he put a hand on her stomach "—and you on Saturday. Don't be late, Doc. I'll be waiting."

"This party's going to be off the hook!" Imani announced excitedly, stepping out of Yasmin's SUV. "There are stretch limos lined up for blocks!"

"Maybe I'll finally get to meet Roy Jones, Jr." Katherine adjusted her strapless dress to reveal more cleavage. "I heard he has a thing for older women."

Morgan shook her head. "You don't want to go there, cousin. I know things about him you wouldn't believe. Girl, he's too much for you to handle!"

Yasmin activated the car alarm and fell in step with Imani, Katherine and Morgan.

"I'm so glad Rashawn invited us." Imani linked arms with her sister, a bright smile on her plump lips. "We're going to have a great time tonight, Yassie. I can feel it."

"I sure hope so." She smoothed a hand over her powder-blue gown. Hoping to impress Rashawn and feeling better than she had in weeks, she had selected a silk empire waist dress that flowed gracefully over her hips and down her legs. "After everything that's happened between us, I'm kind of nervous about seeing him tonight. What if he has a date? Or spends the entire night ignoring me?"

Katherine sent her a smile. "Try not to worry, Yasmin. Rashawn's going to take good care of you. He always does."

The hostess greeted them at the entrance. "Good evening, ladies. Which one of you is Dr. Yasmin Ohaji?"

Confused, she touched a hand to her chest. "I'm Yasmin. Is there a problem?"

Smiling, she reached behind the stand and handed her a bouquet of flowers. There had to be at least fifty long-stemmed white roses. Inhaling, Yasmin buried her nose in the package. The sweet, heady scent was intoxicating.

"They're beautiful." After reading the card, she turned to Imani, Katherine and Morgan, who were all wearing envious smiles. "They're from Rashawn! He remembered my birthday," she gushed, her voice bubbling with excitement.

"Please, follow me," the hostess said.

Yasmin stepped into the lounge. Helium balloons, satin streamers and a banner that read Congratulations hung from the walls. As they entered the main dining room, she noted the oversize flower arrangements, the flaming red tablecloths and the gold-plated china. The soft flickering of floating candles, the dizzying perfume of champagne and the crystal chandeliers reeked class and grace.

"The Laurdel Lounge must have new management," she said, taking in the elegant décor, "because I don't remember it *ever* looking this good."

Singing along with the Anthony Hamilton song playing, she smiled to herself. "Fallin' in Love Again" was her favorite song. The one that had been playing the afternoon Rashawn had burst into her office posing as a new client. It was hard for her to believe they'd only known each other for nine months. It seemed like years had passed since their first date.

"Where's everybody?" she asked out loud. "There are so many cars outside I figured this place would be packed." Her confusion deepened when she heard Rashawn's sleepy, bedroom voice behind her.

"From the moment I saw you, I was at a loss for words, and

not just because you were about to take on a table full of thugs by yourself." His reference to their infamous meeting brought chuckles and giggles from guests.

Yasmin spun around. Her parents, her friends, his family and a hundred or so other people were all wearing smiles, smirks and grins. Glancing around the sea of familiar faces, she saw her father nod, Ms. Bishop wave and Niobie mouthing the word *breathe*.

"I had that crazy, this-could-be-the-one feeling. And as hard as I tried, I couldn't shake it." The crowd parted, and Rashawn emerged. His cornrows were gone and had been replaced with short subtle waves. Without the braids, he looked older, more mature, distinguished even. His tailored milk-white suit was a perfect fit. The swelling in his face had receded, the cut above his eye had healed and he looked more like himself and less like a human punching bag. "Yasmin, you're everything I could ever want in a woman and far more than I deserve."

He walked tall, proud, confident, and stopped in front of her. His scent held power, energy, charisma, and every time Yasmin inhaled it, her thoughts turned to mush. "What are you trying to say, Rashawn?"

Mystified by the sound of his voice, she could only watch as he took her hand in his and squeezed gently. He looked at her expectantly, and when she didn't respond, he said, "What do you think, Doc?"

Gulping a mouthful of air, she gave herself a moment to collect her thoughts. This was all fine and great, but did he mean it or was there something else going on? "Did my parents put you up to this?" she asked, wanting to make sense of his sudden change of heart. Things didn't add up and Yasmin had an awful feeling her family was behind his impromptu proposal. "My dad talked you into marrying me, didn't he?"

"You should know me better than that." His tone was light, but she heard the disappointment in his voice. "No one put me up to anything. I want to marry you because it's what *I* want to do."

"Is this about the baby?" Yasmin heard the ripple of chatter and saw the bewildered looks on the faces of their families and friends, but she didn't let that deter her from speaking her mind. There would be plenty of time to explain later; right now she had to get to the bottom of things. "If you're proposing because of the baby—"

"It's not like that, Doc."

"Then what's it like?" she asked, trying to keep the hostility out of her voice. "I want you to marry me because you love me, not because you feel obligated."

"I'm not gonna lie. I was scared when you told me you were pregnant. I didn't think I was ready to be a husband and a father." He paused, drawing a deep breath. "I was overwhelmed by the responsibility of it all, but when I thought about you and the baby, I realized there was only one thing to do. I love you and I want us to be a family."

As much as she loved him and the idea of being his wife, she didn't want to trap him into a relationship or rush headfirst into marriage without thinking things through. "I love you, too, Rashawn, but are you sure this is what you want? Marriage is—"

He shushed her with a finger to the lips. "Yasmin, I've never been more sure of anything in my life." Sensing her hesitation and worried the night wouldn't go as planned, he took her hands in his. They were cold and clammy and trembling ever so lightly. He sent her a smile of reassurance. "Yasmin, you're strong and inde-pendent and loyal, but what I love most about you is that you've never looked down on me or where I come from. You're not mo-tivated by money or greed and you keep me in line." Rashawn knew his brothers would clown him for getting all sentimental, but he wanted Yasmin to be his wife and he'd stop at nothing to have her. Leaning so close he could smell her cinnamon scented lip gloss, he held her gaze for several seconds. "At the end of the day, there's no one else I'd rather be with than you."

Touched by the sincerity of his words, Yasmin could scarcely speak. "What about boxing?" she asked, searching his eyes for the truth. "Are you going to continue fighting?"

"I've decided to take a year off so I can take care of you and the baby."

"What happens in a year?"

"I'll reevaluate my career and then we'll decide *together* if I should return to the ring. Does that sound fair?"

"Sounds fair to me, bro!" Armondo yelled, drawing chuckles from the boxing fans in attendance.

"Anymore questions?" Rashawn asked, grinning down at Yasmin. "Or can I get on with my proposal?"

Yasmin's heart rattled around in her chest. Praying that she wouldn't faint, she watched Rashawn drop to one knee. A collective gasp rose as he pulled a ring box from his front pocket. Vowing to make her the happiest woman alive, Rashawn took her left hand and slipped the ring up the base of her fourth finger.

"I know it's not Paris, but we can always go there on our honeymoon."

The women in the crowd purred like kittens.

"Yasmin Ohaji, would you allow me the honor of being your husband and make my life complete by becoming my wife?"

The silence was loud.

Yasmin studied the diamond the way a meteorologist studies the sky. It was the ring she had always dreamed of, a three-carat emerald-cut diamond. But how did he know? Unless…a quick glance at Imani, Katherine and Morgan verified her suspicions. They had all been in on the surprise.

"Doc, please?" His voice was bare, vulnerable, stripped of pride. "I'm begging you. Do it for me, do it for our baby, do it for us."

"I'll never forget this moment. All of my dreams have come true," she whispered, cupping his face in her hands. "I have you and the baby. What more could I want?"

"Does that mean you'll marry me?"

"Yes! Yes! Yes!" she shrieked, her voice raising to dangerous heights. Oblivious to the celebration taking place around them, Yasmin flung her arms around his neck and kissed him. Filled with an amazing sense of completeness, she felt tears of joy stream down her cheeks. Wrapped in her fiancé's arms and humbled by the totality of his love, she closed her eyes and cherished the beauty of the moment.

She faced the challenge of her career...

Seducing
the matchmaker

elaine overton

Acquiring world-renowned architect Derrick Brandt as a client is a real coup for Noelle Brown's matchmaking service. Finding him a mate will be no picnic, but as attraction sizzles between them, they wonder if *their* relationship could be the perfect match.

"Elaine Overton does a wonderful job conveying her characters' feelings, their emotional baggage and their struggles."
—*Romantic Times BOOKreviews*
on *His Holiday Bride*

Available the first week of November
wherever books are sold.

KIMANI™
ROMANCE

www.kimanipress.com

KPEO0891108

**Breaking up is hard to do...
even when you know it's right.**

NATIONAL BESTSELLING AUTHOR

first crush

Hudson Godfrey's new wine-making business leaves
him with no time for a relationship, so he breaks up with
one-of-a-kind woman Laila Stewart. Of course, he didn't
realize she would wind up moving to Washington state
and working with him. Or that their heated daytime
glances would lead to sizzling passionate nights. Now
he's starting to wonder if letting this alluring woman go
was the biggest mistake of his life....

*Coming the first wefi of November 2008,
wherever books are sold.*

ARABESQUE®
www.kimanipress.com   KPMKGI131108